ADVANCE RE

THE LAST MORNING

THE LAST MORNING
A Thriller

CAMDEN BAIRD

THOMAS & MERCER

Text copyright © 2025 by Camden Baird
All rights reserved.

Published by Thomas & Mercer, Seattle

www.apub.com

Amazon, the Amazon logo, and Thomas & Mercer are trademarks of Amazon.com, Inc., or its affiliates.

ISBN-13: 9781662530258 (paperback)
ISBN-13: 9781662530241 (digital)

Cover design by Caroline Teagle Johnson
Cover image: © Stephen Mulcahey / ArcAngel; © Cosma Andrei Zalau / Stocsky

Printed in the United States of America

THE LAST MORNING

Camden Bains

SADIE
THE MOM

Day One

It's Emma's first day of kindergarten and I'm racked with nerves. *Will she be okay? Make friends? Will the teachers be nice to her? Will she miss me?*

Allen comes down the back staircase and into the kitchen, where I'm packing Emma's lunch. He's dressed in a blue Oxford shirt and wears a red tie. His blazer's draped over one arm. He reads the tension on my face and gives my shoulder a squeeze. "She's going to be all right." He lays a kiss on my cheek. "Promise."

Emma wanders into the kitchen and Allen bends low to give her a hug. "Have a great time at school today."

Her lips form a pout that is so, so sad. "Bye, Daddy."

I stare at my great-looking husband, wondering how he can be so sure. He's got his hand on the knob to the garage door. "Deep breaths," he cautions lightly, before he goes. His blue eyes twinkle when he smiles. "You'll be fine, first-time mommy."

First time for this, sure. Allen and I have had a series of firsts, all of them moving at breakneck speed. Before I met him, I was more cautious, taking life in baby steps. Then, barely six years ago, we met at a mutual friend's wedding. I fell for him hard and fast. I guess you could say we had a whirlwind romance. Emma wasn't planned. My IUD failed, but we both were in love and wanted our baby.

We married not long after the pregnancy was confirmed. Allen had been single for three years at that point. He'd been married to Teresa for five years, previously. Their ten-year-old son, Forrest, spends half his time with us. I've volunteered tons at Forrest's school, so I know Stonefield Elementary. I'm just not ready for Emma to be there yet.

Ten minutes later, I paste a smile on my face and load her onto the school bus. "Have a great first day!" I nod at the familiar bus driver who's shepherded Forrest to school for eons. Still. This time feels different. This *day* feels different. This is Emma, my little girl.

She lumbers down the aisle, her pale-pink backpack weighing her down. She's so helpless and small. *Why are we doing this?* Maybe we should have homeschooled her? That would have been tricky given the demands of my job, but I might have managed. Maybe I still could if Stonefield's awful for her.

It's a humid August morning, steam rising off the pavement like a muggy cloud. Oaks and magnolias line the road, as well as longleaf pines. The scent of osmanthus cloaks the air.

An older kid sits next to Emma as she peers out the window with sad brown eyes. She's got a new haircut, her honey-blond hair brushing her shoulders. I thought she'd like the change, but she probably would have been happier in pigtails. She's still my baby, only five. Not ready for this step. Or maybe it's me who's not ready for her to be away all day.

Moms of older kids stand nearby, joking about summer's end and their newfound freedom. Making plans for a ladies' lunch with mimosas and toasts. Celebrating. I can't relate and doubt I ever will.

Emma holds up her hand.

A tiny wave.

My heart lodges in my throat and I resist the urge to storm aboard and pull her from the bus. The principal assured us at orientation that the panic will pass. *If I can only get through this first week, first day, these grueling first few hours.*

I blow a kiss and mouth, *Love you.*

She presses her forehead to the window and frowns.

My heart breaks in two.

I busy myself with work to take my mind off Emma and what's happening at school. I freelance as an actuary from home, running numbers for a major insurance company. My home office affords a view of our shady cul-de-sac, but this morning I'm working in the kitchen, where I'm closer to the coffee maker. I've likely overdone the caffeine, but I can't seem to sit still. Refilling my mug gives me an excuse to get up and walk around, so I don't look like I'm pacing.

Not that anyone's here to judge me. Though I *am* slightly judging myself. But all new parents go through this, right? I can't help loving my daughter and having these protective instincts surge to the fore. She was a preemie and we almost lost her. I've hovered over her ever since. Maybe too much, I know. But better to do too much than too little. The world's a scary place.

Even in Chapel Roads, North Carolina, where the crime rate is low and the sense of community's strong. Young couples come for the hip village vibe and stay for the awesome amenities. The Research Triangle's booming, and real estate's out of control. When we put in our bid on this house in a great family neighborhood, four other buyers vied for it simultaneously. We paid above market price to secure the deal, but it was worth every penny. For us. For Emma.

I check the time on the kitchen clock against the display on my computer. Eight twenty-five. Emma should have arrived at school by now and is probably having fun in her classroom's play area. Maybe her teacher's welcoming the kids to school? Reading them a story? I envision the classroom bubbling with laughter and happy smiles, kids being kind to each other. Sharing. *Yeah, right.* I push thoughts of bullies and mean girls from my mind and return to my spreadsheet, digging in.

At eight thirty-eight, I receive a call from the school. My nerves skitter. *Emma.* Something's wrong. "This is Stonefield Elementary," a woman says dourly. I think she's chewing gum. "Can you tell us why Emma's not in school today?"

My heart—stops. I grip my phone so hard my knuckles ache.

What? Nooo. "There must be some mistake." My mouth's dry cotton. It's hard to speak. "I put her on the bus this morning."

"All right. I'll double-check. Please hold."

I stare at the backyard, my pulse pounding. It's huge and ringed with leafy trees. Allen put up the play set last week. I focus on the details. Yellow slide. Black swing seats. A sandbox shaped like a blue tugboat on one side. A cardinal lands on the helm of the ship.

"Mrs. Wilson?"

I hold my breath. "Yes?"

"No, that's correct. I spoke with her teachers. She's not in class."

My soul's ripped from my body so fast it burns.

A mom's worst nightmare.

Emma never made it to school.

SADIE
THE MOM

Day One

I'm rushing out the door with my purse and car keys when a police car pulls into the drive, parking in front of my garage. The police told me to sit tight and wait, but if I wait another minute my heart will explode. I've got to get to the school, have to find Emma.

Two women officers exit their vehicle and stride toward me at a brisk pace, their name badges glaring back at me. Rodriguez has her dark curly hair pinned back and a dimpled chin. Patel wears a tight bun and has amber eyes. They're on the young side.

Rodriguez speaks first. "Mrs. Wilson?"

I nod.

"We got a call about your missing daughter, Emma?"

A couple of neighbors on the street have stopped to discreetly stare. I recognize one of them as a mom from the bus stop. The women pretend to be walking their dogs and chatting with one another, but I can feel them watching me. Wondering about the police car in my driveway. Thinking I might have done something sinister. Not that I'm a victim myself.

That my child's missing. Dammit.

My stomach churns. This can't be happening. *How* is it happening?

"Yes, I put her on the bus at seven fifty." My breath comes in fits and starts. I'm growing lightheaded. I hold on to the hood of my SUV for support. "But then something must have happened on the way, or at Stonefield."

The milky-gray sky seems to spin, puffy dark clouds circling each other. A crow flies by overhead and caws. I blink and stare at the officers. "I got an absence report she's not there."

"What time did that call come in?" Rodriguez stands closer in a position of authority. I get the impression she's in charge and that Patel is newer, maybe in training.

Great. We need experienced people on this. Not rookies.

Rodriguez seems to read my face. "Just confirming what you told the dispatcher earlier."

I try to calm myself. Maybe youthful energy is good. Maybe they're extra sharp and superb at their jobs. Will try harder to prove their mettle than somebody older might. Someone who's tired of investigations. Burned out.

I pull my phone from my purse to check it. My hands shake so hard I have trouble searching incoming calls. *There.* "Eight . . . eight thirty-eight."

Rodriguez writes this down. "We need you at the school ASAP." She indicates her squad car. "You can ride with us. Do you have a recent photo of Emma on your phone?"

My heart stutters. How many times have I heard those words on police procedurals? This can't be happening in real life. Not in my life. Not in Emma's. "Yes." I have *at least* five hundred, undoubtedly more.

"Have you called your husband?"

My eyes burn hot. *Oh my God, Allen. He's so freaked. So upset. Neither of us can believe this.*

"Yes, he's"—I struggle to catch my breath—"on his way to Stonefield now." I scrub my fists across my eyes when the tears gush out. I've got to keep myself together. Need to cooperate with the police. *They're here to help me, help Emma.*

Rodriguez flips shut her notebook, surveying the house. "We'll need something of Emma's. A piece of clothing she's recently worn?"

I shudder inside knowing what that means. They'll use her scent to track her down. Maybe if they find her quickly enough, she'll be okay? But they've got to get to her in time. Every second counts, and this is taking too long. I'm not helping. My feet are frozen in quicksand. Fuck. *Move. Move.*

"Mrs. Wilson?" Rodriguez says.

I grit my teeth and push through the glass wall of my terror. It shatters around me, slicing my wrists, cutting my face and arms. Blood runs down my hands, seeps between my fingers. *"Okay."* I catch my breath and dash into the house, darting upstairs and into Emma's room.

Her stuffed lovey sits on the bed waiting for Emma.

My heart snaps like a twig in the ravages of a storm that's only growing stronger. Mercilessly wrapping my emotions in a black funnel cloud. Hurricane-force winds batter my heart, but I fight through my tears and grab Emma's nightie from beneath her pillow.

ALLEN
THE DAD

Day One

I sit in the principal's office numb with fear. The police are here. Sadie looks oddly disconnected, like her soul's left her body. I've never seen her so pale. I'm not even sure what she's wearing. I think those are her pajama pants. Her blond hair's knotted at her nape, but lots of strands fall loose.

We're seated in chairs facing the principal's desk. The police officers are standing. For an elementary school office it's awfully stark. The pressed-board bookshelves are mostly bare, and the room hums with fluorescent lighting. The flagpole's visible through the window at Principal Rand's back. So is the circular drive fronting the school. The drive that school buses pull into. Where Emma should have gotten off the bus. What the hell happened?

"In cases like these," Principal Rand says, "we have certain protocols." I've never taken to Principal Rand. She's polished in a gray suit jacket and skirt, but I've only seen her smile once—at parent orientation. And then it looked forced. I didn't attend parent orientation night when Forrest started kindergarten. Teri went by herself. Maybe Rand also smiled then.

"Cases like these?" My voice cracks. "You've had them before?"

Principal Rand shuffles papers on her desk, stacking them on their ends and knocking them against her desk until their alignment's even. I get the impression this is a nervous habit. Not that she's doing anything relevant. "Not missing children, no. I meant irregularities."

"My daughter's not an irregularity," Sadie snaps. "She's a child." It looks like she's catching her breath, finding it hard to breathe, while grabbing the arms of her chair. "How could this happen?"

"That's what we're here to find out," Chief Claremont says. She's fortyish and tough looking, with short red hair and a square jaw. She's got a younger guy with her, Deputy Chief O'Reilly. Beefy arms and a buzz cut. His vibe says ex-military. I like the two of them at once. They're on our side. On Emma's.

Chief Claremont addresses Principal Rand. "We'll need to see camera footage. Whatever you've got. Hallways, classrooms? Exterior shots of the building?"

Principal Rand's mouth puckers up like she's tasted a sour lemon. "Of course."

I can tell she's calculating the damage, weighing how this situation will reflect on the reputation of her school. Will it make the papers? Cause her administration to fall under intense scrutiny? Will she be admonished for allowing this to happen on her watch? Will she be investigated? Lose her job?

What the fuck, lady? We're talking about my little girl.

I drag a hand down my face. "What about the school bus?" I ask. "Any cameras there?"

Principal Rand nods primly. "We've already put in a call to the bus driver. He's headed back this way."

"Good," Claremont says. "We'll need to speak to him, and everybody who works at Stonefield."

"All of them?" Rand rubs her forehead, sounding taxed. "I can't pull my teachers out of class." She goggles at the police like their request is unreasonable. *Seriously?* Wow.

Claremont and O'Reilly exchange glances.

"Then we'll take them one at a time," Claremont says decisively. "Starting with the staff who were out front greeting the buses this morning." She questions Rand. "Do you have a complete roster of your employees here?"

Principal Rand sighs. "I'll have my secretary print one out."

Sadie watches their exchange intently. "You think it might be one of the teachers?" she asks. "Somebody here?"

"We intend to canvass them all thoroughly," Claremont says. "And we aim to get started right away."

Sadie collapses back in her chair. "Thank God."

My insides are torn to pieces. I want to rant and roar at them. I know—everybody knows—the longer a person goes missing, the harder it is to find them. "Isn't there a way to hurry things up?"

O'Reilly speaks. It's the first time he's opened his mouth, other than to greet us and say he's sorry about the circumstances. "We've got squad cars in circulation. An Amber Alert's in force. That started the moment we took your wife's statement giving Emma's particulars."

An Amber Alert is *something* but not enough. Nothing is enough. "I want to see that school bus footage," I insist.

Sadie leans forward, hugging herself with her arms. "Me too."

"We'll let you know if we discover anything of note," Claremont says.

"The best thing you folks can do," O'Reilly adds, "is go home and—"

"*No,*" Sadie and I say together.

Chief Claremont turns to us and says kindly, "She could wind up back there? Besides, you two need to be home in case someone calls or comes by. Maybe a neighbor or a relative knows something?" I concede she's making sense. Sadie seems to think so too. "The minute we learn *anything,* we'll let you know." Claremont's eyebrows arch. "I promise."

We exit the school as the canine unit pulls up. Police personnel unload two police dogs from a van, and other officers direct them toward the school. Sadie cups her hands beside her mouth and starts yelling wildly.

"Emma!" Her scream's tense and raw. "Emma!" She races to the edge of the sidewalk and calls into the woods, "*Emma!*"

A wail so visceral it slices to my bones.

Teachers appear in the windows facing the flagpole and students scurry over to peer out the glass. *Oh my God. There's my boy, Forrest.* I'm going to have to talk to Teri.

I wrap my arms around Sadie as teachers referee kids away from the scene.

"Shit, Allen. *Shit.*"

I hold Sadie close, and she sobs on my shirt.

Her body shakes so hard, the earth trembles.

I can't see which way is up and which is down.

I think it's raining.

Fuck, no.

Those are my tears.

I hold her tighter and sob too.

SADIE
THE MOM

Day One

I can't stop shivering. I'm so, so cold. My fingers are turning blue.

Allen grabs a blanket off the couch. He wraps it around my shoulders, swaddling me snugly. "You're going into shock." He pulls me closer using the blanket in his grip and peers at me. "I'm going to make you some hot tea, all right?"

But I don't want tea. I want Emma.

I feel like I'm floating outside my body. There's nothing here I recognize. The objects in the living room are foreign to me. Wait. I see Emma sitting on the piano bench, her small hands on the keys. I only signed her up for piano lessons last week. She hasn't taken one lesson yet. Am I hallucinating?

The phantom image dissolves and a million terrifying scenarios race through my mind.

Is Emma being hurt? Something worse? Tortured?

Vomit surges in my throat and I heave onto the hardwood floor. It splashes warm across my feet. I'm in my pajamas I think. Slippers. Did I run out of the house like this?

"Jesus." Allen's voice, distant, strange.

I think I'm going blind. All I see is white.

"Here," he tries to soothe me, "let's get you to the couch."

My stomach convulses and I hold my mouth.

"I'll get a trash can." He eases me down so I'm sitting and stares into my eyes. "Sadie." Dark pupils in a sea of blue. "Sadie, can you hear me?"

My chin won't move. I'm paralyzed. Is Emma paralyzed too?

Oh God. Have they restrained her?

She can't be dead. My mind won't allow it. I would feel it if something that horrible had happened to my child. I have a mother's heart. Whatever she's going through, no matter how harrowing, we'll overcome it together. Get her counseling, enlist specialists, screw the costs. We'll take out loans if we have to. Mortgage the house, sell our cars.

Just please, God, please. Let Emma come home.

"Maybe I should take you to the hospital." He rakes a hand through his hair, anguished. "Get you checked out." He settles the powder room trash can next to my elbow.

"No." I grab his arm, digging in with my fingers. Maybe if I hold on, the room won't sway. "We have to find her." I want to spring into my SUV, get behind the wheel, and drive and drive and drive. Ransack warehouses, assault buildings, turn the whole damn town upside down. Maybe she's someplace the police haven't thought of, in a location the dogs can't track?

"We will," he says surely. Still. His voice shakes.

I wonder how much he believes it. If he's weighing odds, considering every outcome like I am. Knowing full well we might not find Emma at all. We could live for years and years in this hell. Spiraling and spiraling into canyons of despair. Never learning the whole truth, whether she's dead or alive. Whether someone else has taken her and is raising her as their own. My heart weeps. Or whether she's lying in a cold dark grave—alone.

I can't imagine who would want to harm us, or hurt Emma. We're good people, a nice family. Normal, unassuming. We're not confrontational, don't engage in road rage. Allen and I have no enemies. Neither

13

does Emma. Emma's done *nothing* to deserve this. She's a child, for goodness' sake. When the police arrived this morning, I was so sure this was a nightmare, but the nightmare lives on.

Allen's cell phone rings. "Hang on." He holds it up to his ear. "Yes? What? Now?" A pause. "Okay."

"Let's clean you up," he says, staring at my pajama pants. They're streaked with puke. "And get you into some real clothes. You change and I'll mop up the floor, but hurry. We've got to go."

"Where?"

He darts a glance at the front door. "Chief Claremont wants us to come down to the station," he says. "They've found something."

ALLEN
THE DAD

Day One

We're at the police station in some sort of interrogation room. I am *barely* holding my shit together. Claremont's here and she introduces a man in a suit and tie. "This is Special Agent Lance Mercer from our FBI field office."

He walks over to shake our hands. He's got dark hair with a neatly trimmed beard and mustache. He's probably in his early forties. Sadie and I sit together on one side of a table. "Sorry about the circumstances." He gives us his card and I take it. The bottom drops out of my stomach. *Child Exploitation and Human Trafficking Task Force.* I tuck it in my shirt pocket, the room spinning.

Sadie blanches. "You don't think?" She stares at Claremont and Mercer.

"We've got to cover our bases," Claremont says.

Mercer nods. "Trust me. I'd love to be out of a job."

Sadie reaches over and I squeeze her hand. I don't know what I was hoping for. Maybe that some local woman abducted Emma out of loneliness, meaning her no harm. *Not this.*

Sadie's eyes are wide. She looks terrified. "Is that why you brought us here?"

"We questioned a person of interest earlier," Claremont says, "someone who lives near the school, but he's got a solid alibi."

"Who was it?" Sadie asks.

"He was cleared," Claremont reiterates.

"Yes, but." I purse my lips. "Why was he a person of interest to begin with?"

"He's on a national registry," Mercer explains.

Of sex offenders, he means. Shit. "Who is this guy?" I ask.

Claremont holds up her hands. "We can't release his name. So far as we can tell, he hasn't done anything wrong. He denies being near the school. Denies seeing Emma."

Sadie folds her face in her hands. "Oh my God."

I served on a jury once during the trial of an ultimately convicted sex offender. It was after I divorced Teri but before I married Sadie, seven years ago. I never mentioned it to Sadie because it was a complex case, and not the kind of experience you brag about, exactly. While I didn't have school-age kids then, it's a bit spooky now that he was a teacher at Stonefield Elementary.

"What about other sex offenders on the list?" I'm careful not to say too much, because if Sadie knew, she'd be so upset. Feel like I'd withheld information. I'd nearly forgotten about the Walsh case until now. It was a one-day trial, open and shut.

I don't even know if it's relevant.

"The registry is one of the first places we looked," Claremont assures us. "There was only one individual living nearby, and he's been cleared. The others either have certifiable alibis or are incarcerated."

Apparently not.

"Great," Sadie groans. She looks around the room, hunting for answers. I want them too.

Mercer takes the lead. "We think it would be a good idea if you spoke with the media. Get information on Emma out there. These first forty hours are critical." He studies my eyes then surveys Sadie. "Do you think you two would be up to giving a statement to the press? It would be great if we can do that soon. We can get them here shortly."

Sadie and I immediately concur. "Of course."

Claremont captures Sadie's attention, and mine. "Meanwhile, we'd like you to take a look at this. Unfortunately, there's no audio."

She lifts a remote and nods at a screen mounted on the wall across from us. She flips on the video and it's a bit grainy and in black and white. Wait. That's the inside of a school bus. My eyes burn. That's Emma climbing aboard. She leans her head against the window and the bus drives away. "And this," Claremont says.

She fast-forwards through the clips, and Sadie squeezes my hand tighter.

Claremont hits pause. The bus driver's on his feet staring at the back of the bus. The bus door is open. Claremont hits play. The bus driver strides to the back of the bus, walking past Emma. She turns her head to watch as he admonishes some kids who were acting up. Wait. Movement at the front of the bus.

Here comes Forrest, then a woman.

Holy shit.

Sadie gasps. "That's Teresa."

TERESA
THE EX-WIFE

Seven days before.

I pull up to the house and my gut wrenches. It's got a stone facade, a white-columned porch, and bay windows for Sadie's office. Storybook beautiful with a landscaped yard, but my tale didn't end happily ever after. It ended in heartache.

I inhale deeply and shut my eyes. Although she's always kind to me and Forrest, seeing Sadie's never easy. It hurts to walk into her home and world. I'm like an alien on a distant planet, someplace far beyond the stars. In a universe I've heard of but can't know. There's no oxygen for me here, only darkness. *Okay.* I open my eyes and grip the car door handle.

I can do this. I'm doing this for Forrest.

She answers the door looking pretty in shorts and a V-neck T-shirt. Sadie always looks good, but why wouldn't she? She's got Allen, and this life. "Hey!" She checks her watch. "You're early."

"Lecture ended and you were on my way." I lift a shoulder. "So." The lecture was mine at the university and I expected more questions. I like to think students were blown away by my musings on black holes, but there's an equal chance they were bored. Only halfway through the week, and they've already got partying on their minds. I work at the campus's telescope. It's amazing and vast, and I run my own program. What I didn't run so well was my life.

"Come on in." She smiles pleasantly. "I'll get Forrest." She calls up the stairs. "Forrest! Your mom's here!" No answer. "I think he's gaming in his room."

Some kids should be so lucky as to have two rooms. Others would be luckier to have a full-time dad. Sadie starts to take the stairs, and a set of pocket doors to the living room slides open. It's Forrest. Shit. He's been in Sadie's office. He knows better. "Oh, honey," she says. Her frown's compassionate. "You shouldn't go in there."

"Forrest," I say in exasperated tones.

He shrugs looking guilty, his head bowed forward. His blond bangs cover his eyes. I swear he's grown two inches in the past *week*. "Sorry." He's been this way ever since he passed his tenth birthday. I sense the rebellious teenager building—bursting to come out, with only a short stop at the tween stage for a respite.

I can't wait.

Sadie picks up his duffel bag by the door and hands it to me. Shared custody stinks. "We enjoyed having him," she says. I believe Allen did and I know Sadie tries. It's Emma that Forrest can't stand. I'm sure he's jealous. That makes two of us when I'm being honest, but I can't share that with anyone but myself.

Emma wanders into the front hall from the kitchen. She's got a popsicle in her hand. "Hi, Mrs. Wilson." Is it sad I didn't change my name? I considered it for a nanosecond, but I had Forrest to think of. Life would be easier for him if I didn't. I'd published professional papers besides. Loads of them. Allen and I met in grad school. But he didn't study the stars. He got his MBA. We met at a bar near the campus. The rest, as they say, was history. Until *we* became history.

I glance around the house at their fancy furnishings and art. Allen's work as a wealth manager pays well. Then again, so does Sadie's job. My gaze lands back on the child. *His* child and *hers*. A wave of nausea roils through me. Of course they have a sex life. Allen was great in the sack. I scrub those images from my brain and say pleasantly, "Hi, Emma. How are you?"

"Good." Her big brown eyes are Sadie's, but her straight-across eyebrows are Allen's. She furrows her forehead. "Are you staying for dinner?" *As if.* Sadie's invited us before out of courtesy. Particularly for holidays. I don't know how I could sit through the meal with Allen's new family. Rationally, I understand Allen's happy, and I should accept that. What confounds me is how easily he turned his emotions *off*—like a tap.

I know it's pathetic to keep hoping, but I do.

The truth hits hard.

I still love Allen.

ALLEN
THE DAD

Day One

Chief Claremont holds the remote as the video continues playing.

What the fuck is Teresa doing on that bus?

Forrest takes a seat and Teresa calls out to Emma.

Emma smiles, glad to see a friendly face.

Mercer meets my eyes. "Your ex-wife, right?"

He can't seriously be implying—*shit*. Teresa holds out her hand and takes Emma's backpack, reaching over some taller kid. The bus driver wheels around. He's angry, pointing toward the exit. *No parents on the bus*. Teresa returns the backpack to Emma and raises her hands. She's saying something, explaining and inching away. Claremont hits stop.

"We've got her here." Claremont glances at Teri on the screen. "Brought her down to the station for questioning. O'Reilly's talking to her now."

Teresa? My Teri? No way. It can't be her. Teri's not some lunatic, for God's sake. She's an astrophysicist. "She can't be involved in this." Doubts niggle at me. She always wanted another child. A girl. But *our child*, mine and hers. She would never take Sadie's. She couldn't possibly have. "She was at work when Emma disappeared."

Sadie's breathing hard. "What did the bus driver say?"

Mercer crosses his arms. "Something about she was returning an iPod?"

"So *that's* what happened to it." Relief washes over Sadie's face.

Claremont sits across from us and motions for Mercer to join her. "Care to explain?"

Sadie's shoulders sink. "My iPod's been missing these past few days." She avoids looking at me. "Forrest must have taken it when he came over. I caught him in my office, and he wasn't supposed to be in there. He's been getting into things lately."

TERESA
THE EX-WIFE

Day One

I don't like the way this guy, Deputy Chief O'Reilly, is looking at me. Sizing me up like I'm a *suspect*, for the love of Pete, and why? Because I'm Allen's ex-wife and that somehow makes me culpable for kidnapping Emma? He's making a big deal of my being on the school bus and talking to Emma. Taping everything I say. Fine. Let him tape away.

They've got nothing on me. No proof. Zip.

I don't even have to be here, technically. I'm speaking to O'Reilly of my own accord. Maybe I should just stand up and leave? If he pushes my buttons one more time, I will.

"It was an *iPod*," I say for the umpteenth time. "Just ask Sadie! She'll tell you it was missing. I was trying to return it so Forrest wouldn't get into further trouble. I stuck it in an envelope and enclosed a note, an apology from my son. That's what I slipped into Emma's backpack."

O'Reilly scratches his chin. "Odd method for returning the item."

"Not so odd, really." I adjust the collar on my polo shirt. It feels like it's choking me. Like the V on the V-neck's not quite wide enough. I wear one of these and khakis most days when I'm teaching. Otherwise, I'm in jeans. "Forrest gets on the bus a few stops after Emma."

"So then," he says like a smartass, "why not give it to Emma on the kid's way home?"

"*Because*," I say, growing exasperated. "I'm not home in the afternoons. I already told you I work until six. Forrest goes to aftercare at school when he's not at his dad's."

O'Reilly's taking notes. "How often is that?"

"Two weeks there, two weeks with me. We're on a rotation."

Not that it's any of your business.

I sigh.

But I suppose it is.

I'm so past ready for this questioning to be over.

Why did I agree to it in the first place?

Oh yeah. Because *not* doing so would make me look guilty. Though it's apparent O'Reilly thinks I'm guilty anyway. *Why is it always the jealous ex-wife? That's such an archetype, so unfair. Even when there are grains of truth to it.*

He nods and makes a few more notes. "You couldn't just drop it by?"

"Of course I could, but why?"

"Why trust a five-year-old kid with an iPod? You apparently couldn't trust your ten-year-old." He's very glib at turning a phrase. He's also pretty good at pissing me off. So.

I stand and grab my purse. "I don't have time for this."

He waves me back down. "I'm afraid you do."

There's clearly no one else in the room. I haven't been read my Miranda rights or been given the opportunity to consult a lawyer. None of this is official. He's bluffing. Trying to get something out of me gratis.

Sorry, buddy. You want my cooperation, you're going to have to fucking pay. Pony up for a public defender at least.

I set my chin, still standing. "Am I being charged with something, Deputy Chief O'Reilly?"

He braces himself against the table with his hands. "No."

I meet his stare. "Then I guess I'm free to go."

He gestures grandly toward the door with his large hands, and I stride out. The man is enormous. Very built. He clearly works out. He sure put me through my paces.

Asshole.

Sadie and Allen are in the hall. I rush toward them, reaching for Allen first. It's like muscle memory—I do it instinctively. I take him in my arms. "Oh my God, I'm so sorry!"

Allen hugs me tightly and I melt into his embrace, wishing so badly that none of this had happened. That *we* were still a family. If we were, there *never would have been* an Emma, and no one would be enduring this trauma now.

He releases me with a haggard frown. "Thanks, Teri." A knife twists in my heart. He's the only one who calls me that.

The only one who ever has.

"You must be devastated," I say to Sadie.

Despite the horror she's going through, I can't help wishing it was me by Allen's side. That I was the one there to comfort him, and for him to wrap his arms around for more than just a few seconds.

She answers me, zombielike. "We are."

"Any leads?" I ask, holding my breath.

I'm wondering what they know. What the police have learned, hopeful it will drive suspicion away from me.

Allen shakes his head. "Nothing yet."

SADIE
THE MOM

Six days before.

I'm unloading boxes when a woman knocks on the french doors to our rear patio. Our den connects to a sunny breakfast area and the kitchen. We're mostly settled in except for a few knickknacks here and there. Filling in bookshelves. I set the books I'm holding down on the love seat and answer the door.

"Hi," the woman says, "I'm Cass Thomas." She's got a friendly smile. Her wavy blond hair's pulled back in floral-design clips on either side. "Your neighbor to the south." She nods over her shoulder at our back gate. Only a portion of her yellow house is visible through the green screen bordering our yard. It's smaller than ours but seems nicely kept. She hands me a tall, narrow gift bag done up with a bow. "Welcome to the neighborhood." She leans closer and whispers. "It's wine."

I invite her in. "How nice! I'm Sadie Wilson."

She wrinkles up her face. "You *do* drink?"

"Oh yeah." My face warms. I didn't mean it to sound like *that*. I'm not super lushy. I pull the bottle from the bag to peek at the label. It's a French bordeaux. Looks expensive. "Thank you." I set the gift bag down on an end table beside Allen's recliner. It faces a gas fireplace. The fan-shaped window above the mantel frames our woodsy side yard.

Emma rushes down the back staircase. She can't get over the fact that this house has *two staircases*, one leading directly upstairs from the foyer and another in the kitchen connecting to the upstairs hall and her playroom over the garage.

"Careful, Em!" I caution, and she holds the rail.

"Okay!" She gets near the bottom and jumps down the last three steps, nearly colliding with a built-in cabinet. My heart lurches. We've lived here less than three weeks. I'm not eager for a trip to the emergency room.

I shake my head and ask Cass, "You have kids?"

"Just one." She smiles at Emma skipping toward us.

Emma stops next to me and stares at the stranger. We've cautioned her against speaking to people she doesn't know unless we're with her. "This is Emma."

"Hi, Emma," Cass says, "I'm Mrs. Thomas from the house behind yours. You'll have to come over and play with Bobby sometime. Bobby's about your age. Maybe a few years older." She hazards a guess. "Four?"

"Five," I answer. "She starts kindergarten next week."

"How great. Bobby's entering first grade."

I figure it might be good for Emma to know at least one kid on the bus. "I suppose Bobby's at Stonefield too?"

"No, private school." She sinks her hands into her shorts' pockets. She looks athletic. "Our Lady of Our Savior." I've heard of it. "I work there as a gym teacher." She whispers behind the back of her hand. "They give us a break in tuition that way."

I laugh, my tensions easing. Cass seems like a nice enough person.

"Do you work outside the home?" she asks.

"I work from home," I tell her, "consulting." I've tired of explaining actuarial science to people. A lot of folks ask but then their eyes glaze over when I dive into insurance risk allocation and mortality rates. Cass spies the books on my sofa. One's a yearbook.

"No *way*." She gapes at me. "You went to Braxton High? Go Bulls!"

"Not me, my husband, Allen."

She crosses her arms and squints. "What year?"

When I tell her she grins broadly. "He was a few years ahead of me, but sure, I remember him. Played basketball? Soccer?" She chuckles. "*All* the girls had major crushes."

An unsettled feeling creeps over me, but I brush it off. Silly.

"Small world!" I say.

"Yeah," she agrees. "Small world." She looks around. "Is he here? I'd love to say hi."

"No, he's gone out. But we'll have to invite you and your husband over for a drink. Maybe some of that yummy wine you brought us?"

"It's just me," she says. "Richard and I divorced."

I strive to be inclusive. I hate it when people leave others out who aren't coupled up. That's so unfair. "Just you then! I'm serious. Once we're settled in. You can bring Bobby with you so he can meet Emma."

Emma looks excited at the prospect of a friend.

"Why don't you let Emma come to my house first?" Cass says. "There's always so much to do with a move."

I consider her offer, but I don't really know her. Then again, she lives right behind us. She also *kind of* knew Allen. "I don't want to put you out," I hedge.

"No bother! Bobby would love that. When's good for you?"

A bit pushy.

She's probably just being kind. Still.

Something prevents me from committing right off the bat.

"Let me check my calendar," I say, "and get back to you."

KATE
THE TEACHER

Day One

A policewoman named Claremont sits at a kids' worktable in my room. She's the local chief of police. School closed early and students have been dismissed. All the buses have pulled away. Staff and faculty are being released one at a time after getting questioned by the police. The scuttlebutt's been going around Stonefield with whispers in the faculty lounge and in the hallways, and cell phones, set to silent, blowing up with text message alerts.

Everyone wants to know what happened to Emma. Who's behind her disappearance and who's covering it up? Some speculate Principal Rand might be involved—in a cover-up, that is. She's such a bitch. Who would be surprised? Rand would throw anyone under the bus to save her own precious hide. That's no secret. Rand thinks she's hot stuff and that everyone here loves her. *As if.* Nobody likes Rand. Not even the parents. That's sad.

This table's low to the ground and the seats are tiny. Still, Chief Claremont manages. She's not a large person herself. She folds her hands together on the tabletop and begins. I notice she's wearing a wedding band. No engagement ring, no fuss. Her nails are neatly trimmed and tidy, unpolished. I've heard about her, of course, and have seen her on the news, but have never met her in person.

"I know this must be difficult with Emma being one of your students," she says, "but I need to ask you some questions." She's not a bad-looking woman, minimal makeup and a straightforward demeanor. "Anything you remember might help us." She opens her notebook and takes out a pen. "Where were you at eight fifteen this morning when Emma disappeared?"

"Right here." I sweep my hand around the classroom that should be teeming with life right now, and not dead silent. A fly buzzes against the window facing the playground, stupidly trapped against the glass, buzzing and buzzing against it.

The sound is more annoying than it should be with no other noise to drown it out. "I was preparing for the day with Dotti. She's my teaching assistant." Dotti was one of the earlier ones cleared. "She left to go home thirty minutes ago."

Chief Claremont nods. "Yes. Deputy Chief O'Reilly spoke with Mrs. Gilmore earlier. She verified that you were in your classroom when she brought the kids in from the buses." She glances at the door. "Anyone other than your teaching assistant see you here at eight fifteen?"

The fly throws itself against the window again.

Buzz-buzz, buzz-buzz.

Fuck.

Katherine bristles inside me, but I maintain my outward calm. Cross my ankles. Run a hand through my hair. "Sure. Mitra Parikh, the art teacher. She's right across the hall. One of my student name tags fell off the desk, and I couldn't find my masking tape. Someone must have taken it."

The fly takes a brief reprieve from the window and buzzes by overhead. I wave it away when it zigzags too close to my face. Irritating.

"Does that happen often?" Claremont asks, ignoring the fly. She either doesn't see it or is so laser focused on her job she doesn't rank it as a priority.

"We teachers occasionally borrow supplies from each other," I respond politely, "but it's no big deal. Somebody clearly used my tape and forgot to return it. I asked Ms. Parikh if I could borrow some of hers and she said of course, to help myself. When I got back to my classroom, Dotti was already bringing in the group of kids who'd gotten off the bus."

"I'm sure you'll understand if we check out your story with the art teacher?" Claremont asks. She closes her notebook and tucks it away like she's already decided something about me. Finally. I'm ready to be cleared and for this part to be over.

I smile blandly. "Of course." I'm confident the art teacher will verify my whereabouts. Same as Dotti did.

The fly's back at the window.

Motherfucker.

Buzzing. Buzzing.

Each buzz growing louder in the quiet room.

Katherine wants to throw a book at it so hard it cracks the glass. But no, that wouldn't do. Displaying a temper in front of Claremont.

"Excuse me." I get up and cross the room, opening a small closet and grabbing the flyswatter. In an instant, I'm at the window. I give the flyswatter a whack and the fly smashes into the glass. I leave it there hanging and turn to Claremont. "Sorry, that was distracting."

"Yeah," she says. "Bothered me too." But I have a feeling it didn't. Her gaze is oddly pinned on me. My stomach knots. She's wondering if she judged me too soon. If I could do to a child what I did to that fly. Whether I'm a cold-hearted individual who's capable of murder. She'll never get anything on me though. Nobody will.

I sit back down at the table and smooth the creases in my skirt. Claremont takes her notebook back out and writes something down. Crap. And there I thought we'd finished. "When did you first meet Emma Wilson?" She stares into my eyes, questioning how much I know and what I'm willing to reveal.

I sit up straighter to reply. "At the school open house."

"And Sadie and Allen Wilson?" She looks up when I pause.

"It was at parent orientation." Which is true about Sadie. There's only so much Claremont needs to know about my past affiliation with Allen. I'm no dummy. I understand how that would make things look. It would give me a motive to harm his child.

KATE
THE TEACHER

Five days before.

It's parent orientation night at the school. I'm a bundle of nerves, but my bright smile belies the fact. My teaching assistant, Dotti, helps me run my classroom. Dotti's been working at Stonefield longer than the principal. She hears and sees everything, and children love her. She wears stretch pants and huge colorful shirts every day, always with a funky pair of school-themed earrings. Tonight she's wearing erasers, but she's got crayons and apples, and funny bookworms too.

"Cute," I say, pointing to her jewelry when she walks over. She's short and plump with a thick gray braid. Dotti places a hand behind her head and poses like a siren.

"Thank you." She bats her eyelashes and I laugh. This is our second year working together and my third at the school. I've passed the midpoint in my probationary period. At the end of five years, I'll be tenured.

The parents are in the auditorium receiving an address from Principal Rand, while we prepare the classroom. We've got name cards on the desks, and they're arranged in stations of four or five. I've got a rocking chair for reading in the corner and there's a soft carpet for the kids to sit on. An abundant play area's been established by the windows, with dress-up clothes, like medical scrubs and fireperson hats, and a plastic log cabin with a double-hinged door. We've got three classroom pets: two guinea pigs and a turtle.

I hear a commotion in the hall.

Dotti's eyes twinkle. "Sounds like they're coming!" She loves meeting the parents. I like them *okay*, but I'm way more focused on the kids.

Children make the world go round in my book. Adults just fuck it up. And if they're not fucking things up now, they most assuredly did at some point, more than likely when they were teenagers. Nobody reaches adulthood unscathed. Only the youngest kids are perfect. They haven't gotten far enough along in life to have endured, or inflicted, damage.

I'll meet the little ones soon enough at the school open house. They'll see their room and receive a tour of the school. Parents are invited too, of course, along with other family members, like grandparents or siblings. I had siblings once myself, but *that* changed.

I've tried not to stay angry about it, I have. But I've never been great at subduing my emotions. What *I am* good at is keeping them from showing on my face. No one can look at me and tell what I'm thinking. My boyfriend is a case in point. He's the smartest man I know, and even he can't read me.

A loud group rounds the corner, and several adults filter into the room. A few are on their own, others in pairs. Allen walks in, and my heart beats unsteadily. When I saw Emma on my student roster, I didn't expect it to be this hard. He's very handsome with sandy-blond hair and blue eyes. Sexily built and muscled.

I catch other teachers snatching glances at him occasionally, appreciating his great looks and body. His wife's pretty, too, but I know it's his second wife on account of Forrest. Forrest is Emma's older half brother. He was already in the second grade by the time I came to Stonefield.

Allen may not know a lot about me, but I've got the goods on him. Though he hasn't connected the dots, our two families go back a long ways. We used to take vacations together, rent summer cottages, but that was before our parents stopped speaking to each other.

The line inches up as people pause to shake my hand. When it's Allen's turn, his grip is firm. "Ms. Davis." He smiles. "Nice to meet you. I'm Allen Wilson and this is Sadie."

Sadie grins. "Emma's dad and mom."

"Yes." I nod and shake her hand. "Good to see you both. I'm excited about having Emma in my class."

While Allen's seen me at the school in passing, there's never been a probing glance or any hint of recognition. I've changed so much, he's never guessed. I went by Kit-Kat then and he scarcely paid attention to Mark's kid sister.

I paid attention to him, though.

Allen's got secrets.

SADIE
THE MOM

Five days before.

Allen and I sit together in the den, drinking the bordeaux Cass brought over. Tomorrow's Emma's playdate with Bobby, and I can't help being uneasy about it. I'll feel a whole lot better once Emma and I meet the kid.

I've kept my eye on Cass's house but haven't seen a boy playing in their backyard, which strikes me as strange. Allen says he remembers Cass from Braxton High but only vaguely. She was a nondescript ninth grader, and upperclassmen rarely noticed the younger students.

We tucked Emma into bed half an hour ago, and she drifted right off to sleep, holding Night Doggie and worn out from playing with her teenage sitter. Tonight was parent orientation night at the school, and we hit a gold mine with our next-door neighbors. The family has two young teenage daughters, perfect babysitting age.

The windows in this back part of the house aren't covered. There's not much need for window dressings here. We're mostly surrounded by woods. And now it's dark outside, glimmers of moonlight threading through thickets of trees.

Allen sips from his glass and says, "Hmm, this is nice." He leans back in his recliner relaxing, with his feet propped up. We don't hang out much anymore and just do nothing. He's got some music playing in the background through his high-end speakers, sultry jazz. It's nice mood music. We're always watching movies or going somewhere. It's kind of fun to just sip wine and talk. Enjoy our pretty new house. We're all settled in now and I love it.

I let a taste of wine settle on my tongue, appreciating its nuanced flavors. Cherry. Tobacco. Leather. "Yeah, it's good."

I glance out the french doors at the patio and beyond that at the gate to Cass's yard. Her whole house is dark. Maybe she's not home. But why would she be out at this time of night when she's got a young kid? What about Bobby? I remind myself about the divorce and Bobby's dad. Of course. Bobby could be there.

Allen swirls the wine in his glass and settles deeper into his comfy chair. I'm on the love seat, cozy under a sofa blanket with my knees bent up. It feels nice to snuggle in with the air-conditioning blasting. It topped ninety degrees today. "I think parent orientation went well," he says, "don't you?"

I rest my wineglass on my knees. I wasn't totally thrilled about it. "It went—*okay*."

"Come on, Sadie," Allen cajoles. "Kate Davis seems nice enough and so does Miss Dotti."

"Yeah, Miss Dotti seems nice." She's got a great reputation at the school, and I've seen her in action with the kids. I innately trust Dotti. It's the lead teacher I have my reservations about. She's friendly enough but something about her grin looks glassy. She got one of those smiles that doesn't quite reach her eyes.

I fan my fingers around my wineglass holding it under my chin. But I can't share my feelings about Kate Davis with Allen. He'll think I'm overreacting. He knows I'm worried about Emma starting school.

He keeps urging me not to hold her back, to allow our little girl to spread her wings. But I'm hesitant about her ability to fly so soon.

I'd be happier if she stayed at home in her nest with me. At least for a while longer. She's so small for her age, and still catching up. I don't mean to be overprotective. I just want Emma's life to be different from mine. Better.

I lost my own family young. My mom died from melanoma when I was in elementary school, and then I lost my dad to lung cancer while I was still in college. He had one of those rare cases where he'd never smoked, so it was extra tragic. I had no one to cheer for me in the stands at the stadium when I received my diploma. Bring flowers or gifts to graduation.

I wanted a different sort of life for Emma, complete with a happy home and a loving mom and dad who would stick around, *stay*. When I met Allen, I knew he was the one. We matched physically, spiritually. All of it. When Emma came along, our world only got better. And sometimes when things are really great, you're scared to rock the boat. Upset the perfect equilibrium. I know it's only kindergarten. Still.

It's *so hard* letting her go.

I see movement outside the window. A dark shadow crossing the lawn. Wait. My pulse skitters. Was someone in our backyard?

"Allen," I say. "Did you leave the gate open?"

"Who, me? What? No. Why?"

He peers out the window, and the gate swings on its hinges.

"It's open now."

SADIE
THE MOM

Four days before.

Cass answers her front door and invites me and Emma in. She's dressed casually in athletic pants and a sporty V-neck top. It's midafternoon and she's asked Emma over to play for a few hours after her teacher workday at school.

"Thanks so much for that wine." I smile warmly. "It was great. Allen and I enjoyed it last night."

"Nice! I'm so glad you did." She glances at Emma. "I'm happy we can get the kids together." Her house is very bare bones compared to the outside. She's got almost no furniture, and—odd—nothing on her walls. The floor's bare too. No rugs. "Still decorating," she says when she notices me looking around.

Embarrassing. "Oh! Sorry. I didn't mean to stare. I know it takes a while. How long have you been here?"

"Two years."

O-*kay*. I cling to Emma's hand, my heart hammering.

Cass shrugs. "But then with the divorce . . ."

Ah, got it. The ex took things. I feel guilty for judging her. "Of course." The place is eerily quiet. I peek around the corner and peer up the stairs. "So Bobby?"

Her grin sparkles. "Will be here in a bit."

The rational side of my brain says Bobby's probably with his dad, who's dropping him off. I know how shared custody works through Forrest. Cass's situation probably isn't much different. Still, tension stirs in my gut. I can't leave my daughter here to play with some kid I've never met before. What if he's horrible? A mean bully? Someone who might pick on her? And why isn't he already here anyway, since Emma's been invited over to play?

I protectively lay my hands on Emma's shoulders. "We'll come back later," I say, wondering if I should call the whole thing off. None of this is sitting right with me.

She stops me from opening the door. "Bobby won't be a minute. You can leave Emma with me if you'd like?"

Right. With many other people and under different circumstances, I might believe that, but not with her. Something about this feels off to me. Something about *Cass* feels off. "You know." I check my watch. "I'm really sorry to do this, but I just remembered something."

Her face hardens. Suddenly, she's not the sunny neighbor. "Oh yeah? What's that?"

My pulse skitters. *Think, think, think.* "We, uh, have dental appointments."

Emma wrinkles up her forehead. "We do?"

I wince apologetically. "Yeah, sweetie. I'm sorry. Mommy forgot."

"That's too bad." Cass frowns. "Bobby will be very disappointed." I can tell she's upset about the last-minute change. Her steady perusal makes me antsy.

I lay my hand on the doorknob.

"Thanks so much for the invite, though. Another time!"

I whisk Emma into my arms and hurry her away, carrying her through Cass's backyard and toward our gate. I glance back at her house and she's staring at us through her kitchen window. What in God's name was that about?

"Why couldn't I play with Bobby, Mommy?" Emma asks as I jiggle her along.

I get a sickening, creeped-out feeling.

Listen to your instincts, people say.

I hug Emma tighter.

Maybe there *is no* Bobby.

ALLEN
THE DAD

Four days before.

Teri asks me to stop by her house on my way home from work to talk about Forrest. I don't tell Sadie I'm going. I make up an excuse about new client demands and staying late at the office. Teri and I have had to consult with one another a lot lately about Forrest and I'm weary, frankly, of Sadie feeling like she needs to give her input. *Of course* she's his stepmom, but Teri and I are trying to figure this out together. We created Forrest together and try to coparent him as best we can. We're apparently failing.

The other reason I didn't tell Sadie about seeing Teri is that I suspect Forrest's misbehavior might have to do with Emma. I thought he'd gotten over that phase but maybe I was wrong. He's been jealous of his half sister ever since she was born. He was scarcely Emma's age, right around five, when he took her out of her crib somehow and I caught him holding her at the top of the stairs.

Tension stirs in my gut and anxiety courses through me. "Forrest?" I ask gently so as not to startle him into dropping her. "What are you doing?"

Sweat beads my forehead and dribbles down my neck. He's holding her lopsided in his cradled arms with her head lower than her feet. If he lets her go, she'll plummet down the stairs. The fall for an infant that age would be fatal.

"She was crying." He looks up at me with big blue eyes. "I'm going to feed her." He takes one step toward the stairs—and my heart slams against my rib cage.

My hand shoots up and I steady my voice. "That's so nice of you, Forrest, very thoughtful."

I take one slow step toward him, and he inches away. Shit.

"But you can only feed the baby when Sadie or Dad is with you." Sadie's at her six-week postnatal appointment and I'm here with them by myself. If something disastrous happens while I'm in charge . . .

Fuck me.

He squeezes her against him, probably hanging on too hard, and she sputters a cry, whimpering softly, cranking up.

"Why don't you let me take Emma for now, hmm?"

Another gradual step.

My eyes lock on his so he doesn't pay attention to my feet.

"You can help me feed her later, when we're downstairs settled on the sofa."

Two more careful steps.

I've almost reached them.

"Okay." He slackens his hold and I leap in his direction, catching Emma as she drops into my hands. Fuck, that was too close.

My head reels, my heart pounding.

Thank God she's okay.

I corral us away from the stairs, cuddling Emma against my shoulder and gently rubbing her back. I don't want to scold Forrest for this if his motives were pure. I also don't want him to ever do this again, regardless.

"You shouldn't get the baby up by yourself," I tell him. "It's one of our rules. Okay?"

He frowns. "Okay." His blue eyes glisten. "Am I in trouble?"

42

"No. Hey." I extend an arm and he walks toward me. "Come here."

He does, and I hug him against my leg. "I love you, buddy, and always will."

He looks up, his eyes pleading. "More than Emma?"

Crap. I was hoping his actions weren't about that. "I love you both very much," I say. "And here's the thing about love." I smile down at him. "The more you give, the more it grows."

"Like watering a plant?" he asks.

I warmly squeeze his shoulder. "Yeah, like that."

That might have been the end of it had I not caught Forrest tossing his toys down the stairs the next day, hurling them one at a time and brutally shouting, "Die! Die!" A chill ran through me so deep it iced my veins.

I talked to Teri, then Sadie. Sadie wanted Forrest to get pediatric counseling and for us to keep him away from Emma in the meantime. Teri reluctantly agreed, and after a year or so, it seemed like we'd gotten everything under control. But then there were other things.

Three years later, Emma couldn't find her special lovey, the stuffed dog she sleeps with. Sadie and I searched the house for over an hour while Emma cried in her bed. Ultimately, Forrest admitted to hiding Night Doggie in the dryer. The next year, Emma got a dollhouse from Santa, and some *really bad elf* smashed in its roof before she found it on Christmas morning. Sadie and I both knew it was Forrest.

Forrest always got punished for his misdeeds by receiving time out, or having his privileges revoked. I thought he was finally getting better. At least with regard to Emma. I know Sadie's been working extra hard at having the two of them get along. She's tried to engage them in joint activities with her, like crafts or building gingerbread houses. Emma's all in. Forrest is extremely bored.

I've been trying too, challenging them to Jenga matches and helping them build boxcars. Teaching them about the wilderness while taking them on hikes. Sadie and I are super careful to never show any kind of favoritism between them, and we do tons of fun family stuff together. Go to amusement parks, the state fair, on camping trips, to the movies. But the fact remains that Emma lives here all the time, and Forrest doesn't.

Maybe whatever Teri wants to see me about has nothing to do with Emma this time? One way or another, we'll find a solution to the problem together. Teri and I are both smart people, and I love my son very much. A very deep—and private—part of me still loves Teri too. How can I not with everything the two of us have been through together? Teri's a good person and a great mom. She gives Forrest all she's got, and she always has.

She just never made enough space in her heart for me.

TERESA
THE EX-WIFE

Day One

I drive to the observatory and enter my office, getting things organized. I open filing cabinet drawers and pull out color-coded folders, laying them on my desk. My fingers tremble as I open my laptop. This is not where I thought things were going last week.. I've got to make accommodations for my job. And quickly.

Shit.

I need to make arrangements for Forrest too.

I've got an interior office with no windows. There've been times where I've valued my privacy. Today, the four walls feel confining, closing in on me so I can't breathe. Nobody will understand my actions at this point. Not even Allen. *Crap.*

Maybe with time. When all this passes.

Maybe he'll forgive me.

Maybe I'll find a way to forgive myself.

I open my university Blackboard account, downloading my syllabi and lesson plans. I download detailed notes on my research in progress too. My talented lab assistants can keep up my work, and the school will get someone to fill in with my classes.

It's an emergency. They'll understand.

"Dr. Wilson?" Henry stands in the open doorway. He's an older grad student and my senior research assistant and wears large round glasses with a plaid button-down shirt and jeans. He smiles. "Didn't expect you here today. Aren't you teaching?"

"Ah, yes!" I smile brightly. That's one class the students will be glad to miss, I'm guessing. "On my way there now." I tidy up some paperwork and shut my laptop, shoving things into my satchel.

"That's good," he jokes lightly. "Wouldn't want to run late."

Ha. Wouldn't want to run at all.

Except.

I may not have a choice.

Fucking cameras.

SADIE
THE MOM

Three days before.

I'm at the grocery store shopping for the week and Emma's open house tomorrow. She's not enthused about going, but Allen and I have been trying to put a good spin on the evening, saying it's going to be so much fun to see her room and meet her teachers. There are various things students are supposed to supply and deliver at the open house, like boxes of tissues, and rice for math projects. I purchased other items on her list—colored markers, a pencil sleeve, and marble notebooks—at an office-supply store earlier.

She sits in the well of the shopping basket in her pink shorts and pink-and-white striped shirt, her knees bunched up in her arms. Even though she's small, she's a bit big for the baby seat up front, and I don't want her walking beside me. It would be too easy for her to slip away. Too simple for someone else to snatch her while my back is turned.

A shiver tears through me and I think of Cass. Maybe I made too much of things, and misjudged her? I'll probably never know. I doubt she'll invite Emma over a second time, and I'm not inviting Bobby to our house—ever.

If there is a Bobby. Twisted.

I go through my shopping list, picking out things for our different dinners, Emma's school lunches and snacks.

"Mommy?" she asks, pointing to the stationery aisle. "Can I have a sticker book?" She's such a sweetheart and almost never misbehaves. I can't help spoiling her. I feel the urge to spoil her extra much today, since she's so worried about school and the open house.

"Of course you can!" I wheel the shopping basket over so she can take a closer look. She selects something with ponies on the front cover, pointing with her tiny finger. I lift it from the rack and hand it to her. "Madam," I say with a flourish. "It's all yours."

She giggles. "Thanks, Mommy."

I don't think any more of it until we're checking out with the cashier.

Our bagger's thin with light hair and light eyes. He's got a long bushy beard and tattooed arms and is maybe in his late thirties? He looks out of place here, like he might be better suited to a different sort of job. Something corporate or professional—if he shaved.

I smile at him but don't let my gaze linger.

Until I see him staring at my child. Hairs prickle the back of my neck. I get the same goose-bumpy feeling I did with Cass. Like this person can't be trusted around my child. Maybe no one can. Maybe I shouldn't be sending her to school. Maybe we're making a mistake.

"Ooh, My Little Pony," he says, dropping the sticker book in a bag. "Good choice!" My insides go squirmy. He cocks his head at her. "What's your name?"

"Thanks!" I say, interrupting. "I'll do that."

I scoot my shopping basket to the end of the checkout counter and begin bagging things myself. I'm fumbling with the groceries, making an awkward mess of things, but I don't care if I'm being rude. Those alarm bells went off so shockingly loud in my head I can still feel the blast. I was not much older than Emma when a middle-aged man approached me and my best friend, Amy, in our neighborhood when we were outside playing alone. He smelled of booze and wore a loosely fitting trench coat. Even at six, I knew that was an odd choice for July.

"Hey, girls, how are y'all this morning?"

He leans forward to peer into my eyes and Amy's.

I don't like him. He's scary.

"What're your names?"

It's then I see his trench coat's open, and he's got no clothes on underneath it. His naked body's disgusting. All fat rolls and glistening sweat. Something weird's clutched in his fingers. His arm moves up and down.

A bolt of terror shoots through me and I grab Amy's hand. She hasn't seen what I have. I yank her harder. "Let's go!"

My heart pounds, and my tummy feels sick.

We run and run and run, but never tell our parents. I don't know why. We're afraid. Think we'll get in trouble.

"Don't talk to strangers," our parents said.

We didn't.

Sometimes strangers speak to kids.

My forehead's hot as I cram things into bags.

The cashier shrugs. She's older and matter of fact. "Be grateful for the break," she tells the bagger. He shakes his head and glares at me—a moment too long.

My heart beats like a kettledrum, but I act like I don't notice.

"Not cool, lady," the bagger grumbles and walks away.

Maybe I overreacted due to my past. Or maybe I'm still freaked from the failed playdate episode with Cass. But a mom can't be too careful these days. Everybody knows that. It doesn't matter where you live. Scary people are everywhere. Even in the nicest stores, best neighborhoods, and finest schools. Sometimes they're right under our noses, where we least expect.

ALLEN
THE DAD

Two days before.

We have dinner at the kitchen table. Hamburgers and curly fries, Emma's favorite meal. The sun drops lower outdoors, casting a golden hue over the backyard as twilight approaches. I'm proud of the play set I built.

Emma's on it almost all the time. Swinging on the swings, barreling down the slide, climbing across the monkey bar structure on top. I put lots of crushed tires underneath it to provide a springy cushion in case of any falls. But Emma won't fall. She's very lithe and has always been extremely coordinated, like a miniature gymnast.

She takes a fry and hangs it playfully from her mouth. "Look, Mommy and Daddy," she mumbles, trying to clench it with her lips. "I'm eating a worm." The springy morsel bounces against her chin.

She's such a goofball, but I love that about her. Having kids is fun. They're always full of surprises.

"Em-*ma*!" Sadie shouts, but she's laughing, holding her sides with her hands. "Stop that!" I love Sadie's laugh. It makes her appear even more beautiful than she already is, and that says a lot. I fell for Sadie on the first day I met her at our mutual friend Pat's wedding. I've been head over heels for her ever since.

I sidle up to the bar at the reception, standing next to a very attractive blonde. The event's being held at a fancy country club. There are at least five hundred people here and the room is crowded, peppered with chitchat and the sound of glasses clinking, laughter.

"Are you with the bride's side or the bride's?" I ask as we wait for our drinks. We've sandwiched ourselves in between several others vying for the bartenders' attention.

She laughs and her eyes twinkle. "I'm Patricia's friend. You?"

"Yeah? Me too."

My grad school friend Pat is marrying for the second time. Her new partner's Andrea and I swear I've never seen two people so happy together in my life. If I were the weeping sort, I'd have cried buckets at their wedding.

Sadie flips back her honey-blond hair, pushing it over her bare shoulders. She's in a strapless blue dress. Tasteful but very sexy with strappy high heels. She's got dynamite legs. "You're not Allen?" She covers her mouth and gasps. "Oh my gosh. You're that guy!"

I rake a hand through my hair, unsure if I should be pleased or affronted. Nobody wants to be "that guy" unless that guy is a good guy and the right guy. "Which guy is that?"

"Pat's 'very handsome friend.'" She makes quotation marks with her fingers. "The one Pat's been trying to introduce me to."

I laugh and lay my hand against my chest. "Guilty as charged, I guess." I'm curious about this beauty with big brown eyes. "How come Pat's never told me about you?"

She shrugs flirtatiously. "Maybe she was waiting to see how I felt first?"

Our drinks arrive and we both pick them up. "And how do you feel?"

"I feel like—I might be tempted to dance if you ask me." The music's loud and pulsing. There's a live band. The dance floor's packed.

Oops. "Uh, no. Sorry. No can do." *I hold up one hand and speak above the noise.* "Dancing's not my thing."

She sets one hand on her hip. "It's not an Olympic sport, dude." *She cutely rolls her eyes. How can I resist her?* "It's just moving to the music."

"What if I step on your feet?"

"You won't."

"You seem awfully confident about that."

"That's because I plan to keep a wide berth," *she teases.* "Leave at least eighteen inches of space between us. Room for Jesus, as the Baptists say."

I belly laugh at her joke.

She huffs out a breath. "It's not like we'll be slow dancing, for goodness' sake." *She says it like a dare, baiting me. Waiting to see how I'll react.*

I stare straight into her eyes. "No?"

Electricity crackles between us.

Her cheeks turn pink. "Of course not." *She sounds breathy.*

I know then and there I'll move heaven and earth to hold her. Jesus will just have to step aside. We're slow dancing by the end of the evening, and kissing. A lot. The flowing champagne helps. We wind up in bed and I'm sure I've found my other half. The very special part of my heart that I didn't know I was missing.

Emma slurps the curly fry into her mouth and giggles. "It's yummy." It leaves a trail of ketchup on her chin and Sadie reaches over to wipe it off with a napkin.

"*Emma,*" she chides lightly, but it's all in fun.

We're eating early with the school open house being tonight, so Sadie and I are skipping our usual dinnertime wine. Maybe we'll finish the bordeaux Cass brought by when we get back and once Emma's in bed.

Sadie's experience with Cass was odd, but there's probably a logical explanation for her kid not being home at the time Sadie and Emma came by. Sadie's always been protective of Emma, but she seems to be going overboard with her mama bear instincts these days. I know it's about Emma and her first day of school. Once school's underway and Emma's happily acclimated, Sadie will feel better.

"I like your new haircut," I tell our girl. "It's very grown up." Sadie says the style's called a lob, longer in front and shorter in back. The front part hits Emma's shoulders. Her hair's honey yellow, the color of straw.

She pouts, acting ornery. "I don't want to be grown up. I want to live here forever and ever with you and Mommy."

I chuckle. I know this is a childhood thought. She'll be eager to move out once she gets to high school. Maybe from the time she turns sixteen and gets her driver's license. "Don't you want to have your own house someday?"

She stubbornly crosses her arms. "No." When she becomes defiant, she looks just like Sadie. My two stubborn girls. How did I get this lucky? My life is blessed.

"What about a husband," Sadie asks sweetly, "or a partner?" She glances at me and winks. "Kids?"

Emma grins from ear to ear like she's arrived at a new idea all on her own. "We'll all live here with you!"

Sadie lifts her iced tea glass and takes a sip. "Well *that* would be lovely."

I lean toward her and quip, "And crowded. I mean, come on. Our house is big, but it's not a mansion." Only four bedrooms, and one's my study. We've got our master and Emma has her room. We've only got one guest room.

Sadie plays along with Emma. "We'll manage." She thoughtfully narrows her eyes. "Maybe we'll remodel the playroom and make it a kids' room with double bunk beds?" She turns up her hands. "Possibly convert the garage into a second master suite for Emma and her mate. We can put in a whirlpool tub like the one in our bathroom."

Emma raises both fists in victory. "Yay!" She's such a munchkin. So cute.

"Those sound like options," I tease Sadie. Then whisper, "Expensive ones." We're not exactly hurting for money, but we're not rich either. Just comfortably upper middle class, and I'm great with that. I've got everything I've ever wanted right here within these four walls. My gorgeous wife, my perfect kid, my family.

Sadie laughs and swats my arm. "Oh shush." Waning sunlight washes in through the window, spreading across the table as dusk blooms. Sadie and I both work on finishing our dinners, aware we'll need to head out to Stonefield soon.

I tap my watch with my finger as a signal, and Sadie nods.

Emma sinks her teeth into her hamburger, noting our parental exchange. "Do I have to go to the school open house?" she moans.

We know she'd love to get out of it, but we're not letting her.

Sadie and I both say, "*Yes.*"

ALLEN
THE DAD

Two days before.

I walk Emma over to see the teachers Sadie and I met at parent orientation night, Kate Davis and her older assistant teacher, Dotti Gilmore, whom the kids call Miss Dotti. Both are friendly, and the other children take to them instantly. When I lead Emma toward Kate, she resists. It's embarrassing to feel like I'm dragging her along like a puppy balking on her leash. Tugging back, trying to get away.

"You must be Emma?" Kate smiles but Emma doesn't. "I can't wait to have you in my class." Emma's hand trembles in mine, and my heart thuds. She's really terrified of coming to school, poor kid. I hope she gets over it on the first day.

Kate senses her reluctance and bends toward her, resting her hands on her knees. "We're going to have so much fun, you and I," she says cheerily. "I promise." She motions toward a grouping of four desks. "Why don't you go find where you're sitting and maybe go over to the play area?" Other kids are there, banging in and out of the plastic log cabin's door. One boy sticks his hand in a terrarium and takes out the turtle.

"Ah, ah, ah," Miss Dotti says warmly. "Let's put Timmy the Turtle back for now. You'll get a chance to hold him later." She's got both hands on her hips, a staunch protector of classroom pets.

I'll bet she's a lot of fun. Someone who gets down on the floor to play with the kids. The older woman and the young teacher seem to balance each other well in the classroom. They make a good team.

The boy looks up. "For real?"

"Really and truly!" She's got on a large colorful blouse and interesting bookworm earrings and seems grandmotherly but firm. "As soon as we learn the rules."

The kid obeys, setting the turtle down gently. "Okay."

"Look, Em!" Sadie finds her desk. "This is where you're sitting."

We meander that way and Emma frowns.

Sadie and I exchange glances. Her brow is furrowed. She's worried. She's been worried about Emma going to school for weeks.

"Maybe she's too young, Allen? She's small for her age. Maybe we should hold her back?" We're at the breakfast table completing Emma's first-day-of-school paperwork. They need her medical information, names and numbers of doctors, and emergency contact persons.

We list Pat and Andrea. They say they're happy to fill that role and we trust them. They don't live close by, but close enough to get here if need be. In the meantime, Teri can fill in. We asked her too, and she said of course. She lives as close to the school as we do, and the observatory's not far away. She could be there in a flash.

I understand Sadie's concerns but the time to address them was when we signed Emma up to begin with, not now. The day before her open house and less than a week before the start of school. "Don't you think it's a little late for second-guessing?" I ask her. "Emma's so bright. Academically, she's ready."

Sadie's brown eyes glisten. "It's not academics I'm worried about," she says. "It's the social aspect. She was a preemie, Allen. Still catching up in some ways."

"That's true. But we discussed this."

My parents were big sticklers about commitment. They drilled it into my head that when you agreed to do a certain thing, you stuck it out. Didn't change your mind and back down. A promise is a promise, that kind of thing.

I stare at my child wondering if I was being too pigheaded about that. Maybe I should have listened to Sadie, and we should have talked it over more. But we're already here and have brought Emma this far. Changing our minds would only confuse her at this point. Set the wrong example. We Wilsons honor our commitments. That's what we want her to learn.

"Hey, Emma," I say, seeing a few kids playing dress-up. "Why don't you go over there and try on the fire hat?" She does, but it's evidently only to please us.

Sadie whispers fretfully, "Do you think she'll be okay?"

I understand her nerves, I do. This is a big step, Emma going to school for the first time. Our little girl's growing up. *But that's a good thing.* I draw in a deep breath and release it. What we both need to do is take a chill pill. Relax.

Emma tamps a fire hat down on her head and stares at us. Miss Dotti walks over to Emma and squats down, saying something to her. After a few minutes, Emma giggles. She nods at Miss Dotti as they carry on a quiet conversation.

At last. A big grin.

I aim to reassure Sadie as much as I need to reassure myself.

I give her hand a squeeze.

"She'll be fine."

KATE
THE TEACHER

The day before.

I leave my classroom and turn off the light. Everything's ready for tomorrow, the first day of school. I'll be here bright and early, so I'd better get my rest tonight. Tomorrow's going to be a long day for everyone concerned. As a teacher, I'm not supposed to feel this way, I know. I'm supposed to remain impartial and care for all my pupils equally, but I can't help already hating one of the students in my class.

I would say *dislike* because that sounds milder, but *dislike* is not really a word in my personal vocabulary. I don't *like* and *dislike*. That's so tame. My passions run to greater extremes than that. I further wish I could say I *love* as well as hate, because that would lend symmetry. Make me seem more like a normal person.

I'm skilled at turning the face to the public they want to see. I use the same one in my personal life with my boyfriend. It makes things a hell of a lot easier not having to switch back and forth. I'm either my fake self or my true self. The trick is nobody sees my true self but me. I'm superb at hiding her. I've been doing it for years. In college, boys thought Katherine was weird. Maybe because she kept to herself and didn't smile much—as in ever.

Katherine's roommate, Miriah, said she probably wouldn't land a job unless she faked being cheerful, which made Katherine angry. So angry she stole Miriah's phone and smashed it against a rock, before chucking it into the woods. Katherine despised Miriah's upbeat music, forever bleeding out of those crappy earbuds that never fit properly. Almost as much as she hated Miriah's lilting laugh and shining eyes. Katherine also rationally conceded Miriah had a point.

She'd seen all those peppy teachers during her student teaching assignments. They acted like they were constantly on uppers. Oh sure, she saw them grumble, sometimes curse, when parents weren't around and the administration wasn't looking. But as soon as someone of note walked into the room, they changed. The metamorphosis frightened Katherine at first. But then she began practicing in a mirror herself, and she discovered "faking cheerful" wasn't honestly that hard. Faking cheerful had other benefits too, like attracting boys.

By her senior year of college, she was a regular social butterfly, flitting from one sweet source of sugar to the next. But it was also tiresome. Some nights her face literally *hurt*. Yet when she didn't smile, people asked her what she was angry about, which severely pissed her off, making Katherine want to do bad things.

I could sense Emma being wary of Katherine at the student open house, and she had decent reasons for being afraid. While Allen's past is not exactly Emma's *fault*, sometimes the sins of the father *are* visited on the children. *What goes around comes around,* and all that.

Whether he's aware of this fact or not, Allen's got one hell of a lot coming back around to him in the karma department. Being responsible for someone's death is as good as murder.

And no one should get away with murder.

No matter how long ago it was.

SADIE
THE MOM

The night before.

I tuck Emma into bed, my nerves churning. She'll be okay. Of course she will. I can't let her see how worried I am about releasing her into the big bad scary world. Can't transfer this fear. That would be stupid. Self-serving. I need to be the adult in the room, for goodness' sake. Set a positive tone.

I mentally focus on the future. The bright light at the end of this tunnel. As scary as it will be to let her go, my comfort lies on the other side. The knowledge she'll come home. I don't need to dwell on what will happen in between and make myself crazy with worry. I need Emma to feel confident, unafraid.

Emma snuggles down under the covers and I kiss her forehead.

"Excited about school tomorrow?" I smile softly, channeling loving energy.

All good vibes, Sadie. All good vibes.

She shakes her head. "I want to stay here with you, Mommy."

Her sad puppy dog eyes make my heart weep.

"I know you do." I gently stroke her cheek, and her skin's as smooth as satin. "But you'll have fun at school. Make new friends."

"I have Forrest." She's so genuine and sweet. Attaching herself to him like a clinging vine, but he wants to shake her free. Maybe their bond will strengthen over time.

I've been trying every way I know how, although the five-year age gap between her and her half brother presents challenges. I knew this wouldn't be a cakewalk, a blended family. I wanted it just the same. I wanted Allen, and therefore Forrest. I try to love him as best I can. Open my heart when it clamshells shut, saying he's Teresa's son and not mine. That's not true. He's my child too. One day I hope he'll trust that.

I've come to love so many things about him. His strength, his physicality—he's so great at sports—and his sneaky smarts. Even when he's being naughty, I know he's learning and growing. For heaven's sake, he's just a kid. He's Allen's kid too. Because I love Allen, I love his son.

It's honestly not a struggle. The feelings flow naturally like water over a dam, or a river into the ocean. Loving Forrest feels right. It's the natural course of things with family. That's what holds my heart open. The force of emotions rushing through it. It's not always easy but it's worth it. Who wants to live with a closed heart?

Not me. I want to live with a full heart, forever and ever in this house with Emma and Allen. In my adult way, I share her childhood dream. Though I understand her growing up is bound to happen, I want it to be here with me.

Emma presses her tattered stuffed animal against her cheek. It's supposed to be a puppy but stands upright like a teddy bear with stubby legs and arms. Possibly a beagle from its markings? So much of the fur has worn off from her nightly hugs, and it pitifully has no tail.

She loves him to the ends of the earth and won't sleep a wink without him by her side. He was a gift from her auntie Pat.

"Can Night Doggie come to school too?"

I'm tempted to say yes, finagle a way. But I don't want the other kids to laugh at her, or have the teacher mark her as a problem on the very first day. I make a saddy face, pulling down my lips with my fingers. "I think he wants to stay here and keep the bed warm."

She frowns but I pick Night Doggie up, prying him gently from her grasp.

"What's that?" I hold his goofy nose to my ear. It honestly resembles a piggy snout. "You'll do what? Okay!"

I grin at Emma. "Night Doggie says"—I hold him up in the air and place one hand on my hip—"that he wants to wait right here and save your spot."

She giggles and ducks her chin under the covers.

"My spot?"

Her eyebrows shoot up and I lightly bop her on the head with the toy.

"Right here"—I wiggle him down beside her—"in your cozy, warm bed."

She peeks up at me. "Won't you make the bed?"

"Naturally." I set my chin. "But Night Doggie will stay tucked in."

Her eyes sparkle happily. "Okay."

She picks up Night Doggie and says sternly, "Save my spot."

TERESA
THE EX-WIFE

Day One

I need to get Forrest out of here. I've been questioned by the police. Things could only get worse. Who puts cameras on a school bus, for crying out loud? Call me clueless. I should have known. They've got cameras everywhere these days. In dressing rooms. At rest stops. *Fuck.* Thunder rumbles in the distance. A storm is coming.

I call my mom in Virginia.

"Oh my God, Teresa," she says. "I was going to call you. My neighbor saw the news online and told me about the apparent abduction. *Emma*, of all people. How are you holding up?"

I'm in my kitchen with only a few lights on. Shadows stretch across the adjoining great room with exposed wood beams. This A-frame structure is more of a high-end cabin than a house. Allen and I built it this way, our cabin in the woods on five acres. Plenty of room for a child to explore and play. Forrest was only thirteen months old, and the future looked bright. Then Allen left, taking the sunshine with him.

Rain pings against the windows, making sharp ticks against the glass. Double sliding doors lead to the deck, and my gaze roves to the thick cluster of trees. Winds wail and their branches sway sideways. My heart constricts. Emma's out there in that.

"We're not great here," I tell her honestly. "Forrest is having a hard time. I think it might be good for him to get away from all this for a while."

"What about school?" she asks.

"I can write to his teachers, see if they'll provide remote assignments. I know it's an imposition—"

"Don't even think about it," she butts in. I feel her motherly hug from across the miles. "Of course he can come here. Probably good for him to be away from the commotion."

"Yeah," I admit. "I'm worried about what other kids might say to him at school." Forrest has made no secret among his friends about disliking his half sister. What if they make jeering comments? Suggest he helped her disappear?

My pulse quickens.

What if the police intensify their questioning?

Turn a blinding spotlight on me?

"Do you want me to come and get him?" she offers. She's retired from her job at the bank. I know she has the flexibility.

My dad still works as a heart surgeon, but that didn't stop him from breaking her heart. My mom and I have our divorced statuses in common. The difference between us is she's glad to be rid of her husband. I'm not. Allen never cheated on me the way my dad did on her. I guess I cheated on Allen more, emotionally. I was just too myopic about my career to see it.

I'd never do that to Allen again, given a second chance.

"That would be great if you really don't mind?"

"Not at all," she says. "I'll come first thing tomorrow."

We hang up and I climb the wooden stairs to talk to Forrest. He's in his room sitting on the floor, his back against his bed, his knees bent up and head bowed forward. Glued to something on his phone. He hears me come in and looks up.

"It's all over the news," he says. "About Emma." His face is drawn, his eyes weepy, though he doesn't cry.

"I know, hon." I sit down on the floor beside him and lean back against the bed. "It's a really scary time."

"I didn't do it." His voice cracks with a sob and he sniffs.

"Of course you didn't," I say gently.

He stares up and me and through his bangs. "Did you?"

My heart kicks into overdrive. Shit.

"Forrest," I ask quietly. "Why would you think that?"

"Because I know, Mom." He stares right through me with the frightening wisdom of an old sage. "I'm not stupid."

He swallows past a lump in his throat.

"You hate Emma too."

SADIE
THE MOM

Day One

I creep into Emma's room and turn on her dresser lamp. The lamp has a pink-and-white pony base with gold threading that looks like a horse on a carousel rearing up on its hind legs. A plush lavender cushion lines the window seat facing the street. The area's crowded with stuffed animals of all kinds and a kid-size bookshelf teems with storybook classics, some of them from Allen's childhood and mine.

There's a large dollhouse in one corner, but no dolls to go with it. It's the sort filled with miniature furnishings that Emma likes moving around. Emma's not big on dolls. She loves animals, horses especially. Small stables stand in the corner opposite the dollhouse. She has a collection of toy horses with tiny grooming equipment. All have realistic-looking hair and manes, bridles and saddles. Allen and I have discussed letting her take riding lessons when she's older.

My heart catches in my throat. The uncertain future fills me with dread.

Lightning crackles across the sky outside her window and thunder booms.

Rain pounds the roof, devastating my soul.

She's alone in this. Afraid.

I want her to have shelter, to be safe and warm. I need for someone to be taking care of her. Somebody gentle and caring. Not some monster with who knows what kind of intentions. I'm sick again at the thought. I've got a permanent knot in my throat that won't move up or down. I don't know how I'm breathing. I can barely swallow. Drinking water hurts.

It's after eleven o'clock but the day's been interminably long. It's unfathomable that it was only this morning that I put Emma on the bus. Allen and I went through the motions of eating diner. We fixed sandwiches. Neither of us ate much. We tuned in to the late-night news and watched our news conference in silence.

It was surreal.

"So please," I say on the screen. I try to hold in my tears but fail. I sniff and dab at my eyes with a tissue. My face is so puffy I'm almost unrecognizable. "If you see anything or know anything, contact the police."

There's a photo of Emma transposed above us on the screen. A box beside it gives Emma's name, height and weight, her birthday.

"Even anonymously," Allen adds, because that's how O'Reilly coached us. He said that way we'd get more leads, even if some are from crackpots. "Please help us find Emma." Allen looks like he's been through a war, but our battles aren't over yet. We both know that.

Emma's bed is made with a fluffy lilac comforter settled on top, but the top sheet and blanket are folded back. Pink and purple heart-shaped throw pillows cozy up the spot where Night Doggie sits tucked in, staring. Waiting.

Waiting for Emma.
Saving her spot.
Oh God.

Oh God.

Where's my baby girl?

I take the stuffed toy and hold it to my heart. Anguish detonates inside me like an atomic bomb, blowing my insides apart. My organs ignite, my lungs fail, radioactive. Charred, so I can't breathe. *She was so terrified of school, but we made her go. She wanted to stay a child, but I pushed her. Cut her hair.* I clutch Night Doggie harder and wail. *I was out of my mind to put her on that bus. How could I? I'm the world's most horrible person. The vilest creature on earth.*

I know I'm screaming but my eyes are shut. They're swollen and sting. I'm racked with sobs. My shoulders shake.

"Sadie?" Allen's arms around me. Strong, warm. "Come here."

His heart drums against mine.

We're on an island of shattered dreams and fear.

"Allen?" I sob and sob again. "Why?"

His embrace tightens. "I don't know."

O'REILLY
THE COP

Day One

I come home from work beat, and glad to get out of my uniform. We've got a nice apartment in an old converted house built somewhere in the nineteen forties and less than a mile from the campus. There are only four units here, two upstairs and two down. We're on the second floor, overlooking the street. A streetlamp glows beyond the drawn shade and I hear college kids chatting loudly and meandering toward the bars on the cracked sidewalk below.

The neighbors like that I park my cop car on the shady street. It makes them feel secure. Still, stuff happens. Maybe not as much as it would otherwise. It's not easy keeping the world safe. I learned that in the Marines. Semper fi.

Kate walks into the bedroom as I strip off my shirt. "Hey, babe," I say. "How're you holding up?" I know her day was crap like mine. She must feel horrible about a kid in her class getting abducted. Jesus. She's dating a cop. What are the odds?

She sighs. "Eventful." A second later she frowns. "And sad." She's casual in shorts and a tank top, out of her teacher clothes, and her hair's in a ponytail. It's chestnut colored like her eyes. Kate's got pretty eyes and a beautiful face with long eyelashes and heavy eyebrows.

It's good she was cleared of any involvement so quickly. Claremont would have my head if she knew I'm dating Emma's teacher, which is why I'm not telling her. Anything changes, I will. I'm not morally bereft. I'd always come down on the side of the kid.

Though it stretches the imagination to believe Kate could have anything to do with Emma's disappearance. She's a teacher for Christ's sake. She loves kids. That's one of the things I find so attractive about her. Kate's got a good heart. Besides which, why would she do anything to harm Emma? Just some random kid in her class? No. It's completely nonsensical.

We had a big thunder-boomer about an hour ago, and all I could think of was that little girl being out there somewhere in the dark, and frightened. Missing her mom and dad. Crying to go home. I heave a sigh and sit on the bed to remove my shoes. "Yeah. Same."

I drop one on the floor and then the other, and yank off my socks. I've already removed my duty belt and locked my weapons away. The vest comes next. I stayed late at the station combing through leads generated by the press conference. Unfortunately, none proved useful. I'll speak with the neighbor, Cass Thomas, tomorrow. Claremont didn't have to ask—I volunteered.

We finish the press interview, and the television news crews stroll away. Reporters were here from the local paper and a large regional paper. A radio interviewer too. The Wilsons both made heartfelt pleas for Emma's return. I don't know if it will help, if anything will help, but we've got to try everything. No stone unturned.

"It's been a long day," Claremont says to Sadie and Allen. "You two should go home and get some rest." They're exhausted and it shows, but they probably won't sleep. Maybe they'll never sleep again. "We'll be in touch the

minute there's news. Meanwhile, if you think of anything, or anyone else we should talk to?"

Sadie looks like she's on the verge of saying something. Now's not the time for self-doubt. She needs to spill it. "Yes!" *She stops Claremont before we go. The chief and I turn back around.* "I've got this neighbor." *I can tell she feels stupid about sharing this, like she's grasping at straws.* "I think she's kind of weird."

If everyone reported those . . .

I rake a hand across my buzz cut. "What makes you suspicious of this one, exactly?"

"I've got nothing concrete." *Worry shows in her eyes.* "She asked Emma over for a playdate, but then her kid wasn't home." *She shrugs, wondering if she's making too much of it. She's not. If a mom thinks it's important, it probably is. Every detail counts.*

"Give me her name," *Claremont says.* "We'll look into it." *Both she and I are aware there could be reasonable excuses for the kid not being there at that specific time, but the situation does seem fishy and worth investigating.*

Sadie nervously gnaws at her lip. She clearly doesn't want the police showing up at Cass Thomas's after she's apparently ratted her out.

"Discreetly," *Claremont adds to reassure her.* "She doesn't have to know you said anything about her to the police. Emma's disappearance is public knowledge now. We'll say we're speaking with the neighbors about what they know."

"Great, thanks." *Sadie sighs and Allen wraps his arm around her shoulder. They seem tight. Like they're together in this, but I'm not cementing any judgments yet. You never know.*

Kate comes and sits beside me on the bed. "Nothing on the kid?" she asks. I know she's concerned, as any reasonable individual would be.

I shake my head. This is my least favorite part of the job. Coming from a big Irish Catholic family, anything to do with kids being endangered puts me through the wringer. Every one of them could be Rosie, or Kayleigh, or Declan. I'd rather chase down drug-dealing thugs any day. At least then it's a fair fight. With these kids, they're outmatched.

Someday when I've got kids, I want to teach them to be badass. Really tough, you know? Like we were growing up in Philly, so nobody messes with them. I bet lots of parents feel that way before their kid goes missing. Crap. This is hard. I saw Sadie and Allen outside the school and her shouting Emma's name into the woods. Tear my heart out and burn it, why don't ya? Just torch it. Come on. Don't hold back.

Kate drags a hand down my arm, appreciating my muscles. "Penny for your thoughts?" The bedroom's kind of messy. The rest of the apartment is too. Neither Kate nor I are neatniks and that's okay. In that way, we get along. We don't leave dishes lying around though. That's our cardinal rule. The bugs are fucking huge in North Carolina. Warm winters and plenty of sunshine. It's the South.

My mind returns to the case, and Emma. "I can't say much. You know that."

"I know, but at least tell me they've got a suspect." She's being awfully curious about this, but I guess I can't blame her. If I were in her shoes, I'd want to know too. She tickles the crook of my arm with her finger.

"Stop!" I laugh and grab her hand.

"*O'-Reilly.*" The way she says my name gives me a hard-on. She loves that I'm a cop, and I *love* that she loves that. "I've got a stake in this too."

"I know, babe." I kiss her. She's so sweet and caring. "Still. Procedure."

"Procedure, smocedure." She gives a huff that blows back a strand of her hair. She's a very beautiful woman, no matter what she's wearing. She's also fucking cute. She cracks me up with her antics.

"For a teacher," I say, "you're awfully good at making up words."

"That's what teachers do!" She squares her shoulders, looking proud. "We're creative."

I lean toward her, my arm brushing hers. "Yep. You're that. And smart. And gorgeous."

"Oh please, oh please, oh please." She fakes going breathy. "Tell me more."

I chuckle and thumb her nose. "What'd you have for dinner?"

"Burritos," she says like she prepared filet mignon. "I saved you some."

She makes me happy just looking at her. It's like being in the presence of the sun after wading through the darkness. I wrap my arms around her in a bear hug. "I'll burrito you."

"Shane, stop!" She laughs but she's squirming, trying to get away. Maybe sex will take the edge off and help me focus on what's good and right. Today wrung me out like a rag and tomorrow could be even tougher, depending on what we do—or don't—find.

I bring my mouth down on hers and she stops trying to get away, sliding her palms up to hold my face. She kisses me good and hard, and I return it, all tongue and fire. I know we're going to have sex and it's going to be good. Sex with Kate always is. Heat pulses through me as I ease her back on the bed.

Christ, what a day.

I hope the kid's okay.

SADIE
THE MOM

Day Two

I wake up in the middle of the night, thunder booming. The timbre of the rain's deafening, drowning out the drumbeats of my heart. Galloping like a million horses' hooves against the roof. Lightning tears up the room and a jagged white bolt crosses Allen's face. His cheeks are sunken, his eyes hollow. Allen stands by the window staring outdoors.

The blinds are raised, and rain curses the glass, obscenities rage in the wind. The world's angry, railing against us. It takes me a moment to know where we are. In our bedroom upstairs. In our new house. "Allen?" I'm groggy, my mind coming into focus. "What are you doing?" Then I remember.

Emma. No.

The truth slams down on me like a ten-ton weight. Our child is missing, kidnapped. Someone horrible has taken her away and it's all my fault. I fed our child to the wolves, turned her loose in the wild. *How could I?* I clutch my heart, my breath catching. I think I might suffocate. My lungs collapse like a bellows suddenly squeezed shut.

I'm in a car that's gone over a bridge and plunged into the frigid depths. Plummeting down, down, down to the rocky bottom of the sea. A graveyard of lost hope and missing children. I crash with a jolt and stare down at my clothes. I'm still dressed, wearing what I put on yesterday. I don't remember crawling into bed. Did I fall asleep somewhere else?

Yes.

I'm in Emma's room, lying on her bed. Curled into a fetal position, Night Doggie pressed to my chest. Sobs rack my breath. My tears soak her pillow. Who's taken my baby girl? I wish I could know who. Please, let it be someone kind. The right kind of people looking after her and not—oh God.

Her dresser light's turned on, but all I see is blackness. The deep, deep well of my despair. My cries echo endlessly as I fall into the pit of the earth. Dirt caves in around me. Damp. Wet. Smelling of worms.

"Sadie?" Allen's gentle touch on my shoulder. "Come on, hon, let's go to bed."

But I'm not leaving here. Not leaving Emma. I'm waiting with Night Doggie, saving her spot. Growing dizzy, feeling faint. A shovel digs in with a crunch, and earth pours on top of me. Moldy and wet. My eyes burn and sting. My fingers grip her stuffed toy, as I weep and weep and weep. I think I'm dead.

And then, I'm here.

"Did you move me?" I ask Allen.

He turns away from the rain-streaked glass. It's been storming off and on all evening. I'm aware of that somehow, even though reality seems to have slipped away. "Yeah." Is he really only thirty-eight? He looks so much older somehow. We've both aged exponentially in one day.

"What time is it?" The room is cloaked in shadows.

"Three a.m."

"Have you slept?" I ask, knowing he hasn't.

He hangs his head.

"Allen?"

"I just want to bring her home." The tremor in his voice shakes me to my core.

My heart breaks for both of us. "Me too."

He rakes both hands through his hair. "I feel guilty," he says. "Like there's something more I should have done. Like I've let her down, you know?" His face is haunted with remorse, the ghosts of his failings. I've had mine too. *So many* and they gut me.

"You couldn't have known." But I get what he's saying. I feel exactly how he does.

"The police seem to think it's someone we know." He says it like he can't believe it. A lightning flash. Thunder. More rain drumming.

"What do you think?" I ask softly.

I have the feeling he's thinking about Teresa.

"I hope they're wrong."

KATE
THE TEACHER

Day Two

I lie in bed next to Shane listening to his deep rumbling snore. It's not loud and annoying, but soothing and low, normally lulling me to sleep. But tonight I'm restless thinking about Allen and the damage he's done. Shane shifts under the covers, pulling me closer, spooning me in his strong embrace and cradling my back against his rock-hard chest. I feel bad about him being caught up in this mess. Shane's a good guy and this case is eating him alive. I can see it.

The whole town's been stood on end, with everyone in a tizzy over Emma's disappearance, fretting about the well-being of the missing child. But they don't know her dad the way I do. Can't see how he deserved this. People talk about losing a spouse or parents. God forbid, losing a child. And sure, that's tough. But no one ever talks about losing a sister. *About children losing children.* No one prepares you to handle that when you're eight years old.

When Diane died, people sent flowers to the church and cards to my parents. Nothing ever came for me or Mark. Diane was one year younger than Mark and he took her death very hard. Looking back, I guess Mark and Diane were more than siblings. They were good friends.

Things would have been okay if Allen hadn't gotten between them, and messed things up. Mark self-destructed after Diane died.

Mark was supposed to be college bound, but he started doing a bunch of drugs. He's a junkie now, and in and out of halfway houses. I only heard from him periodically over the years, and then he completely lost touch. I don't even know where he lives anymore. Last time I heard, he'd moved to Florida. It's like I've lost him too.

That's not *all* on Allen, I know. *But* the burden of blame *is* his. If he hadn't been with my sister that night, Diane would still be alive. My home wouldn't have broken up with my parents constantly attacking each other.

After the divorce, my dad remarried and began a brand-new life with a brand-new wife. I hate it when people do that, erasing the kids they had before. Now Allen's done the same thing. Oh sure, he's here for Forrest, but he doesn't love him the way he does Emma. I can tell. Everyone can tell. It's obvious.

When I officially met Allen at parent orientation night, the memories came rushing back. I wanted to blank them out like a terrifying nightmare. Hold back the floodgates. But Katherine couldn't. Katherine used to fantasize about how she'd get even. How she'd settle the score on behalf of our sister. Then Katherine saw Emma on my new-student roster for this year and she sensed an uncanny opportunity. The universe aligning itself in just the right way. She wanted Allen to *pay* for Diane losing her life.

TERESA
THE EX-WIFE

Day Two

My mom arrives super early. She left Virginia in the middle of the night, fueled up on candy bars and coffee. She texted me she was leaving at four a.m. She's always been here for me. Such a good mom. Even when she was still working, she was the kind who would come at the drop of a hat. I've always wanted to be that kind of mom for Forrest, but now I don't know if I can. I've made such colossal mistakes, I'm afraid they'll bury me.

But I don't want them to bury Forrest.

I need my child to live.

"Mom." I hug her when she gets out of her car. "You didn't have to do this."

Dawn is just breaking, sunlight spreading through the trees. Mourning doves call from the roof, and birds chirp on tree branches. The sky's clear blue with white cirrus clouds pulling themselves apart like wispy threads of cotton candy. The scent of yesterday's rain rises from the earth. A fresh start after the storm.

She squeezes me in her loving embrace. "I know. But you've probably got work today, yeah?" She holds me by the shoulders and stands back to scan my face.

I look a lot like her, or at least a lot like she used to when she was my age. She's cut her hair to her shoulders, and it's layered. Colored dark brown with auburn highlights like mine. Wrinkles settle around her mouth and eyes. "Tell me about Allen," she says, keeping her voice down. "I don't want to ask in front of Forrest when we're in the house. How's he handling this?"

"I guess as well as could be expected." I wipe a tear that leaks from my eye, aware of the pain he's going through. Wishing I could be there to hold his hand. Reassure him that dark days will pass. After this storm blows over, maybe we'll get another chance.

I didn't believe I could have one until a week ago when Allen gave me hope. I hang onto that hope like a life raft on a tortured ocean, possibilities and fear cresting like white-capped waves. If things break one way, we could start a new life together in our safe harbor. If they break another, I'm lost at sea.

"Oh my gosh, honey." She frowns and strokes my cheek. "You still love him?"

I sniff. I can't lie to Mom. She always knows, and so I tell the truth. "I do."

"You don't think there will ever be a way?" she asks. She searches my eyes. "Not with this tragic situation?" She stops dead in her tracks and stares at me. It's like she's crawled into my head and knows what I've been thinking. Shit.

"Teresa." She gasps. "You didn't have anything to do with it?"

"For God's sake, Mom," I testily reply. Better to sound angry, hurt, than reveal my vulnerability. "I expected better of you."

She blinks back her tears. Rubs my upper arms with her hands. "I'm sorry, hon. That was a stupid thing to say. Forgive me."

How could she think that?

Why would she think that?

My gut wrenches.

My ten-year-old son thinks that too.

It won't take long for the police to form the same conclusion.

And if they start looking too closely, I'm fucked.

SADIE
THE MOM

Day Two

I open my eyes and it's the morning. The blinds on one of the windows facing the backyard remain raised. Bright glimmers of sunlight blind me. I shield my eyes with my hand and scoot myself upright into a sitting position so the sun's not on my face. It hits the bunched-up covers near my pillow instead and I swing my feet to the floor, getting my bearings.

I feel guilty for sleeping, even if it was only for a few hours. How could I sleep at all? I need to find a way to undo this thing. To get back Emma. I should have never put her on that bus. Never, never, never, never, never.

I remember waking in the middle of the night.

Allen said it was three a.m.

He comes away from the window and sits with me on the bed.

I stare at him numbly, my mind still fuzzy from my labored sleep. "This can't be happening, it can't."

"I know." He hugs me close, and I hold him tightly.

We both give way to our tears.
At some point we lie down, and he nestles me in his arms.
"We should probably change out of our clothes," he says.
His voice is drifting. My mind is drifting too, fading away into a no-man's-land where time and space dissolve.
All of me is weighted down, heavy.
My arms, legs, eyelids.
My body's a bag of sand.

I stare down at what I'm wearing and see that I slept in the clothes I threw on hastily yesterday before going to the police station with Allen. They're rumpled and uncomfortable, my bra pinching at my back below my T-shirt and the waistband of my jeans creasing my midsection. I must have dozed off again from sheer exhaustion.

Allen's not in our bed. I wonder if he got any sleep or whether he spent the rest of the night downstairs, or maybe in Emma's room. I find him at the kitchen table, drinking coffee and staring at his phone. "Anything?" I ask and he looks up.

He shakes his head. "No word yet."

Shit. Why haven't they found her? Why isn't anything happening? One night was enough hell—for my poor baby girl.

For us.

It's just past seven o'clock. Early. But kidnapping honors no timelines. It's merciless in its assault of emotions, and yet. I catch my breath. I'm here and safe in my house and in my kitchen. Allen's safe. *Emma's not.*

The grass outside glistens from last night's heavy rain. The lid to Emma's sandbox is open, turned upside down and lying on the ground. Rainwater pools inside it and droplets gleam on the yellow slide. My heart aches. Did Emma spend last night outdoors? Did she break free from her abductor? Steal into the woods? I hope she found shelter.

Somewhere dry. Even if she did, she must have been terrified. Must still be terrified to be away from her parents, her home.

Rationally, I know it's fantastical to think Emma's gotten away, that she's somehow escaped her kidnapper. You hear tales of children who do, but those children are older, often teens with greater physical strength and ingenuity than Emma. She's just a little girl. So tiny. Fragile like a porcelain doll teetering on a shelf.

If I could reverse her circumstances I would. Sacrifice myself for Emma. Make a bargain with God. Maybe I'll go to church. Talk to a minister or a priest, anyone who will help and listen. Someone with an inside line to the person upstairs. But I can't deal-make our way out of this. I know it. I couldn't save either of my parents from cancer, and Allen couldn't keep from losing his in that boating accident, either.

I hate that Allen lived through such a difficult time, and the knowledge that his parents' death might have been suspicious. The mere *thought* that someone could have been out to harm them intentionally, the way someone's targeted Emma, crushed him intensely. But no, their case was different and, upon investigation, was ruled as an accident. *How the hell did we get to be orphans in our thirties? Our lives are fucking cursed.*

Allen hands me a coffee mug. "Here."

I didn't even notice him standing from the table and walking over to the coffee maker. I'm living in a twilight zone. I feel like a lamp that's been unplugged with no current running through it. I'm not sure how I'm functioning, able to speak or walk. My actions seem robotic. Like I'm running on autopilot. Not fully aware of what I'm doing, or what's happening around me. I accept the coffee mug as Allen sits back down at the table. "Thanks."

I manage a sip and then another. My throat's tender and raw but I force the hot liquid down. I need to be awake to face the day. Alert. For Emma.

We stare out the kitchen window at Emma's play set and my soul whimpers.

Will she ever use it again?

I see her on a swing, gliding happily back and forth with a big sunshiny smile on her face. The wind blows back her hair but she's still wearing her blond pigtails, pumping her legs and calling, "Look at me, Mommy! Look at me!" propelling herself higher and higher like a kite floating toward the heavens, trying to reach the stars.

Emma loves her new play set, and she loves our new house. Her room's crowded with toys, and the playroom above the garage holds even more: a kiddie kitchen set with a table and four chairs, a sturdy playhouse with blue window shutters and a pink door. An indoor slide, a trampoline. Beanbag chairs and a cabinet full of games.

We've spoiled her, I know, but she's our only daughter and it's unlikely we'll have another. We had enough difficulty having her and her birth was traumatic. Her umbilical cord got tangled around her neck during delivery, and she almost didn't make it. If they'd known in time, they would have taken her by cesarean section. Because they didn't, the forceps they used to extract her caused severe uterine damage.

Afterward, she had breathing issues due to having been born early and spent five days in the neonatal ICU. It was touch and go for the two of us, with Allen and I holding each other close while shedding quiet tears in my hospital bed. Still, I wouldn't change those tense early days for the world.

Allen and I pulled through that dark storm together and landed here on the other side. With our wonderful child in this amazing house in probably the best family neighborhood in all of Chapel Roads.

Allen's gaze fixes on the gate at the rear of our yard. It's not quite latched. Did one of us leave it open? Maybe it was me when I hurried away from Cass's house carrying Emma in my arms? No, that was days ago, and I distinctly recall latching it then. I remember thinking I saw someone skulking across our lawn the night of parent orientation, and I shiver. Has she come back to spy on us again? Was it Teresa, or maybe Cass?

"Do you really think she had something to do with it?" he asks. "Cass Thomas? That's so hard for me to believe. In high school, she seemed normal enough."

My mind snags on his phrasing. "I thought you didn't know her at Braxton?"

"I didn't." He centers his fingers around his coffee mug. "I meant, from what I saw." Why do I feel like he's hiding something? Like I'm not getting the full story?

"Well, if you didn't really know her then it's hard to say, isn't it?"

He frowns uncertainly. "Guess so." There's something he's not telling me about high school. Something he knows about Cass.

"Allen," I say. "If you two had a history—"

"Jesus, Sadie," he says sharply, "why is it always about that?"

My mouth hangs open. "About what?"

"We did not have a *history*, okay? She was several years younger than me, and in the ninth grade. I was a senior. We barely talked at all."

I lean toward him. "So you did talk?"

He stares at me exasperated. "Once or twice, sure. Maybe in the hall in passing. Or at a pep rally? I'm not sure. It wasn't a huge school then. And anyway, I don't really see why me having gone to high school with her has *anything* to do with Emma going missing, *or* what happened between the two of you concerning that playdate."

"Sadie, listen to me." He's very serious now, speaking with his eyebrows lowered. "There actually could be a Bobby, you know. You might have gotten that part wrong."

I stare at our rear gate, swinging open on its hinges.

Might have, but I don't think so.

O'REILLY
THE COP

Day Two

We're in the situation room getting briefed by Chief Claremont. There are no windows, only cinder block walls. The air is musty and stale, like we're in a warehouse basement reeking of mildew and sweat. But we're fully above ground, on the first floor in a building near the center of downtown, steps from the art gallery and less than half a mile from city hall.

A large video screen's mounted on the wall behind the chief. She presses a remote and the screen retracts, rolling up into a sleeve and exposing a giant bulletin board. She's got a photo of Emma tacked to it in the center, along with five other photos around the periphery.

Any one of these people could be responsible for Emma's kidnapping. Could be holding her hostage, or worse. It's up to us to determine which one. Every person in this room knows it. Feels the pressure, and the pressure is immense. We've heard from the mayor and the governor. They want action. They want answers—*now*.

So do the parent groups who rallied at the school last night, holding a candlelight vigil for Emma, until their efforts were rained out by the torrential storm. The police aren't being heralded for our efforts, we're being lambasted for not achieving results.

Which is fair. I feel guilty for going home last night. For sleeping. Christ. For having sex with Kate. Maybe I shouldn't have done any of that. Maybe I should have spent all night at the station. Burned the midnight oil. Worked harder.

Even though we had patrols on the street, even with an Amber Alert in force. Even with Rodriguez and Patel pulling all-nighters. I should have been here with them, pulling an all-nighter too. This is not the kind of case you take a break from. This is one you stay with until it's solved. I rub my forehead when it hurts. But who am I to complain about a headache? I've got the fucking luxury to take a painkiller, don't I? That kid's got no luxuries at all.

Mercer's here, leaning his shoulder against the wall near the back of the room, his arms crossed. He's good at hanging back and behaving like he's not important. But the chief and I understand how critical his role is. He's our tie to the feds and a larger cache of resources we can't access in this small community on our own. He's also got great insight into these things. It's very sad to think he's worked a number of these cases. This is my fourth and each one was horrendous. None of them ended well.

Emma's case is going to be different.

Just before the meeting, Mercer called the chief and me aside, sharing an update.

"We've been getting no chatter on our child-trafficking networks," he says. "Which I think bodes well for Emma."

"So the chances of her being caught up in that?" I ask.

Mercer rubs the side of his neck. "I can never say zero, but I'd say we're looking at narrowing the search closer to home."

Claremont and I look at each other knowing what this means. The closer to home we're able to keep this investigation, the more likely it is we can retrieve Emma safely. I'll take all the good news we can get.

I've got a question for Mercer since he's a guy in the know. "I want you to be honest with us." He's clearly worked a number of these cases. "Realistically, what are our chances of finding Emma?"

"Realistically? Fifty fifty." He directly meets my gaze. "Starting tomorrow, our odds go down."

"I don't think I have to tell any of you time is critical," Chief Claremont says. "We're closing in on twenty-four hours." She stares around the room. There are maybe two dozen officers sitting at desks. The station's midsize and this space is also used for training and instruction.

"This is what we know so far. Emma's mom put her on the bus in their family neighborhood at seven fifty a.m. Bus camera footage shows Emma on the bus when it arrived at Stonefield Elementary at approximately eight fifteen a.m. She stands holding her backpack and slips it on her shoulders before becoming engulfed in a sea of taller kids in the aisle. We assume she got off the bus at that point, but none of the school staff can attest to seeing her." Claremont's got our rapt attention. "I think it's fair to say Emma didn't literally disappear. Someone took her."

"School officially starts at eight twenty-five a.m.," Claremont continues. "Attendance is submitted electronically by the teachers on their classroom computers by eight thirty-five a.m. The school office secretary automatically receives the class attendance lists and begins making her calls, starting with absences in kindergarten and working her way up to the fifth grade. The school phone log syncs with Sadie's report that she received the call about Emma being absent from Stonefield at eight thirty-eight a.m."

Claremont points to the bulletin board. "These are our persons of interest."

She taps a photo of a slim brunette with bangs. Attractive, high cheekbones, late thirties. "Ex-wife, Teresa Wilson. Works as an astrophysicist at the observatory. She and Emma's dad, Allen, had one kid together, Forrest. He's ten and also at Stonefield Elementary, where Emma is enrolled. But in the fifth grade. Teresa's the one we've got footage of talking to Emma on the bus. O'Reilly interviewed her." She meets my eyes and I clear my throat.

"Right." I step forward to address the group. "Camera footage shows Teresa on the school bus, taking Emma's backpack and tucking something in an envelope inside its front pocket. The bus driver was interviewed and said his back was turned when that happened. When he saw Teresa on the bus, he demanded she get off at once. She claims she was returning an iPod her son Forrest had lifted from Sadie's office when he was over for a custodial visit. But her story seems fishy. Why not return the iPod to Sadie some other way?

"Plus, she was in a big hurry to get out of the interrogation room. I had the very strong sense she was hiding something, but I had nothing and couldn't hold her. She says she was at work and in her office at the time when Emma disappeared. She was unclear about whether anyone could corroborate her story."

Some of the officers are taking notes. Several will be on patrol today, others here at the station manning their desks.

Claremont points to a second photo of a woman with wavy blond hair, midthirties. "Cass Thomas, the neighbor. Lives directly behind Sadie and Allen. Wife, Sadie, thinks there's something off about her. Cass claims to have a kid, but Sadie hasn't seen him. Cass tried to get Sadie to leave Emma at her house for a supposed playdate when her son wasn't home.

"O'Reilly's headed over there this morning to check her out." She pauses and looks around the room. "We also found a past connection. Cass and the dad, Allen, went to the same high school together. Braxton High. Not sure anything's there. Who wants to look into it?"

A hand shoots up. "Me, chief." It's Rodriguez. She's seasoned and solid. Great investigator.

Claremont nods. "Thanks." She drinks coffee from a paper cup with a lid. She temporarily rests the cup on her lectern.

The next photo's of a guy with shaggy blond hair falling past his shoulders and a long dark bushy beard. I'm guessing in his late thirties.

"Caleb Walsh," she says, lifting her cup toward the screen. "Registered sex offender living near the school."

People exchange glances and she sighs, pulling the photo off the board. "Ironclad alibi. He was at his job. Coworkers vouch for him, so does CCTV."

"What about the parents?" Rodriguez asks. "With missing kids it's often one of them."

"More often than not." Claremont casts a glance at their pics on the board, indicating the pair. "Allen and Sadie Wilson. He works in wealth management. She's got an insurance job she does from home. We've talked to them together. Today, we'll do it separately. Though honestly?" She shakes her head. "I don't see a motive there. Let's dig deeper."

"What about the husband and the ex-wife?" Patel asks. She's a new recruit, and eager. I have a feeling she'll go far. "What's their relationship?"

"Seems cordial," Claremont answers. "Not close. You never know." She scans the group. "Another volunteer to go down the observatory to talk to some of Teresa's coworkers? Cleaning personnel? Someone who can verify Teresa's story? We need to make sure Teresa was where she said she was when Emma disappeared."

Patel waves.

Claremont gives her a thumbs-up.

"Someone else to corroborate the husband's and wife's stories?"

"I'll take Sadie," I say. "I'm going to be in her neighborhood anyway."

Claremont nods. "It's unlikely it's the wife," she tells the room. "There wasn't a lot of time for her to have taken Emma off the bus and then rush home to place the nine-one-one call. Officers Rodriguez and Patel"—she glances at them—"arrived on the scene within minutes."

Mercer pushes himself off the wall and straightens his tie. "Let me work on Allen." His suits are high end but always a touch rumpled. Like he pays for the best brands but then doesn't bother with the dry cleaning.

"Thanks," Claremont says. "Could be a random stranger." She briefly hangs her head and looks up. "Then we're SOL." Officers are recording madly, getting the details down. Some write on paper, others type on their phones.

Rodriguez has another question. "People at the school? Teachers? Custodians? Cafeteria workers? All cleared?" God, the woman's brainy. I'd probably ask her out if I didn't have Kate.

Claremont answers, "O'Reilly and I spoke with everyone who might have encountered Emma at Stonefield. Others corroborate their fellow employees' stories about them being at their posts or in their classrooms at the times they've claimed. But great question, Rodriquez. Thanks for asking."

Someone's won some brownie points today. The smug look on Rodriguez's face says she knows it. We need more people like her.

There's a low murmur as officers confer with one another.

Claremont reins them back in. I know her job's not easy, but she never shows the stress. As far as any of us is aware, she's got no personal life. No partner. No kids. Though I doubt that's true. She just doesn't want this life hemorrhaging into that one. I don't blame her. If I had a family, I'd probably feel the same. Move heaven and earth to protect that sanctuary from the dark shit that goes down in this world.

She squares her shoulders, hands on her hips. She's tough as nails when she needs to be. Everyone respects her because of it. "I want my patrols out there with *eyes*"—she makes a V with her fingers and points to her eyes—"and ears"—her hands cup her ears—"*open*. Pay attention to everything. At this point, we don't know if Emma's dead or alive."

A lump forms in my throat.

"I'm banking on alive." Claremont sets her jaw giving us each a steely stare. She individually meets our eyes, leaving no one out. She's bringing us all on board, building her team. And we'll follow her, she knows that. All the way down the line.

"Let's bring that girl home."

SADIE
THE MOM

Day Two

I sigh heavily finishing my coffee. "I wish we could talk to Cass ourselves." Allen doesn't think she's involved, but I have my doubts. I also have my doubts about Teresa, but I don't voice those again. Every time I do, Allen gets angry, defending her. I'm concerned about the timing of Emma's disappearance. How could it have happened so fast, and why was Teresa *really* on the bus? My gaze flits across the backyard and skims the gate, slightly ajar.

While I was horribly, horribly afraid of Emma being at school, it never occurred to me that something might happen to her *before* the day even got started.

The *second* she got off the bus.

"Yeah, but no," Allen says about us talking to Cass. "Best to let the police handle it." I understand why the police want to conduct any interrogations themselves. They don't want us interfering and possibly making a mistake. But it's brutally painful to wait on the sidelines. I have to do something other than sit around checking my phone.

"Maybe we can make up flyers?" I say to Allen. "Put up a posting online?" The police are doing their part, but they gave us a list of support organizations we can reach out to. The more we can speed things along, the better.

"Great idea." Allen's phone buzzes with a text message. "That's Mercer." He looks up. "He wants me to come in."

"Okay." I take a quick sip of coffee. "I'll get ready." I need to shower quickly and change. My hair's still a mess from yesterday. I'm a mess in general. "I won't take long." I need to stay on top of this investigation. Every instant means more time away from my baby girl. The police have to find her. Why haven't they found her already?

"Not you," he says seriously. "Just me."

"What?"

Allen pushes his chair back from the table. "O'Reilly's coming by to talk to you after he sees Cass. So maybe it's good for you to stay put. You'll want to be here in person to hear what he's learned." Before he goes, Allen kisses the top of my head. "I know it's hard, but we've got to stay strong." He gives my shoulder a squeeze. "For Emma."

It's probably standard to bring in the FBI when kids go missing, but Mercer's involvement fills me with dread. I can't imagine our baby being sucked into something as scary as human trafficking. I see the signs on mirrors at rest stops. Notices urging civilians to stay aware and advise the police of suspicious activity. Maybe the Amber Alert will come through? I cling to the hope that Emma's okay. That whoever's taken her is kind, and not malicious.

I dart a glance at the backyard, feeling creepy about Cass. Could she really have taken our child? I would *sense that*, right? *Feel it*—if Emma were so close? I can't shake the feeling that something's wrong with Cass. That she's jealous of what we have. What I have. Allen, Emma, a family. Is she the one who left the gate ajar? Did she come into our yard to peer into our windows? Keep tabs on us? See how we're handling our trauma? At least if Cass has Emma I can hope that my baby's unharmed. That Cass is looking after her like her own. Like "Bobby."

Hoping for the least bad scenario makes me sick with fear. It's better to dwell on that than the alternatives. My mind and heart can't handle examining those frightening scenarios. Allen's right. We've got to stay strong for Emma. She's going to need us both in one piece when she comes home.

The morning's warm with steam rising off the grass, raindrops giving way to dew speckling Emma's play set. I need to get dressed before O'Reilly comes by, but before he and I speak I want to check something on the internet. I'm not thrilled there's a sex offender living near the school. I'm also not thrilled they let him off so easily without telling us who he is. Maybe I can figure out who he is and then get more details from O'Reilly?

My laptop's on the table. I go online and locate the national registry for my state. It's easy to run a search. I enter my address and select a five-mile radius, as that puts us in the same zone with the school. Icons load on a map. I click one and my stomach roils as I read the description of his offense and the age of the victim at the time.

I shut the window and narrow the range, checking another.

This person's less than a mile from the school.

No, one quarter mile.

Oh my God.

I blink and stare harder.

That face.

My skin crawls.

It's the bagger from the grocery store.

SADIE
THE MOM

Day Two

I'm shaking so hard I almost can't see my computer screen. I steady myself against the table, holding its lip with my hands, and stare at convicted felon Caleb Walsh. Seven victims, all elementary school age. Fourth grade? I don't know what *corruption of minors* means but it doesn't sound good. And the police let him off? Why?

Because he invented some alibi? Alibis can be faked. The police can be wrong. Everybody knows that. I recall the way he looked at Emma in the grocery store and I shiver, his words playing back in my head, *Not cool, lady.* Was he so angry with me for publicly shaming him that he decided to enact payback? Take it out on my little girl? Is this all my fault? Did I piss the wrong person off? *Oh my God.*

Emotion sweeps through me, pulling me left and right. My head's a jumble as I try to figure out what to do. I should call the police. No. Go to her. *Emma.*

I hear her voice calling me: *Mommy! Help!* Pitiful. Scared.

She's locked behind a door. Banging and banging and crying to get out. Or worse, she's tied up, abrasions on her wrists from her restraints. Maybe even gagged so she can barely breathe, her big dark eyes weeping.

A wave of nausea crashes over me but I will it away. I've got no time for that now. No time for being weak. I need to be a fierce warrior for my child.

I've got his address right in front of me. I can locate his house. It's not far from the school, not far from here. Every minute counts. I've got to hurry. I don't care that I haven't showered and look a wreck. My baby won't care either. She needs me.

I have to get to her *fast*.

I call Allen. It goes to voicemail. *Shit.*

He's probably with Mercer. Good. I'll text him.

SADIE
Please call! Urgent!

I take out the business cards the police officers gave me. They're wedged in the front pocket of my jeans. Crumpled. I lay them flat on the table, pressing out the creases with my fingers so I can read the numbers.

I try Claremont first.

She doesn't pick up.

Good God.

The seconds tick away like a time bomb winding down in my head. How close is it to going off? Is he about to hurt her? I've got to get there before he does.

My thumbs fumble on the keypad.

Come on, come on.

I try another number. O'Reilly's.

Voicemail.

Nooo.

I take a pic of the address on my computer screen with my phone. If I leave it to the system and the system's too late, I'll never forgive myself for not getting to Emma in time.

I'm a *mom. My child needs me.*

Forget what the police say. I can't wait any longer. I've got adrenaline on my side. My knees wobble when I stand, and I grab the back of my chair. I visually search the kitchen for a weapon. Something I can take with me. A knife? *Who am I kidding—he'll only turn it back on me. Maybe use it on Emma. No.*

I text everyone where I'm going, grab my car keys and purse, and *go.*

ALLEN
THE DAD

Day Two

"I need you to level with me, Mr. Wilson," Mercer says. "Where were you at eight fifteen the morning of Emma's disappearance?"

We're in an interrogation room again. It's claustrophobic. There's no one here but the two of us and all those cameras. Plus the double-sided mirror. I wonder if there's someone watching, sitting on the other side. Is it Claremont? Rodriguez? Patel? Will they confer about this later, each weighing in with their opinion on my innocence or guilt?

When Mercer asked me to meet him, I stupidly thought he had news. Possibly something traumatic he wanted to run by me first before talking to Sadie. Not that I was going to be treated like a suspect myself. I can't believe this. He's out of his fucking head. "Am I a person of interest, Agent Mercer?" I ask incredulously.

He stares at me without answering. I notice a plaster crack in one of the walls behind him. This room looks like it hasn't been painted in the past ten years. Maybe not since the building was built.

"For God's sake, I'm Emma's dad! Why on earth would I want to hurt her?"

"I never said that she'd been hurt." It's like he's laying a trap. Waiting for me to walk into it. So he can string me up by one ankle in a snare.

My heart beats erratically. "Then she's okay?"

"We don't know where Emma is, which is why I was asking *you* where you were." Sweat forms at my brow. I wipe it discreetly, pushing back my hair with my hand so he won't notice. I should have figured they'd come to me eventually. My alibi's as weak as they get.

"I was on my way to work," I say, repeating the story I told the police earlier. I can tell he doesn't believe me. He wouldn't be asking unless he knows. Unless he has some kind of evidence. My palm's damp. I wipe it on my slacks. "The moment I got the call from Sadie, I turned my SUV around and headed to the school as fast as I could."

"Your daughter's life could depend on your being truthful, Mr. Wilson." He taps his pen against his notepad, like he's growing impatient.

What the fuck? I'm the one who's growing impatient here. Fed up with his insinuations. I should stop answering. Get up and walk out. "Where I was has nothing to do with Emma going missing."

"Doesn't it, though?"

He's peering at me in a knowing way.

Did they find footage?

Did somebody see?

Tell?

Has a witness come forward?

My phone buzzes in my pocket but I ignore it.

"Mr. Wilson," Mercer asks flatly. "How long does it take you to drive to work?"

"On a normal day?" My face feels hot. "Fifteen minutes, maybe twenty."

"And you weren't home when Sadie put Emma on the bus?"

"No, I'd gone by then."

"Mr. Wilson." His stare grows more intense. "Are you aware of what time that was?"

I grip the arms of my chair recalling what Sadie told the police. "Seven forty-five? Seven fifty?"

"So, you would have gotten to work by the time Sadie phoned you at eight thirty-eight or thereabouts, after she'd heard from the school."

Shit.

"What route do you take to your job?"

My temples throb like my brain's exploding. "Um, the bypass, but it was very backed up that day. There was an accident." I'm babbling now, making shit up. Stupid. He can verify the information about local traffic conditions with the police. "Fender bender, really. Police weren't involved. The two drivers seemed to be trying to settle things themselves."

He picks up a remote and clicks on a video on the screen behind him, turning to view it fully. It's camera footage of a road. Two lanes in either direction.

I recognize the intersection. I am so fucked.

"There are cameras on the stoplights along your route," Mercer says. He flips to another reel and then a third. "Traffic seems to be moving along smoothly. There also—oddly—doesn't seem to be any footage of your SUV's make and model passing through any of these intersections at that approximate time. So."

He turns off the video, and the screen goes black.

"It appears you weren't on the road at the time you said you were, which means you were somewhere else." He cocks his head. "Where was that, Mr. Wilson?"

Jesus Christ, this is looking bad.

"Not—not at Emma's school."

He nods like he anticipated that answer. Then he lowers the boom. "Mr. Wilson," he says in a very calculating manner. "Are you sleeping with your ex-wife?"

My world starts spinning and spinning.

I try to stop it, grab control.

"Do I need an attorney?"

"Nobody's going to prosecute you for infidelity," he says.

Sweat dribbles down my back and soaks my shirt.

That has nothing to do with *anything*.

"Then, no."

SADIE
THE MOM

Day Two

I drive to Caleb Walsh's house clenching the steering wheel so hard my fingers go numb. I glare at the stop sign ordering me to slow down. I look both ways and floor the pedal, speeding through it. If he's harmed her, I'll kill him. I'm not sure how but I will. I don't care what the consequences are.

I'll drive a stake through his heart. I'll find one somewhere. A fireplace poker maybe, or smash his skull with something heavy and blunt. A sculpture? A lamp? Anything I can lay my hands on? Dammit. I should have brought a knife. I can't believe I'm plotting murder, but it doesn't seem like murder in my head. It feels like justice.

I pray that things won't have to go that far. That he's left her unharmed. Maybe he's just holding her to psychologically taunt me. What if he's exposing her to something awful? Lewd? Not even touching her but showing her things a child her age shouldn't see? Perverted things that no decent person should be exposed to?

I've got to stop this now. Stop *him.*

I arrive at the address and park by the curb in front. It's only two blocks from the school. Wait. I've driven by here before. Many times on the way to Stonefield Elementary from our former house. Allen and I took this street every time we attended one of Forrest's school events. How many houses like this are out there?

Normal looking. Nondescript, hiding a threat to society inside? It's a smallish rancher, with a fresh paint job and a manicured yard. It can't be bigger than two bedrooms. Maybe he's got Emma in one of them.

I climb from my SUV and slam shut my driver's door, my adrenaline surging.

Nerves skitter through me and my stomach knots.

No. I have to be strong—for Emma, my baby girl. I telepathically will her to know I'm coming. That everything's going to be all right. I ball my hands into fists and march toward the door with long strides. I've got my keys gripped in my right fist, my heaviest key protruding. It's solid enough to use as a weapon.

If Emma's here, I'll punch him in the eye. Blind him temporarily, grab Emma and run. If he tries to stop me, I'll fight him.

I am so fucking ready it hurts.

I ring the bell with the hand not holding my keys.

My right fist tenses. Taut.

No answer.

There's an old-model hatchback in the drive.

I roll back my shoulders and knock.

The door slowly peels open. It's him.

"I already talked to the police." He pushes the door toward me, but I shove back with my left hand. I'm so mad I'm seeing red. My heart's exploding.

"What have you done with Emma?" I seethe, pushing into the door. I throw all my weight against it, but he holds it back, angling in with his shoulder.

"Look, lady"—he peers through the opening—"I have nothing to do with that."

He doesn't look particularly strong, or in shape. I work out, do yoga and aerobics—I can take him. A child would have trouble. A sweet, good girl who wouldn't fight back. A child who does what she's told.

Anger rears up inside me like a dark stallion, blinding me with fury. "The. Hell. You. Don't!" One giant shove with my shoulder.

The door swings wide.

ALLEN
THE DAD

Day Two

My phone buzzes again, a third time. "I need to check this," I say. "Might be Sadie."

Mercer takes out his phone and checks it too. "What? Seriously?"

We both scramble to our feet.

He points at me. "We're going to finish this."

What? About Teresa? Fine.

I can't think about that, and the fallout, now.

All I can think about is Sadie.

She's gone *where*?

Dammit, Sadie.

Mercer leaves at a fast clip, and I trail him.

He grabs his suit jacket off a rack. "You can ride with me."

SADIE
THE MOM

Day Two

Walsh stumbles back a step. "Holy hell, lady!" The house smells acerbic, of cleaning fluids and chlorine bleach. It's got wall-to-wall carpeting in the living room, and the carpet's stained. What the hell has he done to her? What's he been cleaning up?

I storm toward him, and a wave of heat follows me inside. A window-unit air conditioner blasts above the sofa, but hot air engulfs the room. "I saw you at the grocery store!" I yell. "You spoke to her!" The front door's ajar at my back, heat seeping in from outside.

He inches away from me, his face flushed. "Speaking's not a crime, you know." He's guilty as sin. I can see it in his eyes. They're mossy green and shimmery. Freakishly weird. He's got her hidden somewhere. I know it. The monster.

"Emma!" I call toward the back of the house. "Emma!" I search the simple living room and connected dining area. The furniture's threadbare, but the rooms are tidy. There's a short hall in front of me ending in a bathroom. Maybe she's in a back room? Tied up? Unable to scream. I turn in that direction, and he grabs my shoulders with his hands.

A shiver runs through me so cold. Like a mountain stream in January.

"She's not here," he says quietly. He dips his face toward mine to look in my eyes. My breath comes in fits and starts. "Okay?" I so badly need to believe he's lying and that Emma's here. That she's safe and he hasn't hurt her. *Please God. Not that.*

My pulse threads unevenly through my veins. "Then where is she?"

"I don't know."

He lets me go and I brush off my shoulders like I'm wiping the filth away. I dart around him, and he tries to catch me, grabbing my arm, his hands clenching around it like a vise.

I tug my arm free, and it burns—ripped from his hold.

I lunge forward and race into the hall, my breath catching. My hands on my knees. My stomach turning over. The hall flips a quick revolution. The light on the ceiling appears on the floor. I think I'm dizzy. I think I might fall. A kitchen's to my left and two bedrooms on the right. Their doors are open.

I check one and then the other.

My heartbeats slow to a crawl.

One-two. One-two.

One.

I cover my face with my hands and sob.

They're empty.

O'REILLY
THE COP

Day Two

I'm in Cass Thomas's front foyer. I identified myself as the police making local inquiries about a case concerning her neighbor and showed her my badge. She let me step inside, but only by a few feet. She has the strap of an athletic bag swung over one shoulder. Car keys in her other hand. There's a Jeep in her drive. She's a medium-sized woman and in shape.

"I really can't talk," she says, holding the bulky bag against her side. "I'm headed in to work."

"Where's that?" I'm canvassing her house while we speak.

There's not much to it. Two soccer chairs and a folding table in one of the front rooms. A short couch and a TV on a stand in the other. There's a kitchen in the back with a bay window facing the backyard. Looks like a card table in front of it with metal chairs. No photos on the walls or elsewhere. Zero mounted mirrors or art. Only overhead lighting, no lamps. My first apartment at eighteen looked better.

"Our Lady of Our Savior." She glances at the door, looking like she's in a hurry. Or maybe she's anxious. Hard to tell.

"This won't take long," I promise, taking out my notebook. "You may have heard a child's gone missing from Stonefield Elementary. Emma Wilson. Her family lives behind you."

She frowns. "Yes. So sad. I saw it on the news."

"Do you know the Wilsons?"

She shakes her head. "Not well. Although Allen and I knew each other in high school."

"And Sadie?"

"I've met her a couple of times, and Emma."

I pause, pretending to write something down. Instead I'm listening for any odd sounds. Indications of another person being here. Maybe a hidden child. This house doesn't look right. Doesn't feel right. Although feelings aren't enough to get me a warrant. I'm well apprised of that fact. Maybe she'll give me something.

"We're talking to the neighbors," I tell her. "Asking for help. If anyone's seen or heard anything, even if it doesn't seem relevant."

She checks her sports watch. "I wish I could help you, but—like I said—I don't even know them all that well."

"You got kids?"

She blinks, clearly broadsided by the question. "Why?"

Red alert. "I was just thinking they might have heard something around the neighborhood? You know, from their friends? Other kids?"

"That's doubtful," she says. Her eyes are cold, a blank slate. "Haven't got any."

"Haven't got any . . . ?" I ask.

She sets her jaw. "Kids."

Alrighty. This has gotten weird.

I'm tempted to mention the failed playdate with Emma, but we promised Sadie we wouldn't tip Cass off to her having said anything about that.

"Sorry." My gut knots when she adds, "Got to go."

There's something wrong about this house. Something odd about *her*.

"Just out of curiosity," I ask, putting my notebook away, "where were you at eight fifteen the morning Emma disappeared?" I'm aware she doesn't have to answer, but if she's innocent, why wouldn't she?

"At work."

"Anybody there who can vouch for you?"

She visibly bristles. "What is this, Deputy Chief O'Reilly? Am I a suspect *in the disappearance of a missing child*?" She says that last part like she can't believe it. Insinuating I've got some nerve. She huffs out a breath and I hold open my hands, waiting for her to answer.

She gives me a steely glare. "I was alone," she says, "okay? At school, setting up the gym."

"All right, ma'am. Thanks for your time."

She shuts the front door and I glance back over my shoulder, thinking she might exit right after me since she was in such a big rush to get to work. She doesn't. Instead, I see her peering at me through the glass in one of the sidelights by the front door.

Creepiness crawls over me like a nest of tiny spiders.

I've got to find a way to search that house. I climb into my squad car and check my phone. I've got a missed call. I listen to my voicemail.

Christ.

Sadie's in trouble.

SADIE
THE MOM

Day Two

Walsh walks up to me and hangs his head, his hands on his hips. His large beard bushes out around his face. I note the tats on his arms. One says "Delia," another's of a Celtic cross. "I'm sorry," he says. His tone is earnest, coarse. "Sorry about your little girl."

I draw in deep breaths, sucking air into my lungs. I don't know how my legs hold me. I can't feel them. Don't feel anything but loss. I hug myself with my arms and my fist slackens. Keys clank against the hardwood floor by my feet, splaying out in an array of discount cards. One is for the grocery store where Walsh works.

He bends down and picks up my keys, handing them to me.

I take the keys, my eyes burning. "You really didn't take her."

He shakes his head. "I couldn't, wouldn't. That's not who I am."

"What did you do?" I ask on a heavy breath. I right myself so I'm standing. "To those kids?" I'm not sure if I want to know. Still. Another part of me needs to.

He rubs one of his arms, massaging the tat of the Celtic cross. "Nothing." The way he says that, it strangely sounds like the truth. "I was a teacher," he says, "at Stonefield Elementary. Fourth grade." His tone says he's suffering. It's hard to believe he's making this up. "It was a routine day, and class was just getting started. Then the laptop on my desk suddenly went bonkers. All these popups started appearing on the screen. Naked women. Sex shots. Pornography. One nasty pic right after the other."

He sighs heavily and hangs his head. "I was totally shocked. Didn't know where they came from. You know?" He peers up at me and this time his eyes don't look freaky. They look tortured. Like he's remembering something he'd rather not.

"We teachers turned in our school laptops for refurbishing at the end of each year, then checked out new ones in the fall. That's how it goes. You never keep them over the summer. School had only been in session a couple of days, so the laptop they assigned me must have been buggy. Maybe someone was using it illicitly before, and it never got cleaned up."

"Oh my God." If what he says is true, what a horrible situation. To be caught in a spot like that within your own classroom.

"Yeah, it was bad." He turns away and stares out the open front door. Heat still pours in, flooding the place. The single window unit can't keep up anymore.

A police car's arrived, O'Reilly. And a dark sedan, Mercer. They exit their vehicles, briskly striding toward the house. They see me calmly speaking with Walsh and that I'm unharmed, and slow their pace.

"Some kids gathered around my desk," Walsh continues, "mostly boys—and I tried to shoo them away. Every time I closed a box, another popped open. I quickly shut my laptop, but a half a dozen or so had already seen.

"I let the principal know what had happened at once, and I thought she would defend me. Get the whole sordid thing sorted out through IT. But she didn't and the kids told their parents. The parents pressed charges. I was convicted quickly. It was a circus trial. The jury already had its mind made up. I served eight months behind bars."

O'Reilly enters the house. "What's going on here?"

Mercer walks in and stands beside him.

I hold up my hand for them to wait and Walsh ignores them, finishing his story with his eyes on me. I can tell that he wants me to hear it. I'm awash with shame over why. I unfairly faulted him for taking Emma. I understand now I was wrong.

"Things might have gone better for me," Walsh says, "if the school had had my back. But they didn't. The principal was more than happy to scapegoat me and get me out of the way. It was an inconvenient scandal, something she wanted quickly swept under the rug."

"The principal?"

Walsh spews bitterly, "Principal Rand."

ALLEN
THE DAD

Day Two

O'Reilly and Mercer escort Sadie out of Walsh's house and the door shuts behind them. I leap from Mercer's black sedan. Not knowing what he and O'Reilly would find inside, Mercer insisted I wait there. For Sadie's safety and possibly Emma's.

I run toward Sadie across Walsh's yard. "Jesus, Sadie!" I wrap my arms around her and hold her close. "Are you okay?"

She nods but I can tell that she's been crying. Her hair's stringy and her clothes rumpled. I think she's been wearing the same thing since yesterday. I give Mercer and O'Reilly a questioning glance. Mercer frowns and O'Reilly shakes his head.

My heart squeezes to a stop.

After a few short breaths, it begins beating again.

Emma's not here.

Mercer talks to O'Reilly. "Mr. Wilson shared something on our way here." We're outside Walsh's house and standing by the curb and near our vehicles. "He and Walsh have a past connection."

Sadie's startled and it shows on her face. "What's that mean?"

"I was on a jury years ago." I glance toward the house and the blood drains from her face. "Walsh's trial."

Sadie's aghast. "Allen, why didn't you say something?"

"I had no reason to think about the trial until yesterday. And then, when the police said no one on the registry could have possibly been involved, I fully believed he'd been cleared."

"That's still the case," O'Reilly says, "despite this development. Walsh may have had motive, but he didn't have means or opportunity, as far as we can tell. We've got no reason to hold him or charge him in Emma's kidnapping."

"Oh my God." Sadie surveys O'Reilly and Mercer. "Do you think Walsh knew? Made the connection between Emma and Allen?"

"After the fact?" O'Reilly asks. "Maybe." He spreads open his hands. "Even if he did, that doesn't change the fact that he couldn't have been anywhere near the school at the time Emma disappeared."

"I didn't even think he was guilty," I go on to explain. "That's the irony, but I got outvoted by the other members of the jury. For most of them, the case was open and shut. But I kind of felt for the guy, you know?" I shrug. "It was almost like he was framed." I consider my impression of Principal Rand. "If not that, at least scapegoated by the school."

"Walsh probably doesn't know that you believed him, though," Sadie says.

"True. I was the jury foreman. So he probably assumed I agreed with everyone else. I didn't. It was a scary case. One of those everyman things where you could envision it happening to you. Being in the wrong place at the wrong time. Any teacher could have gotten that laptop accidentally. Hell, Principal Rand could have gotten it herself."

Sadie considers this. "Yeah, but she doesn't usually have a bunch of students in her office, like teachers do in a classroom."

O'Reilly blows out a breath. "What a messed-up world." He turns to Sadie and says seriously, "I know you acted out of concern for your daughter, but confronting Walsh like you did was not a good move. We can't have you or Allen putting yourselves at risk."

She scoffs at him. "Don't tell me you wouldn't have done the same if it were your daughter."

He sets his hands on his duty belt. "Fair point. But still. I'd ask you to be more cautious in the future. For your sake. For Emma's." He takes out his car keys, jangling them in his hand. "Just so you're informed, I chatted with Cass Thomas this morning."

"And?" Allen asks.

"I've got nothing concrete," O'Reilly says. "But something about her doesn't add up. When I asked her about her having kids, she claimed she hasn't got any."

Sadie gasps, "Oh my God."

Shit. I bring my arm around Sadie's shoulders. There I went downplaying her story about Bobby being made up.

"Her alibi's also weak," O'Reilly adds. "I'm going to see what I can do about getting a warrant to search her house. Meanwhile, we've got surveillance on it. First sign of Emma being there, we go in."

ALLEN
THE DAD

Day Two

I ride with Sadie back to the station so we can get my SUV. She's still shaken up, so I drive. Mercer and O'Reilly take their own cars. Neither was pleased about Sadie confronting Caleb Walsh out of the blue and all on her own. I'm unhappy about that myself. "Sadie, what were you thinking?"

She stares at me with red-rimmed eyes. "I thought she was there, Allen. I'd convinced myself of it. He was the same guy we saw at the grocery store. The one who made an overture toward Emma. Maybe I can see it was possibly innocent now. But when I found his face on that sex offender registry and recognized him, I snapped.

"I was sure I'd made him angry. That he'd taken Emma in revenge. I tried to call you, Allen. Tried contacting everyone. No one responded. I was worried sick something would happen to Emma if I didn't act fast. If I didn't get to her in time."

I set my chin. "That was still reckless, and you know it. He could have hurt you."

"He's not the violent type," she volleys. "You basically said as much yourself."

"You didn't know that though, did you?" There's a hard edge in my voice, but I don't mean to be cross with her.

I understand how unnerving this is. Neither of us is thinking clearly. Both of us are stressed. I can't have Sadie going off half-cocked, though, and storming into some stranger's house. We've already lost Emma, our baby girl, and are living through the nightmare of trying to find her. I can't have something happen to my wife, as well.

"No," she concedes finally. "I didn't." She stares down at the floor and her feet. After a beat, she looks up. "That's weird about Principal Rand though, isn't it?" she asks. "That she's somehow connected to both these cases. First Walsh, and now Emma?"

"It's true I don't like her, but maybe she's just doing her job?"

Sadie tugs on her seat belt like it's too tight. "Or maybe she's hiding something? Maybe she's the sort to not want bad press for her school. Maybe she knows what happened to Emma and it was something awful, something that happened right there at Stonefield Elementary on her home turf? Something that could bury Rand if the truth comes out?

"Maybe her stupid job is worth more to her than our little girl?" She's stringing herself out, getting more and more worked up as she talks, wringing her hands in her lap, twisting her wedding band around in circles.

"Maybe we're getting paranoid," I tell her gently. "Seeing shadows around every corner, where none exist."

"Our child is *missing*, Allen."

"I know, and we're going to find her. No matter what it takes."

"You don't think Teresa—?" She faces me, her eyes huge. She's like a dog with a bone on this theme. She won't let it drop.

"Jesus Christ, Sadie. We've been through this. Teri wouldn't hurt a fly, much less Emma."

"Why are you always defending her?"

"Why are you always attacking her?"

"She got on the bus, Allen," she snaps.

"You know it was to return your iPod."

118

"That's what Teresa says," she scoffs. "We don't know that's true."

My neck feels hot. So do my ears. I *know* Teri didn't do it. I can't tell Sadie why.

"Oh my God." She cups a hand to her mouth. "Is there something going on, Allen? Something between you and Teresa?"

"No," I say a bit too empathically. "Of course not."

She sits back in her seat and stares out her window, like she's wondering whether or not to believe me. I think of Mercer's accusations about me and Teri. Will he say something to Sadie about a suspected affair?

I steal a glance in her direction. She seems so worn and frail. Why would he? Sadie doesn't need to know. We've got enough we're dealing with already. Still. The threat of Mercer revealing what he believes is there hangs over my head.

When we get to the station parking lot, Chief Claremont comes outdoors to meet us. Mercer is with her. He got here fast. I roll down the window of Sadie's SUV and Claremont peeks inside.

"Sadie?" she says. "Have you got a minute?"

Mercer looks at me and nods toward the station. Shit. My stomach knots. He wants to talk about Teri again. I need to decide what to say. Then I have to figure out what I'm going to say to Sadie. I know I should tell her, and I will, but now seems like the absolute suckiest time.

She doesn't need to know about my moral-judgment lapse on top of us having a missing child. I was never going to leave Sadie for Teri. Never going to upend our family. *Our lives.* After this is over and Emma's home safe and sound, maybe I'll tell Sadie then? Or maybe that would be a selfish move, and only to assuage my guilt?

Sadie and I climb from the vehicle and shut our doors. As we walk toward the entrance, Claremont says, "Before you both leave, we'll want to call another press conference. We need to keep doing those every day."

Every day until Emma comes home, she means.

Fear grips my heart.

What if she never does?

SADIE
THE MOM

Day Two

I should have known I'd be in trouble for tracking down Caleb Walsh. We're in one of those interrogation rooms with a double-sided mirror and cameras. But I'm not a suspect. Why would I be? I'm the mother. It's crystal clear Chief Claremont is as unimpressed as the others by my act of bravery. "Chief Claremont," I say. "You must understand how I felt. Like things were urgent. She could have been there."

"Yes. But. She wasn't." She clasps her hands together, elbows resting on the table. "We can't have you interfering in police investigations, Sadie." She stares at me seriously. "Taking matters into your own hands. It's too risky. Someone could get hurt."

"Someone's already been hurt. *Emma.*" Panic wells inside me and I grip the arms of my chair. My heart beats erratically. I take a new tack. Claremont's one of the good guys. She's on our side. I want to keep her there. "Are you a mom, Chief Claremont?" I ask, trying to get her to relate. While she's professional, she's not made of stone. If she's a mom, surely she has a mother's heart. Will understand how desperate I felt.

She remains stoic. "Yes."

"Then you must know. Must be able to imagine the sheer hell of this."

She softens her stance. "I do. But Sadie, we don't want you and Allen complicating matters by potentially endangering yourselves." She blows out a breath looking almost like she doesn't want to say what she's going to next. "I hope you understand this is procedure, but I need to ask you a question." I'm not sure I'll like what's coming. "Where were you at eight fifteen yesterday morning when Emma disappeared?"

I feel like I've been hit by a train. She can't possibly believe I had anything to do with Emma going missing. "At home, like I said. In my office." My cheeks grow warm.

She glances at the double-sided mirror and then a camera. "I thought you said you were in the kitchen when you got the school's call?" *Crap.*

My face burns hotter, then I remember the play set. "The kitchen. Yes. That's right. I was there. I had my laptop with me. I was working when the secretary called. Of course it's all a jumble. Anyone would expect that. I don't have perfect recall. Nobody does under stress."

"Any of the neighbors see you?"

"Like who?" I ask sarcastically. "Cass Thomas?"

Claremont frowns. "I don't want you jumping to conclusions about her like you did with Caleb Walsh."

I square my shoulders and respond. "O'Reilly told me you're looking into her as a person of interest."

"We *are*," she says firmly. "But as of yet, she's not a suspect."

"And Teresa?"

She raises an eyebrow. "Why do you ask about her?"

I sigh like it's obvious, because to me it is. "The iPod story." I don't know why others can't see it. Why Allen's constantly making excuses on Teresa's behalf. Unless he knows something he's not saying, and I'm starting to think he does.

"Which you confirmed," Claremont reminds me, though she's got the details wrong.

"I confirmed that it went missing, not that Teresa said she was going to return it to me." I lean toward her, growing agitated. "What if it wasn't an iPod she slipped into Emma's backpack, but something else? Has anyone thought of that?"

She temples her fingers together. "Like what, exactly?" I seem to have piqued her interest. She's listening—good. That's more than I get out of Allen on this topic.

"A key to her house?" I guess. "Or maybe a pass card to her work building?"

Claremont narrows her eyes like she's not understanding the connection. "For Emma to use? A five-year-old child? How would she get to those places on her own without an adult taking her? Neither is walking distance to the school."

The room's constricting, closing in on me. I'm finding it hard to breathe. "I don't know." All I have to suggest Teresa's involvement is my instinct, which I do suppose could be wrong. I have similar instincts about Cass Thomas. It certainly can't be both of them. They don't even know each other. My heart freezes up.

But Allen and Teresa do. *No, he wouldn't. Never. Not do something to his own little girl.* I've seen how Teresa looks at Allen, like she's never emotionally let him go. Like she's still mooning over him and pining for the days when she and Allen were together. I never thought it was mutual, so I was able to set her continued attraction to Allen aside. Tell myself my jealousy's not warranted. Even feel sorry for her.

Not now. Now I'm suspicious.

Claremont lifts a pen off the table and takes some notes. But her scrawl is upside down and tiny, and I can't read it. "For the record." She closes her notebook. "We haven't entirely ruled out Teresa Wilson as a person of interest, and we're continuing to investigate her iPod story. Unfortunately, without our having Emma's backpack, there's no way to corroborate what she says."

My heart twists. *I want more than Emma's backpack. I want my baby girl.*

"Your concerns about Cass Thomas are valid too," she says, "and we're keeping our eyes on her. But I also want to make you aware of certain facts. In cases of missing children, it's often one of the parents who—"

"No." I shake my head. "Not Allen. He wouldn't. Couldn't. He's my husband. Emma's dad. He loves her." Even as I say it, it sounds more like I'm trying to convince myself than her. Claremont's canny. She senses my fear. The doubt that's crept in on stealthy footsteps.

"Sadie," she says softly. "I know it hurts to think that, and I hope it's not true. But I need you to do me a favor for Emma's sake. I need you to keep an open mind about everyone, including Allen, until we've learned more. He might not be involved directly, but it's possible he knows something he's not telling us."

Her suspicions hit hard.

There's something Allen's not telling me too.

I can feel it.

"If you need me?" She stares at me long and hard. "Call."

"I did call." I don't hide my irritation. "You didn't pick up."

Claremont frowns. "I'm sorry about that." She takes out her cell phone and types something in. "I'm setting your ringtone on priority. Next time, I'll do my best to answer."

She sets her phone on her desk. "And Sadie," she says. "I meant it about you not interfering. It's not just your safety we're concerned about. It's Emma's. If you do anything rash, it could set the wrong person off—in the wrong way. You got lucky with Mr. Walsh because he wasn't hiding anything. You don't want to upset someone who is."

KATE
THE TEACHER

Day Two

The bright-orange school buses pull up out front, and kids spew from their open doors like little sea monkeys being released into the ocean. Through the art teacher's windows across the hall, I see them climb down the steps. Piñatas dangle from the art room's ceiling in an array of papier-mâché hot-air balloons, rainbow arches, bulbous suns, and pointy stars. They were a project her students did for Cinco de Mayo last spring. Blue, green, red, and yellow streamers from their Holi project still hang there too, shimmering with sparkly painted designs.

Teachers stand on the sidewalk counting heads as kids get off the bus and dividing them into groups. Fifth graders here, fourth graders that way. There's twice as many staff on hand as usual, and each busload of kids disembarks one at a time to keep things orderly. Hang on.

Where's Forrest? I don't see him with the older bunch. Then again, if he were my kid, I might keep him home from school today too. Maybe I'd never let him return to Stonefield. His sister went missing from here. Who's to say he wouldn't too? For all anyone knows, Emma's kidnapping wasn't random. It was a personal vendetta.

After closing early yesterday, school's back in session and operating today on a delayed schedule. But I'll have one less student in my class. Emma's desk sits in its exact same spot, an ugly blight on the bright aura of my classroom. Even an inanimate object like that piece of furniture seems to know Emma's never coming back.

Missing children don't reappear. They vanish into thin air, leaving their families devastated. Forever searching for answers they'll never find. The police interviewed everyone at Stonefield and cleared them of involvement. That doesn't mean someone wasn't lying. In fact, I know someone was. Dotti covered for me like I covered for her.

Dotti lays her hand on my arm. "How you holding up, kiddo?"

"Okay." I sigh, my heart heavy. "You?"

She whispers hoarsely, "I know this is rough, but we'll get through it."

Maybe so, but it's going to be a long road.

It will be longer for Emma, Katherine intervenes.

"Do you think they'll find her?" I ask, my eye on the new arrivals. Dotti's silent a long while. "No."

ALLEN
THE DAD

Day Two

Mercer's got me back in an interrogation room. Chief Claremont's speaking with Sadie. I should have guessed this question was coming. Prepared for it. Talked to Teri. I know how it will appear. Like Teri and I had something to do with Emma's disappearance. Like we planned her kidnapping together.

Shit. One or the other of us, or *both of us* colluding together.

We're on opposite sides of the table. He's recording. I'm starting to think I do need an attorney. Nobody's charged me with anything. Nobody's read me my rights. But I have the keen sense I'm in the hot seat. Maybe more than *a person of interest*. Maybe an actual *suspect*. Shit. When did all this start? Maybe at the beginning? I know parents are often suspected in kidnapping cases, but those are estranged parents. Not us. Not me and Sadie.

"Shouldn't you be out there looking for real suspects right now?"

He leans back in his chair, his eyebrows arched. "Did somebody call you a suspect, Mr. Wilson?"

"No." I tug at my shirt collar. "But I feel like you're treating me like one."

"I'm simply trying to get to the bottom of what happened to your daughter."

"You can't possibly think that I had something to do with it."

"We were talking about you and Teresa," he counters.

I read his eyes. He knows that we were involved. He knows we slept together. *For fuck's sake.* He *does* think I had something to do with it. "Look, Agent Mercer. I don't know what you're getting at, but you're wrong. Teresa and I would never do anything to harm Emma. I'd cut my own heart out first." *So would Teri.* I want to believe that about her so badly. She said some things, but she didn't mean them. Not like that.

He scratches the side of his head. At length he says, "So there *is* a you and Teresa."

Sly bastard.

TERESA
THE EX-WIFE

Day Two

I watch Mom drive away with Forrest riding shotgun in the front seat of her sedan. My kid sticks his hand out the window and waves. Hurt coils inside me like rusty barbed wire, every bit of it piercing. I'm heartsick at him leaving. My baby boy.

I was greedy for wanting Emma too.

And now I'm paying the price.

But when it happened between me and Allen, I believed I could have it all.

I invite Allen over to talk about Forrest. He's getting into trouble again and I'm at loose ends about how to handle him. Every time I think I've got the kid figured out, he pulls the rug out from under me again. Last week, he pocketed candy at a convenience store. Now he's got Sadie's iPod. I sent Forrest to his friend William's house so Allen and I could talk. Then William's mom invited Forrest to stay for dinner. Ideal.

I ask Allen in, my emotions raw. He's still got the same face, the same build, that I adore. This talk isn't going to be easy. I need courage. "Wine?"

I ask, walking toward the kitchen. Late afternoon light pours in through the skylights and from my big glass doors. I've got an A-frame contemporary set back on a wooded lot. It's private out here, peaceful. I liked it more when Allen lived here with us. He loosens his tie and follows me.

"Sure." He checks his watch. "I can't stay long," he says. "I didn't tell Sadie I was coming over here."

Tension flutters in my belly, but I caution myself against becoming hopeful. Of trying to make this out to be more than it is. "Why didn't you?" I ask anyway. I've got an open bottle on the counter.

He shrugs as I pour him a glass of zinfandel. "This is between us."

"Yes." I meet his eyes and feel a buzz. A sensation I've missed so badly. It's different with just the two of us being here alone. Without Forrest. Without Emma. Most definitely without Sadie. He's right, anyway. This is between us. Just because Allen's remarried, that doesn't mean that he and I can't maintain our relationship. That's what relationships are. They're friendships in which you share confidences. And this is about our child, Allen's and mine.

I serve myself some wine too, and we walk into the living area. The ceiling's high with exposed beams. Our view is of the twilight through the trees. Romantic. We used to sit here and have wine in the evenings. Back when our world was good and we were united on everything, from our tastes in music to our choices in film. I think he'll pick his old recliner, but he doesn't. He sits on the sofa, where there's ample room for me. I sit down beside him, holding my wine.

This should feel awkward, the two of us being alone together, but it's not. It's like slipping my hand into a familiar glove. Warm and cozy. Comforting in a way that makes it seem like he's never left. I don't really blame Allen for our divorce. I blame myself. I got so focused on my work, I forgot about him, literally, in so many ways. Forgot his birthday. Forgot our anniversary. Forgot about reservations we'd made to meet up at restaurants. Completely blanked on invitations to parties. He said we were growing apart and that our relationship was no longer my priority. He was right. I wanted tenure more. I thought he'd wait. He didn't.

"So what's going on?" He leans back in his seat, and I smell his body-wash. Sandalwood and spice. He still uses the same brand that he used to when we were married. I remember that scent washing over me. Him taking me in his arms, and in our bed. The way he covered my body with kisses. The way he stroked back my hair. How we made love. I duck my head to hide my blush. God, if he knew what I'm thinking.

I take a sip of wine. "Forrest is acting out again," I tell him reluctantly. "Taking things." I pull Sadie's iPod from my pocket and set it on the coffee table in front of us. "After he was at your house, he came home with this. It's Sadie's. He snagged it from her office when she wasn't in there."

Allen sighs heavily and rakes a hand through his hair. "Great."

"Last week he took some candy from a store, and he's started picking fights with his friends. I'm worried about him, Allen. Worried he's starting this school year on a bad foot."

Allen laughs bitterly. "I'm worried he's starting life on a bad foot."

I peer up at him over the rim of my wineglass. "We could consider family counseling."

"We're no longer a family, Teri."

Ouch, that hurt. I didn't know the wound was so raw, so deep. Okay, yes I did. I've just been trying to ignore it.

I set down my wineglass when my eyes burn hot. "You know what I mean."

"I'm sorry." His voice is rough with emotion. "I didn't mean that how it sounded." I hear his wineglass settle on the table. He's right, though. We're not. My fantasies about things between us being otherwise are just that, all made up in my head. "Teri." He holds my cheek with one hand and my heart stutters. "If I could have changed things," he says, "I would have." His probing stare warms me. Excites me and threatens me at once. I'm endangered by his look, and by what it's saying. What I want it to say.

But no, we can't. Sadie.

"I know." I lay my hand over his and lick my lips, wishing so badly he would kiss them. Wishing we could make the pain and heartache go away. He loved me once—so deeply. Maybe a part of him still does. But we're not *who we were. He's moved on. I do the brave thing. I speak up. "But now you have Sadie."*

He meets my gaze and sensation hums through me like an old familiar song. One I'm desperate to hear again—with Allen. His eyes are lyrically blue like an ocean sonata, gently playing in my heart. His hand stays on my cheek, and he moves closer. "She's wonderful, yes." Something in his eyes says, But she's not you. She's not what we had.

The hope in my heart slays me. Makes me feeble, weak.

His mouth moves nearer. "Allen—"

"Teri." His lips brush against mine, feathery soft. "I'm so sorry," he says. "So sorry about so many things." He kisses me again. Tenderly. "About you and Forrest." Another gentle kiss. "How everything ended. If I could take it all back." I thread my fingers through his and guide his hand, lowering it from my face and holding it in my lap.

My breath hitches. "We can't."

His hand squeezes mine. "I know." A flicker of remorse in his eyes. I think he might stand up and leave, but instead he leans in, kissing me again—and this time I kiss him back. My palms slide over his shoulders and around his back, press against his muscled chest, remembering. Him moving on top of me. Inside me. The two of us as one. Warring emotions course through me. I want him, I do. But not like this. I want him without Sadie.

But Sadie's not here. It's just the two of us. Alone together like we used to be. Before children and our divorce, before we became so lost in our own worlds we fell away from each other. Before I emotionally walked away from him. I'd never do that now.

If I could have Allen back. If I got one more chance, I'd hold on tight and cherish him forever. Maybe that's what this is? A new beginning. A way for us to move forward and beyond the brutal past. We could work things out if we decided to. Together. Love always finds a way.

He nibbles on my bottom lip and flames caress my breasts, lick at my belly, seep lower. His mouth is hungry, hot. I melt into his kisses, losing my soul to his. His hands squeeze my thighs, move between my legs.

My body aches from his touch, ignites. Slowly, like a torturous flame. Lapping at every part of me until I glow like a torch. He shoves down his slacks, and I slide out of my jeans. My shirt and bra are on the floor. His shirt is somewhere. Suddenly it's just us, skin to silky skin, his chest hair teasing my nipples.

"I remember this couch," he murmurs, easing me down in his arms.

I remember it too. It's where we made Forrest.

I don't want to weigh the outcome. I know what we're doing is wrong. I just want him. I lie back and he climbs on top of me. All sexual heat and longing. A serenade to yesterday. He rocks forward and a concerto swells in my heart. Booming. Joyous. I stare out at the woods and pretend like we're making a baby.

Our little girl.

SADIE
THE MOM

Day Two

I stand in my backyard staring at Cass's house. It's late. Maybe close to midnight. I shiver in the darkness, hugging my arms around myself. Crickets chirp under the faint light of the moon, partially covered with clouds.

It's Cass. I know it's her. O'Reilly said she claims she doesn't have kids. Maybe she never had kids to begin with, or maybe she lost one and wants to replace that missing child with my little girl. Was that her goal in taking Emma? I wish I could know that Emma was there. Wish that I could feel it. The fact that I can't fills me with the worst kind of dread.

I have to believe Emma's alive and well somewhere, and that someone is taking care of her, the way I've always done. I've been such a careful mom. Keeping her medical appointments and childhood vaccinations up to date. Making sure she uses her car seat and wears a bike helmet on her two-wheeler with training wheels. Monitoring who she plays with. *Like "Bobby."*

I'm near the fence and the gate, watching Cass's lights go on upstairs. First in one bedroom and then another. Who's the second bedroom for? Maybe I could try a window or a door? See if she's left any unlocked. I could sneak in during the dead of night and prowl through her house. Reality slams into me like a freight train.

Great way to get yourself arrested, Sadie.

I don't need to be charged with breaking and entering, but waiting on a warrant is like lying on a bed of nails. I can't stand the pins-and-needles agony of it one more minute. What are the police waiting for?

"Sadie?" Allen's arms fold around me. He hugs me from behind and sets his chin on my shoulder. "What are you doing out here?"

"Thinking about Emma." The gate in front of me swings toward us, carried by the breeze.

"I've checked that gate," he says. "The latch needs tightening. I'll fix it in the morning."

If only there was such a simple explanation for the dread in my heart. "I can't help the feeling she's watching us, Allen. Spying."

Movement in a window in Cass's house upstairs. A shade goes up, and then she stands there with her hand over her eyes and pressed to the glass. Allen and I back behind the trees. He lowers a branch to peer toward Cass's house. We're concealed in the shadows. "Seems to me like we're the ones spying on her."

"Allen. You can't possibly think she's innocent."

"That would be very brazen of her, don't you think?" He keeps his voice down even though it's doubtful she'd hear us from where we are with her windows closed. "To take a child and keep her so near, right under her parents' noses?"

But I've heard of things like that happening. Kidnapped children being sequestered away at some seemingly innocent person's house, practically in plain view. "What if she's there, Allen?" I fight my urge to call her name, sensing danger. Would that torment her, hearing her mom's voice and not being able to respond? I don't want to think about why she couldn't cry out. Can't face the idea of her being gagged and tied up. My heart shatters at the thought. The same thought that's been ravaging me for these past two days.

"We need to let the police handle this," he says.

"The police aren't moving fast enough, though, are they?" I charge bitterly, although I know that's not true. They've been working as hard as they can. Some of them around the clock. Chief Claremont told me they work in shifts. There are always officers out there searching for Emma. The Amber Alert's in force.

Allen tugs me up against him, holding me close. "You're freezing," he says. "You should come inside." It's still warm outdoors, but he's right. My blood doesn't seem to be circulating properly, traveling from my heart to my extremities. Maybe it's because my heart is barely beating.

"You said the police think it could be someone we know." I turn around to face him. "If it's not Cass, then who is it?" He's been adamant about defending Teresa at every turn, saying it's not her. "Allen," I say. "If the police haven't eliminated Teresa as a person of interest, maybe neither should we?"

"It can't be her, Sadie. She's Forrest's mom, too. She wouldn't do that to him. To Emma. For crying out loud, to us."

"Then who?"

We stare back at Cass's house. She's gone from the window now and the shade is drawn. The internal light beyond it goes off. "Come on, Sadie. It's really hard for me to believe it's Cass. She was a nice kid in high school, not some teenage psycho."

"You said you barely knew her?"

"I mean, from what I saw." He keeps acting like there was nothing there, saying they never had a history. Then why is he in such a hurry to defend *her*—a person he barely knew—the same way he's done Teresa?

A memory surfaces about the night of Emma and "Bobby's" play-date, last Friday. Allen came home late from work. Generally he calls or texts to say he's running behind. That night he didn't.

Allen removes his suit jacket and tie after entering the kitchen from the garage. "Hey. How was your day?" he asks me.

135

"It was okay." I'm making spaghetti on the stove. I pulled the sauce I made from summer vegetables from the standup freezer in the garage. I'm still unsettled by the playdate experience with Cass. "Are you sure you don't remember more about Cass from high school?" Water gurgles to life in the pot I've heated for the noodles, steam rising. I add pasta, small fistfuls at a time.

He shakes his head. "No, sorry." Allen hooks his jacket and tie over one arm, heading for the back stairs. "Hey," he says, evidently remembering, "didn't Emma and her kid, Bobby, have a playdate today?"

Emma plays in the backyard while I fix dinner. I kept her indoors for two hours due to our fake dental appointments, and she was eager for some fresh air. She's got the lid off the sandbox and digs in the sand, filling a bright-green bucket with a shovel.

"Did, as in past tense. Didn't happen," I respond.

He pauses on the bottom step. "Why not?"

"Emma was supposed to go there, but I didn't let her stay. The house seemed empty, spooky. Cass kept saying Bobby was on his way home, and she wanted me to leave Emma there with her. But I got a weird feeling. Said we'd reschedule for another time."

He leans into the railing, holding it with one hand. "Well, Sadie, that could have been true, you know. About Bobby."

"No, Allen." I lay my wooden spoon on a spoon rest and turn toward him. "When we got back from her house, I did some looking online. She does work where she says she does, but I couldn't find anything at all about the kid she claims she has."

"Could be his legal address is with his dad?" Allen says. "Maybe his dad's got a different last name, and maybe so does Bobby? Listen, Sadie," he says reasonably, "lots of kids don't have footprints online. Let's hope to God Emma doesn't."

Allen's making sense. Still. I didn't like the sensation I had while standing in that house. It felt haunted. Part of me worries that I'm overreacting or imagining things. But I can't help being protective of my daughter.

The spaghetti-noodle pot returns to a boil. I stir it. "You're probably right," I say, looking up. I blow out a breath, my mind made up. "I'm still not letting Emma play over there, though."

"I trust your judgment." His blue eyes shimmer. "Your call."

He takes the stairs.

"Long day at work today?"

"Yeah. Had a problem with some clients."

For some reason, he doesn't look at me.

Why do I think he's lying?

I study his face in the shadows, and for an instant I don't know him. Claremont told me to keep an open mind, but I slammed mine shut. A crowbar of doubt pries it open. *What is Allen hiding?* All this time I've been thinking it was about Teresa. What if I'm wrong?

Teresa's not the only one Allen's been making excuses for.

What if he knows more than he's saying about Cass?

KATE
THE TEACHER

Day Two

Shane walks into the bedroom where I'm watching TV. He's had another late night. He doesn't like sharing his emotions, but the stress shows on his face. I hit the pause button on the remote. "Any news?" I ask as he walks over. His got a beer in his hand, which he puts on the nightstand.

He drops down on the bed, dead weight. "Parents gave another press conference." He's shed most of his uniform in the living room and is in his undershirt and uniform pants. "No real developments that I can speak of." He's noncommittal, being vague. A cop through and through. Doing the honorable thing. Keeping his professional confidences.

I push back the covers and scoot over to him, setting my feet on the floor. I hug his arm, snuggling close to him, attempting to win him over with my sweetness. He loves how sweet I am. He finds me charming. I've never been charming to anyone else before, and it's nice being charming to Shane. "Any suspects? Persons of interest?"

"Babe." He unties one shoe and then the other, kicking them off. "You know I can't say."

"She was in my class, Shane." I say it like I'm super distressed and this is breaking my heart. Like I'm the kind of teacher he thinks I am. Concerned. Caring. Someone who would do anything for her students.

His gaze washes over me, so warm and compassionate, it's tragic. For an instant, I wish I could be the person he wants me to be. But I can't. It's psychologically impossible. "Yeah. I'm sorry about that." He leans forward, resting his elbows on his knees. "It's just . . ." He hangs his head. "Very complicated, that's all." I don't like the toll this case is taking on him. I'll be glad when it's over. When they've finally given up. Called it a day. They'll never find Emma.

I try to sound understanding. "I suppose all cases of missing children are."

"Yeah." He glances at me. A tired smile. "What have you been up to all night?"

I shrug. "Streaming shows on TV." I don't say I've been glued to the news coverage about Emma, hunting for clues. I want to know how much the police know. I wish I could find a way for Shane to tell me more. I've been paying extra attention when he's around. Trying to listen in when he gets work calls without him knowing it. Peering over his shoulder when he's on the computer. Stealing peeks at his notebook on the table.

Shane stares at the television screen. I'm in the middle of one of our favorite police procedurals. It's set in Scotland and the scenery's stunning. I'd like to go to Scotland someday, maybe with Shane. Maybe we'll get married? Go there on our honeymoon? Shane will probably ask me to get engaged, and I think I'll say yes. It will be good for my job and make me look settled. Parents will like me even more, believing I'm such a safe bet. Someone married to a cop.

"That sounds like the right idea," he says. He picks up his beer. "Maybe I'll settle in and watch something with you."

"Hungry?" I ask him.

He takes a swig of beer and sets down the bottle. "Not really."

Less than forty-eight hours, and this investigation is already wearing him thin. I hate this for Shane. It leaves him distracted and less able to focus on me. Yesterday, he was upset about Emma, sure. But also more upbeat and hopeful about the prospects of catching the perpetrator, it seemed. We wouldn't have had sex if he'd been *that* down about it, but we did, and it was good.

Tonight, he appears more discouraged, like maybe sex won't be an option. But I can tough that part out for a few more days if need be. I'll be understanding, supportive. Not put an ounce of pressure on him unless he initiates. He can't know what I know. He'd have me out on the street so fast my head would spin. So I guard my secrets, watching it all unfold.

I've got a feeling they've got their eyes on the ex-wife and one of Emma's neighbors. Shane went to talk to her this morning. I overheard his quick phone call with Chief Claremont before he left for the station. I think her last name is Thomas. If she lives behind the Wilsons, I can probably find her street. Figure out which house is hers. No doubt there's a neighborhood directory of some kind. It's *that* kind of neighborhood. I already know where Teresa lives. Her address and phone number are in the parent database at school.

I wrap my arms around his shoulders in a hug. "I know you can't name names," I say as temptingly as I can, "but if I at least knew the police have someone they're looking into, it would make me feel so much better."

He meets my gaze. His eyes are liquid brown, pools of dark chocolate. He's a good-looking guy. So handsome. "All right." He presses his lips together and then says, "We have persons of interest."

Persons, plural. Which is what I suspected, and I'm fine with. As long as I'm not on the list. "Thank God," I sigh like I really mean it.

Shane gives me a funny look and my heart stutters.

He can't honestly be starting to wonder about me and whether I'm somehow involved? I've been cleared. I'm his "Babe." He loves me. He'd never suspect me, never turn me in.

Handcuffs slap around Katherine's wrists, and cold hard metal dents her skin.

She's hauled toward a cop car with flashing blue lights.

I close my eyes and breathe deeply, knowing that will never happen. There's no fucking way they'll ever pin anything on me. If Allen's never connected the dots between the two of us, then no one else will either. I kiss Shane's cheek and warmly say, "Thanks for telling me."

He shakes his head. "Probably shouldn't have."

"It's all right." I hug him harder. "I won't tell."

It's those other things I'm not telling about that might land me in prison. Shit.

Katherine didn't understand what she was witnessing at the time because she was just a kid, but she knows now. Allen was a bad influence on Diane in more ways than one. He led our sister down a dark path, and in turn our entire family. Nobody knew Katherine was there lurking in the shadows. Katherine's the only one who knows the truth.

The only one who saw everything.

The bunk bed creaks below Katherine. Diane grabs her sweatshirt and sneaks out of the room. She's not supposed to be leaving. Diane's fifteen. Katherine's eight.

Katherine creeps down the ladder and follows her. Shadows flood the great room, moonbeams stretching into the cottage. The dark ocean rolls and roars beyond the sliding glass doors. Diane slides one open and slips outside. It's not quite closed when Katherine reaches it. She slips out too and hides. Wind buffets her short nightie, and chill bumps rise on her legs and arms. Still, she follows Diane.

Surf pounds the beach and it's dark, but there's a big yellow moon above.

Katherine sees them huddled together on the sand. Diane and someone are drinking. Wait. That's Mark's friend Allen. He's sixteen. A red ember passes between them.

They're smoking too. Diane will be in huge trouble for both.

Maybe Katherine should tell?

Now they're laughing and pointing at the water. She's stripping off her sweatshirt and he's climbing out of his jeans.

Katherine covers her mouth and giggles—they're naked! And going into the water. Splashing each other, hugging. Kissing. Their glistening bodies bobbing in the water. Gross.

Diane breaks away, splashing water into Allen's face.

He laughs and wipes his eyes.

Wait. What? Where's our sister?

Allen looks around. He doesn't see her either.

Our heart thumps. Then it thumps harder.

Allen's shouting and shouting, trudging through the shallows and screaming her name. He's cursing. Shit! Shit! Yanking up his jeans and racing across the sand.

He slams into the house and darts up the stairs, taking them in leaps.

His parents' bedroom light goes on.

Then our parents' light.

They call it a riptide.

Diane's body is never found.

SADIE
THE MOM

Day Two

I lie in bed until Allen's sleeping, having decided to go through his yearbook myself. I can no longer take his word for it about Cass, or trust what he's telling me about high school. I've never had occasion to study his yearbook before. I didn't really see the point. I didn't even keep mine, but I understand why he kept his. He was a big deal in high school, apparently. Popular. He's modest in how he talks about it, but it's been easy enough to gather from the things he's said.

I asked him about his yearbook once when we were first married and combining the books we owned on our first jointly stocked bookshelves. He flipped through the pages and showed me a few photos of him playing soccer and basketball. Him hanging out with his group. There was nothing unusual in what I saw then, and I'm not sure what I'm looking for now. I just have the sense that I'll know it when I see it. That something will jump out at me.

My stomach churns because this feels duplicitous somehow. Sneaking around in my own house. But I need to know the truth about Allen, especially if there's something he's concealed that could help me find our little girl. When he got home late from work last week, I thought he was lying about those clients, and that he was up to something else instead. Now I'm wondering if his obfuscation had to do with my questions about Cass? He keeps reiterating the fact that he didn't know her well. Looking back, that seems odd. Like he's protesting too much.

I creep out of our bedroom and stop on the threshold of Emma's room. Her night-light's on as it always is, casting a pretty sheen across the pastel pinks and purples of her window seat cushion, frilly curtains, and quilt. I hold my hand to my heart and stare at her bed, where Night Doggie saves her spot.

It breaks me to pieces that she doesn't have him with her. If nothing else, she should have her special lovey to hang on to with all her might. She'd still be scared and so badly missing her parents and home. But at least with Night Doggie by her side, she'd feel safe. Comforted. Not like her entire world has been wrenched away.

I steal down the back staircase in the shadows, pictures of Emma lodged in my brain. My gaze flits to the darkened window by the kitchen table, and I see her on the swings and in her sandbox, playing so happily on a summer's day. I need to believe she's still out there, waiting to be found. Waiting to come home to this house. *To me.*

It's been less than forty-eight hours, and there's still so much hope. Claremont's words about Allen ring out to me like a clanging a gong. Of course I've heard those statistics too and know it's sometimes a parent. But in our case, no. Allen can't be involved. How could he? He would never hurt Emma. He's as broken up as I am about her being gone. And yet. He's very uncomfortable around the topic of Teresa. And now, Cass Thomas too.

I'm starting to think there are things in Allen's past I'm not aware of. Just look at the jury duty connection he had with Caleb Walsh. He didn't mention it at all when he should have, first to me and then to the police. Allen seems to hide things when they're inconvenient or when it makes him uncomfortable to share. I've never considered that about him before, but that truth is glaring at me now like a blinding bright light. Allen's not always been truthful with me. Maybe he's still not being truthful now.

I pass through the darkened kitchen, stealing a glance out the window at Emma's play set. Moonlight glistens on the slide and haunts the hollows of the tugboat, the sandbox lid left open. Loss and longing flood me, sweeping me away on a tide of grief.

Will we dismantle the play set if she never comes home? Or leave it there in homage to her forever? I have to rid myself of these dismal thoughts. They're not helping. I need to focus on my goal of finding Emma. Even if that means the unthinkable. Even if it means suspecting my husband in our own child's kidnapping.

The kitchen's open to the family room, and I walk in.

I find Allen's high school yearbook on the shelf.

SADIE
THE MOM

Day Two

I finish looking through Allen's senior year yearbook for the second
time. I've gone carefully through its pages, one at a time, and Allen was
right. While there are gobs of photos of him due to his activities—and
popularity, I suppose—there's only one that I found of Cass. Her ninth-
grade photo with others in her class.

She wasn't homely like I suspected. Maybe I'd thought she was
one of those ugly ducklings who'd turned into a swan. But no. She was
also cute back then, with smiling eyes and apple-dumpling cheeks, the
words "future cheerleader" written all over her perky face.

Allen dated a cheerleader his senior year. Allen dated a lot before I
met him. He was obviously married too. I don't enjoy dwelling on the
thought of him being with anyone else, and never have, so I push those
annoying thoughts away, flipping back through the yearbook's pages. I
land on the ninth grade and Cass's photo. She was Cass Curtis then. I
guess Thomas came from Richard. If there is a Richard. I'm questioning
everything.

Cass is clearly the type to invent things. Maybe she also invented
having an ex-husband? Allen hints that I'm being paranoid, seeing

shadows around every corner. But maybe it's just that he has certain revelations he doesn't want me to find. As hard as it might be to handle, I need to learn the truth about Allen. Even if that means he's not the man I thought he was. Even if—God forbid—he's connected to Emma's kidnapping. In which case, he'll wind up in jail. If that happens, I hope he rots there and they throw away the key.

I hate thinking bad things about Allen, but he's a grown man who can look after himself. And if he's done the unthinkable in harming our daughter, he'll just have to suffer the consequences. Emma is a child. *My child* and she needs protecting.

I glance up at my backyard and through the trees, I spy a sliver of Cass's house. It sits there in the darkness, and all its lights are out. I'm pained thinking of Emma. Emma can't stand being in the dark. That's why we installed the LED night-light that automatically comes on each evening. It breaks my heart that she's somewhere without her special lovey, but she *will* come home. I feel it. If she doesn't, I might not make it. I'm not sure how I'd continue functioning from day to day. I push those horrifying thoughts away and stare down at my lap. I'm about to give up on the yearbook when I flip through one final time, thumbing with my fingers page after page, until I've passed the final one and—wait.

The last several pages were left blank intentionally because that's where the student autographs are. I start to read them out of curiosity. One's in big swirly letters and written in pink pen. "Can't wait for prom!" It's signed "Jen" with a big heart. My stomach sours. That was the cheerleader. Whatever. She was very beautiful, and she and Allen were supposedly serious then. Of course, it was high school. So how serious could they have been?

It's not like he married Jen, like he did Teresa. It's not like they had a child together. Allen had other girlfriends in college, but he doesn't really mention them. Which is fine. I'd rather not hear about them.

What wife wants to know about all the other wonderful women who captured her husband's heart, and most probably his body in bed?

The very thought makes me ill. I read a few more autographs. Some seem to be in code I can't decipher. Some are from other sports players, with allusions to great games, goals and matches.

I laser focus in on a message. It's not from Allen's cheerleader girl-friend, Jen. It's from someone named "CC."

I want to have your baby!
XOXO

Waves of nausea crash over me.
Shit.
I flip back through the yearbook's pages as fast as I can go.
Ninth grade, *here*.
I press my finger below Cass's photo.
Cassidy "CC" Curtis.

O'REILLY
THE COP

Day Three

We're in the briefing room and it's the first thing in the morning. Most folks hold paper cups of coffee and look tired. We've been pulling long nights. Some here at the station, some on patrol, others working over-time from home. I've already had a double espresso shot myself.

Claremont taps Allen's and Teresa's photos on the bulletin board with a pointer. "We now have reason to believe that Allen and his ex-wife, Teresa, were having an affair. We also suspect the two of them may have been together at the time of Emma's disappearance, but nei-ther has admitted to that. Allen's alibi didn't hold water. He was not en route to work like he claimed, and the timing of his commute and when he received the call from Sadie about Emma not being at school don't add up." She glances at Mercer, who nods, his gaze sweeping the room.

"Which of you went to the observatory?" the chief asks.

Patel stands. "Talked to a couple folks who work in her lab, also one of her bosses. She's got no alibi at the time of Emma's disappearance either. She claims to have been in her office, but nobody saw her come in. A cleaning crew member thought he saw her lights on in her office, but he's not sure. Nothing conclusive and no CCTV."

"Can we maybe go back further?" Mercer asks Claremont. "Track her movements in the weeks leading up to Emma's disappearance? Maybe we can find a pattern? A history of her and Allen meeting up? Or her preparing for a kidnapping somehow? Same goes for Allen?"

Jesus. That would be awful. Though rationally I know somebody planned for this ahead of time. It's very unlikely that somebody taking Emma was a last-minute crime of passion. Her disappearance was calculated. Even if the calculations didn't take long, somebody thought this out in advance.

Claremont sets her gaze on Patel, expecting her to volunteer. She does. "Yes, Chief." She nods, sitting back down.

"What if it's just an affair that they're hiding?" Rodriguez asks.

"Could be," Mercer agrees. He said as much to me and Claremont earlier when it was just the three of us in the room.

"Allen's lying about something," Mercer says. "I'm just not totally sure about what. He confessed to an affair with Teresa but doesn't want Sadie to know."

I turn to Claremont. "What do you think about that, Chief?"

She spreads open her hands. "Let's see how things play out."

"If Allen and Teresa's main alibis are each other," Mercer adds, "then it's eventually going to come out. If I were Allen?" Mercer rubs his beard. "I'll tell Sadie myself first."

Claremont addresses Rodriguez. "Learn anything on the neighbor?"

"Yeah," she says. She takes out some notes and gets ready. This I've got to hear. I want all the dirt on Cass Thomas possible. I'm pretty sure she's hiding something.

"There was nothing in the old yearbooks that stood out," Rodriguez says, "but I started checking around on the school's website and found a link to their electronic alumni magazine. It goes back several years to when Cassidy Curtis graduated. She went by a nickname in high school, CC."

Everyone waits with bated breath.

She's about to drop something.

"There were some reunion photos from different class years. Guess who attended her ten-year?" She grins self-satisfiedly. "Cass 'CC' Thomas with her kid and husband. Kid was a toddler then, probably two or three."

Holy shit.

"Dug through public records." Rodriguez checks notes on her phone. "She and Richard Thomas divorced roughly a year after that reunion photo was taken. A year and a half later, the ex-husband and the boy were in a fatal car accident. It was a shared custody arrangement. Richard was bringing their son back to Cass's house when the wreck occurred." She pauses to let the weight of that sink in. The room's dead silent. That's a big reveal.

Bobby. Fuck. So there *was* a child, but there isn't any longer. It's my turn next but I'm tongue tied. That failed playdate is sounding more than weird now. It's looking fucking scary. Why would Cass Thomas have wanted Emma left there alone unless she had something nefarious in mind? It's at the very least creepy. At worst, we've got a motive for kidnapping.

Claremont stares at me. "O'Reilly? You spoke to Cass Thomas yesterday. Got anything to add to that?"

"Yeah." I pull out of my fog. "I think we need to search that house."

"Probable cause?"

"She lied to Sadie about having a kid, acting like Bobby was still alive. Tried to set up that fake playdate. Wanted Emma to stay with her. Alone."

"That's weak, O'Reilly, and you know it. She could concoct a million and one excuses about that, might claim she never said that to Sadie. Never invited Emma over, that it was Sadie who made up the story. Sadie's word against hers. Any witnesses to the playdate invite?"

I shake my head, recalling my conversations with Sadie. "Only the kid herself, Emma."

Claremont sighs. "Yeah, well. Unfortunately, we can't ask her." She crosses her arms. "Find something more."

Crap. I was worried she'd say that. "One more thing." I address the room. "Principal Rand was involved in another legal matter some years ago involving Caleb Walsh."

"Yes, I'm aware of that," Claremont says. "You think there's a connection?"

"Not sure." I sink my hands in my pockets. "There is a common thread, though. Stonefield Elementary."

Claremont removes Walsh's photo from a folder and holds it up to the group. "Walsh was the convicted sex offender with the solid alibi we removed from suspicion earlier. He's still technically in the clear, but new data has come to light.

"Allen Wilson was the jury foreman at his trial. So Walsh could have had motive for harming Emma. Walsh's life basically blew apart during the intensity of the media coverage following his conviction. His wife, Chelsea, left him, taking their infant daughter and moving out of state. Chelsea severed all ties with Walsh's family after that, and Walsh served eight months in prison. Still, given Walsh's solid alibi, we're missing an apparent opportunity.

"I'm putting Walsh back on the board for now, but over here. Something material will have to change about his whereabouts for him to become a suspect, but I agree the coincidence of Allen having served on his jury is strange." She tacks his picture outside the ring of others. She digs through her file for one last photo.

It's of Principal Rand. She pins Rand's pic up next to Walsh's. "Not sure about the principal," Claremont says, pointing to her. "It's possible, but probably unlikely, she's engaged in some kind of cover-up. Let's keep our eyes and ears open, just in case."

SADIE
THE MOM

Day Three

I'm in the family room with my coffee when Allen comes down the back staircase. I spent half the night on the sofa staring at his yearbook and the other half upstairs in Emma's bedroom, sitting in the dark and holding Night Doggie. How could he hide that about Cass? Why would he? Was he covering up for her the way he's been covering up for Teresa?

I want to have your baby! XOXO, CC

That hardly sounds like a note from someone he barely knew and only passed in the halls. I get that it's a thing girls say, "Oh my God, I want to have his baby!" But they almost never say it to their crushes directly, if that's what this was all about. Cass did indicate to me she'd crushed on Allen in high school, like lots of people did. Still. This new knowledge gives me the willies. What if she wanted Allen's baby literally?

He takes a mug from the cabinet and makes himself a coffee. "You're up early."

I'm aware the dark circles under my eyes show. I saw them in the mirror when I finally showered and washed my hair very early this morning. I can count the hours of sleep I've gotten over the last three days on one hand. I'm on the sofa under a blanket, my knees drawn into my chest. I rest my coffee mug on them. It's nearly empty. "Couldn't sleep."

"I'm sorry about that." He walks toward me and frowns. "The waiting's brutal, I get it." He sits in a club chair nearby and pulls out his phone. "Nothing new this morning from Claremont or O'Reilly," he reports. He shakes his head. "Maybe I'll go in to work today. I don't know." He looks as exhausted as I feel. "Claremont said we should stick to our usual routines as much as possible, rather than sit around fraught with worry. Maybe doing something to distract myself would help." He glances out the window at the gate. "I'll fix that faulty latch first."

I can't believe he's thinking of leaving me to contend with this catastrophe on my own. We haven't found Emma. Haven't solved anything yet, and he needs to give me some answers. "Allen," I say. "Why didn't you tell me about Cass?"

He's broadsided, his coffee mug jerking away from his lips. "What's that?"

"'XOXO'?" I pick up the yearbook sitting beside me and hold it in front of him. "CC?"

"Shit." He drags a hand down his face. "Sadie, it's not what you think. I swear. It was really nothing."

"Oh my God, Allen! 'I want to have your baby!' You said you didn't remember her!"

"I didn't!" His voice cracks sharply. "I swear." He huffs out a breath. "It wasn't until I went back through the yearbook the day she brought the wine by that I remembered, but it was so long ago, and really inconsequential, Sadie. She didn't mean it. She was only joking around."

"Allen!" I throw the blanket aside and set my feet on the floor. "Cass is a *person of interest*," I emphasize, leaning toward him, "in Emma's disappearance."

He sighs. "We don't know where that's going yet." What is it with him? Why can't he see the obvious?

"Oh my God, Allen." My temper flares. "How could you keep that from me? I'm your *wife*. And Cass is what? Another ex-girlfriend? Is that why you've kept this from me?"

"What? Jesus, no." He sets his coffee mug on an end table. "She was just a kid at Braxton. Besides, I had a girlfriend my senior year, Jen. You know that."

"So then," I press, "what's with the message and the 'XOXO'?"

He holds open his hands and shrugs. "She had a crush, I guess?"

"So you remember her then, a lot more than you said?"

His neck colors. "Okay, yes. A little."

My temples throb. "Allen, how could you not tell me? Not tell the police?"

"Because it was stupid stuff, Sadie. Seriously. High school non-sense." I'm starting to panic, thinking about wasted time. How could Allen do this to me? Do this to Emma? Is she there with Cass? Or has Cass taken her somewhere, maybe hidden her at the school where she works? O'Reilly said her alibi was weak. Oh my God, Claremont was right. I can't trust Allen.

I cross my arms, my head reeling. So he *has* been lying to me. And if he's lied about this, then what else? "I want to hear the story."

He rubs his tightly shut eyes. After a moment he opens them. "There was this party, okay? Somebody's parents were out of town. I don't know, maybe Kyle's? It was a long time ago." Images of a wild high school party fill my mind, the unruly sort you see in teenage films.

"What happened at this party, Allen?"

"Nothing all that bad, I promise. I mean, drinking, sure, yeah. But it was mostly seniors. A few ninth graders showed up. I still don't know who let them in. One of them was Cass. I was out chatting by the pool with some guys when she walks up to me and starts flirting."

I squirm inside. "What do you mean *flirting*?"

"Saying things like 'Ooh, it's you, the mega soccer star. It's so great to meet you.' Crap like that. Dillion's there and jokes, 'Hey, Wilson, I think you've got an admirer.' I tell him to cool it and try to politely brush Cass off. She pouts and says there's one problem, she's made a bet with her girlfriends. I look over and see a bunch of them watching. I ask what kind of bet. She says they've dared her to come and ask for my jersey, the literal shirt off my back."

"For God's sake, Allen. You gave it to her?"

"Sadie. It was a stupid thing. All right? High school. She got a charge out of it, and all my friends thought it was hilarious. Okay, except for Jen. She was slightly pissed when she came back with our drinks and found me shirtless."

"I'll bet."

"Anyway, it was nothing. Except I had to pay for a replacement jersey. That sucked." I'm trying to read his eyes and gauge if he's telling the truth. Some people are really great at telling half truths, though. They say a bit of what's real mixed in with lies so it's harder to sort things out.

"What did Cass do with it?" I ask him.

He glances out the window and toward her house, almost like he thinks she's watching us. Maybe she is. "She wore it to school a couple of times. After that, I have no idea."

"You didn't talk after that?" I stare at her house too, but it looks still. I check the clock in the kitchen. It's nearly eight a.m.

"Not really." His face says he's guilty. He's not telling me everything.

"What about the night of the party? What happened there?" There are details he's not giving me. I want them because they could be useful. How could he not have seen this might be connected to Emma going missing? Oh my God.

He shrugs. "After I gave her the shirt, she went back to her girlfriends. They were amazed I'd actually done it. That I'd given her my shirt. One of them shouts—just to embarrass her, I'm sure—'Hey, Wilson! She wants to have your baby!' Cass was totally humiliated, burying her face in her hands. They did that just to razz her, I'm sure. She was new and trying to be one of the cool girls. That's why she came to the party. That's why she took their dare about the jersey."

"How do you know all this?"

He sighs. "She told me later in the hall. She stopped me by my locker, her cheeks all red, and tried to return the jersey a few days later, saying she felt stupid about the whole thing. She was sorry. But at that point I'd already paid for a new one, so I said no sweat, she could keep it. Sadie," he says, "I'm not even convinced she wrote that note in my yearbook. You know how it is. Yearbooks get passed around all the time for various people to sign. Any of her friends could have done it as a joke. That's what I suspected back then. What I still think now. That's why I didn't mention it. It was nothing."

I glance at Cass's house and the gate swinging open between our backyards.

I'm not so sure about that.

TERESA
THE EX-WIFE

Day Three

I email my bosses saying I'm distressed about Emma's kidnapping and need to take a few days off. They understand Allen's my ex-husband and this affects me and Forrest too. I tell them I'm sending Forrest to stay at my mom's house in Virginia for a couple of weeks and want to coordinate with his teachers about providing assignments online, and they are very understanding about me needing the time to pull arrangements together.

What I don't tell my bosses is that I'm planning to take more than a few days before coming back to my job. If I ever come back at all. My heart bleeds when I think of leaving Forrest behind. But my leaving is better than him knowing his mom is behind bars and having to live with that fact among his peers.

I need to wait until I'm in the clear, and then I'll send an email, asking my bosses for extended personal leave. I'm a valued employee and have contributed greatly to the university with my research. They'll allow it. At least for six months, if the police stay off my tail in the meantime. I'll be on the other side of the country by the time my leave runs out. Maybe I'll be out of the country. We'll see how far I get.

Forrest doesn't need this disruption in his life. The drama. Getting a front row view to his mom's being led away in cuffs. I'm glad my mom came to North Carolina early to pick him up. She's a good person and he loves her. She'll look after him for me. For as long as it takes. Even if it takes forever, and it might.

I'm in my bedroom, pulling a suitcase from my closet. I set the rolling bag on my bed and unzip it, packing everything I bought. The clothing I purchased for a small child. Shorts outfits, blue jeans, a pair of overalls she would have looked adorable in. A few cute play dresses with sparkly sandals. Socks and underwear. Matching bows and hair ties to go with everything. I've also got toiletries. Toothpaste and a toothbrush, a comb. Lilac-scented shampoo and soaps. Pajamas, nighties and slippers. I was finally getting our little girl.

I spent a nearly a decade waiting on Allen, never imagining this could happen. Dreaming of a life I thought I'd lost and could never have again. Then when he was here last week, everything changed. After being stuck in remembrances of what *was*, I finally saw a way forward, a way for us to be together again—a family.

But not the family we had—a new and bigger one. One that included Emma. We wouldn't have to share custody and ferry her back and forth. That's been hell on Forrest. How could we do that to another child? Maybe Allen and I could find a way to get back together and keep both Forrest and Emma for ourselves?

I've been spying on Allen and his family this past week. Sneaking in through the back gate and watching Sadie and Allen, imagining myself in her place. In her house. In her life. There were ways for me to make that happen. To give myself all she had.

I just had to organize things strategically so Allen would agree. Devise a neat plan with no loose ends. I had to take the lead. After what Allen said that day, he left me no choice.

After we make love on the couch, Allen holds me. I'm tucked under his arm, my cheek resting on his chest, and we both snuggle down in the sofa blanket.

Trees dance in the breeze outside the window, limbs curtseying toward each other. We know we don't have long, but for now we have this.

"We probably shouldn't have," he says in hushed tones. His lulling heartbeats soothe me as he gently strokes my hair.

This is how it should be. The two of us together. I can't believe how much I've missed him. Being with him now fills that unfathomable hole in my heart.

I release a deep breath. "Maybe not," I say, "but Allen?" I raise my head to peer at him. "Maybe it was time?"

He kisses me on the forehead. "Yeah. Maybe." He says it like this is goodbye, the fond farewell we never had. But that's not how I think of it. I see this as a window opening to the future. Our future, his and mine.

I lay my head back down on his chest and speak to the woods. Somehow it's easier than looking at him directly. What I'm about to say will expose me, make me raw.

"I've been thinking a lot about us, and I don't mean just today." My ankle twines around his, our bare feet brushing. His muscled leg's nestled beneath my thigh. I run my hand across his chest, loving the feel of him. Wishing I could have this always and that we hadn't wasted so many years.

His voice rumbles, "So have I."

My heart swells so large with hope it aches. "Maybe it's not too late?"

He swallows hard. "Sadie," he replies firmly. "She'd never let Emma go."

"Shared custody?" I venture, knowing that's not what I'd want either.

"She'd never go for it. She'd want Emma all to herself."

"What if there was no Emma?" My words hang there in the air, weighty, dark.

His tone changes. "Don't even think that," he barks.

I rush to cover my tracks quickly. "I didn't mean it like that, Allen. Jesus." I meet his eyes and try to smooth things out. "I meant if there never had been?" I soften my tone. "In a different life?"

He rakes a hand through his hair and says, "This is the life we're living, Teri, and I love my little girl." I know then that Emma will always be a part of us. A part of the equation, as long as she's around.

"Of course you do," I say. But he still might never have had her if it hadn't been for me. If I hadn't fucked up the beautiful thing he and I had together by letting him go.

He folds back the sofa blanket and I scoot out of his arms, feeling like I've made a misstep. He's unhappy with me now. After how close we were only minutes ago, it breaks my heart. Both of us dress in silence. I see the iPod on the coffee table, but I don't mention it. Maybe if he forgets to take it now, I'll have an excuse to see him again. Another chance to fix this.

To fix us.

I'm not giving up. What I once thought was impossible is possible again. I just have to find a way. Allen puts on his tie and stares at the rumpled sofa blanket, and then at me. "We should probably pretend this never happened."

I'm on the highway in a head-on collision. It happens too fast—I don't even know I've crossed the line. I grab his arms, holding them through his shirtsleeves. "You don't mean that."

"Yeah, Teri, I do."

The steering column rams into my chest.

I can't think or breathe.

I'm dying.

"No."

"Teri." He holds my face in his hands. "I'm sorry. This was a mistake."

I grip him harder, my world spiraling. How can he not want this too? Everything's changed. We were like we were before. We can bring yesterday back, but better. "Allen, we can make this work. You and me and Forrest and Emma."

"That's a fantasy, Teri." He tries to move away but I tighten my grasp.

"No, Allen. No."

He glares at my hands where they're holding his arms.

My heart pounds and I slowly release him.

Rebar slices through me, a stake in my heart. Blood is on my face and on my hands. He picks up his suit jacket. "I'd better go."

Shards pierce my flesh like broken glass.

I'm a million scattered pieces, all of them screaming.

"Allen, please." I hate that I'm begging. Pleading for my life. "Don't go! Not like this!" I race after him, and he wheels on me in the foyer.

I stumble, grabbing onto his arm.

He pulls me upright with his other hand and his grip pinches. So tight. Like a blood pressure cuff squeezing my upper arm. I think it'll leave a bruise.

He glowers down at me, breathing hard.

His grasp tightens before he lets me go.

Then it tightens some more.

I break a panicked sweat at the gleam in his eyes.

The finality in his stare.

He wants me to believe it's over, but I can't. I won't.

He walks out and shuts the door.

Leaves me lying on the side of the road.

Abandoning me a second time.

I reach into my nightstand and grab one last item.

I lay it in the suitcase on top of everything else.

Sadie's iPod.

KATE
THE TEACHER

Day Three

School is dismissed and the kids have gone home. Dotti's left too. I sit in my rocking chair and stare at Emma's desk. Her name tag's so gloomy, hanging over the classroom like a little black cloud. I've been instructed by Principal Rand to leave Emma's desk intact for a few more days. Then I'm to discreetly remove her name tag and rearrange my seating groups. Principal Rand thinks it's morbid for the other kids to remember a missing student once it's clear that Emma's not coming back.

Everyone at Stonefield Elementary knows Emma's not coming back. Forget about the candlelight vigils being held here in the evenings, like a ritual at eight o'clock. Those do-gooders honestly don't believe Emma will be returned safely either. They just want their faces in the paper, and online, as a show of force for concerned citizens. It makes them feel proactive, like they're *doing* something, like they're protecting their own children by forming a ring of love around the school. *As if.*

No one can protect their children from lurking dangers out there. *No one.* Anyone who thinks they can is delusional. I can see why parents won't face it. Mine never faced it about Diane, or Mark. They didn't even care about losing touch with me. Maybe they considered it a relief when I dropped out of their lives. When I divorced myself from my family. I despised both my parents by then anyway. I also hated my dad's new wife, though not quite as much as I hated him.

It's good Forrest's mom sent him away. Otherwise he'd be privy to the rumors. It's not just employees here who are gossiping about Emma's disappearance and trying to figure out what happened to her—the kids are trading theories too. Many fifth graders think it was Forrest's fault. He hated his younger half sister, as any normal boy in his situation would. But maybe he's not *normal*. I've considered the angle of him being different, like Katherine. Dark and devoid of feeling except for a very few certain emotions.

My heart aches and I'm filled with sadness over the loss of our sister in a way few people would understand. Katherine thought her distress would lessen over time, but it hasn't. Introducing me to the pain only made those feelings worse. We share them now, the two of us, along with poignant memories of Diane. The wound's as fresh as if it happened yesterday, thanks to Allen being present at Stonefield and driving wood splinters into that deep gash. And now, Emma's gone missing, and the police don't have a clue.

I stand numbly from the rocker and walk to my desk, plunking down in my desk chair. I've been hiding something from the police until I can decide how to handle this. Katherine says I can't afford any mistakes. If I slip up, the shit could all blow back on me and I'll lose everything. Lose my job. Lose Shane. I could even be charged with kidnapping if I'm not careful. Go to prison. *Fuck.*

Is accessory after the fact an actual thing, or only something you hear about on cop shows? How did circumstances get this twisted? Before the police decide to give me a second look, I've got to get rid of the evidence.

I take plastic gloves from my first aid kit and put them on before pulling open my middle desk drawer and prying out the envelope concealed beneath my tray of paper clips, a ruler and scissors. It's a teacher note addressed to me, written by hand on a blank sheet of printer paper and sent in a sealed security envelope.

It's not uncommon for students' parents to send notes to their kids' teachers via "backpack express." In fact, we expect it. It *is* a bit unusual to receive an early dismissal request on the very first day of school, but I've seen it happen before. I've just never seen it occur under such suspicious circumstances.

I was shocked when I found this note on that first day of school, and then I had to decide what to do with the information. Since the manner in which I came by it could be viewed as more than a little self-incriminating, I opted to bide my time and wait.

See who came forward as witnesses. Learn as much as I could about case developments. Even glean information from Shane if I could. Allen was getting what he deserved, after all. Maybe this was the world's way of settling the score on our sister's behalf. We didn't have to do a damned thing except for not interfere.

The note requesting Emma's early dismissal was supposedly written by Emma's mom, Sadie, but Sadie's never said anything in her press statements about having intended to get Emma early. And clearly, nobody's mentioned that to me. So I suspect very heavily the note was fabricated by the person who really wrote it.

It's a forgery.

SADIE
THE MOM

Day Four

We made it through our fourth press conference, and each day in front of the cameras and microphones only gets harder. You'd think having practice would help, but no. It's awful to beg publicly for Emma's safe return. It makes us sound vulnerable, pathetic. Pleading with bloodshot eyes and trembling voices. Trying not to cry this time. Failing again. I don't even believe that whoever's taken her is watching.

Somebody else who might have seen or heard something could be, though. That's what the police remind us. As the days unfold, the case will fade from the public's view. We need to keep it present as much as possible, and for as long as possible. That's what Mercer says. The media won't support these press conferences forever. After a while, they'll go down to once a week. Then once a month. Eventually, they'll get spaced out further. Only occurring on special occasions like on the anniversary of when our child went missing.

I'm wrought with fear about Emma's disappearance being never ending. I want it to be *over*. I want us to have Emma here at home with us, safe and sound. I want to bathe my little girl and comb her hair. Help her put her pj's on and get her ready for bed. Read her bedtime stories. Say her prayers. The prayers that should have kept her safe but didn't.

Allen and I haven't spoken any more about Cass, or Teresa. He fixed the latch on the gate and went to work shortly after we talked. Maybe it was good for us to have space. I feel like I'm losing my mind accusing my husband of taking our daughter. Of course he didn't do that. Claremont was wrong. Allen has hidden things from me, though, and I want him to be sorry about that. I want him to apologize. He hasn't yet.

We made sandwiches and watched the news together in silence, staring blankly at our faces on the screen like those distraught parents were strangers, anyone but us. I wouldn't eat if I didn't believe I must. I'm staying alive for Emma. I climb the stairs, headed for her room. I have a nightly vigil of sitting on her bed. Praying. Hoping. Watching the light fade from the sky through the streetside windows and seeing the night-light gradually glow brighter.

I enter her room—and freeze. It looks like a wild tornado's hit it. The whole place has been upended. Torn from stem to stern. Ripped to shreds. Her covers yanked off her bed and heaped on the floor. Dresser drawers pulled open and dumped over. The closet door ajar. Dresses slipping from their hangers. Her clothes hamper turned upside down. For the love of God, her curtains yanked from the windows, a valance hanging from one end.

The carousel pony lamp from her dresser's smashed to smithereens on the floor.

What's happened?

Fear seizes my brain, and I can't think, can't process the scene beyond the guess that this is impossible. It's a nightmare. I'm dreaming, a horrible, horrible dream. No. I shiver and survey the mess. It's real. A wave of nausea crashes over me. I feel so violated. Lightheaded. Someone's been in our house. Are they still here? Oh my God. Who did this? Someone who has Emma? Some unhinged person who's seen us on the news? Broken in?

I open my mouth to call for help. I try to scream. No sound comes out. My feet won't move. I'm mute. I clutch my throat when it constricts, and wheeze. "*Allen,*" I manage, but it's weak. Barely audible. I shut my eyes and clench my fists, forcing power into my lungs and out through my mouth. "Allen!" I shriek. "Allen! Oh my God! Help!"

He comes running up the stairs, taking them in leaps and bounds. I hear his thundering footsteps in the hall. He stops and stands on the threshold, gawking. "What the hell?" His face goes slack with shock as he takes in the carnage.

Emma's window seat cushion is dislodged, and stuffed animals lie in a pile on the floor. Her small stables are turned over, toy horses on their sides, their splayed-out manes and tails combing the carpet. The dollhouse is wrecked. Like a giant hand reached through it and yanked the miniature furnishings out. A plastic kitchen table's missing one leg.

My stomach heaves and I cover my mouth with my hands.

I have an unfathomable thought. My pulse races. I almost can't bear to look. I'm afraid of what I won't find. I whip my view to the bed and the empty spot between Emma's throw pillows. *Nooo.* I dash to the bed and toss aside the pillows, pull up the fitted sheet. Strip back the mattress pad. Pointless. *Shit, shit, shit, shit, shit. Shit!*

My mind races off in a dozen scattered directions. Who could do this? Who would be so cruel? Someone who has Emma? Are they doing this to taunt us? My heart makes an imaginative leap. *Have they taken him for her?*

The room spins but I catch my breath.

"*Night Doggie,*" I say to Allen. "He's gone."

O'REILLY
THE COP

Day Four

There's a nine-one-one call from the Wilsons' house. There's been a break-in. What the hell? When I get there, gloved officers are going through the house. Patel's here and so is Rodriguez. I approach Rodriguez, who's examining the back door that leads to the patio.

"No signs of forced entry here or at the garage door. Front door either," she tells me. "Patel's checking the windows."

Patel emerges from a downstairs office with pocket doors. It faces the street. "Negative on the windows. Everything's intact. Hot day, central AC is on."

Rodriguez glances at me. "It's hard to see how anyone could have gotten in without a key."

"Thanks," I say. "Parents?"

She nods toward the back staircase. "Still upstairs."

The chief's with them talking to Sadie. Sadie's holding herself and shivering, kind of a mess. "Only one thing's missing as far as they can tell," Claremont says when I walk over. "A stuffed toy belonging to Emma. The special dog that she sleeps with." The room is totally trashed. It looks like a drug raid's gone down.

Tension snakes through me. Who would take Emma's special toy unless they knew her well enough to understand its importance? Someone who wanted to help her? "So that's good news, right?" I glance at the chief, Sadie, and Allen.

"Meaning she's okay?" Claremont speculates. She sighs. "Hopefully." Gloved officers prowl around the room, picking up dropped and broken pieces to examine them. Bagging items. Maybe they'll lift prints off something. That would help. Claremont speaks to them. "Anything?"

A few officers shake their heads. "Nothing yet," one says. It's incredible that someone doing this possibly wore gloves. That would take premeditating. That would also mean they'd trashed the room on purpose, but why? Why not just take the dog?

I share what Rodriguez said about no forced entry. "Who else, besides you two, has a key?" I ask Sadie and Allen.

Sadie turns to Allen. "What about Forrest?" Sadie rubs her upper arms. She looks cold. Allen wraps an arm around her. I can tell he loves his wife. What a prick for having an affair, though. Jesus. Guilt must be eating him alive.

"Right," Allen agrees. "He's got a copy for when he comes over." Meaning his mom, Teresa, has access to it too. Interesting.

"And Teresa lives close to here," Claremont states as fact. "Biking distance for Forrest, yes?"

Allen sees what Claremont's getting at. His face turns red. "For crying out loud, Forrest couldn't have done this. He's not even in town. Teri sent him to stay with his mom."

"What?" Sadie gapes at him, pulling herself out from under his arm. She grits her teeth and hisses quietly, "More secrets, Allen? Why didn't you tell me?"

Allen hangs his head.

Trouble in paradise *lost*. I should have seen that coming, knowing what I do about Allen and Teresa. I wonder if he's told Sadie yet. "Any other copies?" I ask them about the key.

"We keep a spare key on the patio for emergencies," Sadie says.

"Who knows about it?"

"Only us." Allen visually confers with Sadie. "Maybe Emma?"

"Yes," Sadie says. "Emma's seen us hide it there." More important information. Emma would know how to tell someone how to get into the house. My pulse hums. This is possibly very great news. This could indicate she's alive.

"Can you show me?" I ask.

I follow her downstairs while Allen hangs back to talk to Claremont.

"If you've got a photo of Emma with that dog somewhere," she says to him, "that would be good to have."

"There's one in a frame on Sadie's dresser in our bedroom," Allen says. "I'll get it."

Sadie and I exit onto the patio, and she points to a flowerpot situated among some others closer to the house. "Under there."

I bend and lift the pot.

There's no key.

Sadie stares at her back gate. It's unlatched and stands open about a foot.

"Deputy Chief O'Reilly," she says. "I need to tell you something about Allen and Cass."

SADIE
THE MOM

Day Five

Allen and I pick up Emma's room, putting it back together. After the emotional exhaustion of coping with the break-in and having the police here, we didn't have the heart to do this yesterday. The police dusted for prints and will let us know what they find if anything. Meanwhile, a car is stationed out front. They'll keep our house under watch as a precaution in case the intruder comes back. I don't think they will. Whoever came in here was looking for one specific thing and they got it.

"I can't believe someone would do this," I say, making Emma's bed. I shake out the top sheet and lay it down, then add the blanket and comforter. "Why trash the room? Why make such a horrible mess of things?" I pick up the dollhouse furniture, setting aside the broken pieces. "Destroy Emma's toys?"

"It has to be good news, though." Allen scoops littered clothing off the floor, folding it neatly and depositing it in Emma's dresser drawers. "Don't you think? Maybe this means that Emma's okay? That someone's looking after her?"

That's what I want to believe with all my might. "I hope so." I arrange bed linens, folding the top portion back and setting down the fluffed pillow. My heart stills as I stare at the vacant spot. An eerie thought occurs. "Someone wouldn't do this just to be cruel?"

He's got a broom and a dustpan now and is sweeping up the broken pieces of Emma's lamp. She loves that lamp and has had it since she was a baby. "Jesus, Sadie," he says, looking up. "I hope not. That would be sick." He stands and dumps the lamp shards from the dustpan into the wastebasket he's dragged over. "And anyway, who would know about Night Doggie?"

"Lots of kids have special loveys."

"Yeah, but someone's taken a very specific one."

My heart bleeds. The one that Emma can't sleep without.

"You don't think Teresa?" I ask. She's a logical guess.

"Please, Sadie."

"Why are you so defensive of her?" I ask.

"I'm not." But the look on his face says he knows he is.

In the old days when he was acting out, I might have suspected Forrest of doing something similar, but never to this level of atrocity. He's messed with Emma's belongings before out of jealousy. But no. This would be like Forrest on quadruple steroids. No child's capable of this. Besides, Allen said he's gone away.

"Allen." He finishes cleaning up the lamp pieces and stands. "Why didn't you tell me about Forrest going to his grandma's house?"

He clips the dustpan to the broom handle and leans them against the wall near the door. He also carries over the loaded wastebasket. "I only just learned today while I was at work. I got a text from Teri, and then you and I had to go to the station. We got busy with other stuff."

I sit on Emma's bed and stare at him, feeling like I need to tell him the truth. Maybe if I do, he'll start being honest with me. "I told O'Reilly about Cass."

He blinks. "What? When?"

"Yesterday evening, before the police left."

"Sadie." His tone's admonishing, but how dare he admonish me? He walks over and sits beside me on Emma's bed. "I don't want us getting Cass in trouble. She could be completely innocent."

"No." I set my chin and gaze at him. "She's lying."

He sighs. "Look. I know that's what you think—"

"O'Reilly shared that the police learned the truth about Bobby. Cass *did* have a husband and kid. They both died in a car accident a few years back. So Bobby wasn't totally made up. He just doesn't exist anymore."

Allen scrubs his fist across his mouth. "Oh wow." His brow shoots up. "That's twisted."

"I know," I agree.

"What are the police going to do?" Allen asks.

"O'Reilly's trying to get a warrant. Meanwhile, they've got surveillance on her house."

"Fuck." He drags his fingers through his hair.

"Allen," I say softly. "I know you've been keeping things from me and it's scaring me. Making me start to wonder." I take a deep breath, gathering my nerve. "Whether you had something to do with Emma going missing?"

"Oh my God, Sadie." His eyes are huge, disbelieving. "How could you even think that?"

"Then why all the lies, Allen? Why'd you hide the fact about Walsh and jury duty?"

A muscle in his cheek flinches. "I already explained that."

"Cover up your former connection with Cass?" I charge.

His shoulders sink. "It wasn't a cover-up, Sadie."

I'm on a roll now, so I continue. "Lie to me about what's going on with Teresa?"

He goes completely white. "What do you mean?"

"Allen." I stare at him long and hard. "Are you and Teresa having an affair?"

His Adam's apple rises and falls. "No." Crap. He looks so guilty.

A blistering-hot arrow shoots through my heart.

He reaches out and takes my hand, and I'm too stunned to resist. My world is crashing and burning around me. So fast. I find the words to speak through my building anger, my hurt, my brimming tears. "I'm not sure if I believe you, Allen." My breath catches. "How do I know you're being truthful now when you weren't before?"

"Sadie, please." His pitiful stare wrenches my soul. He's the man I love, my husband. How could he do this to me? To us? "*Please,*" he begs again. "Can we not do this now?"

I sigh and hang my head, count my heartbeats. How do I still have a pulse? Why am I living? My daughter's disappeared, my husband's been unfaithful. *He's lied.* But we are united in one thing. Our quest to find Emma. Unless. Allen's still lying. Still covering things up.

Doubt rushes through me, flooding the dark corners of my mind. Maybe it wasn't an outsider who took Night Doggie? Maybe it was Allen? He could have messed up Emma's room earlier to throw suspicion off himself. He was home by himself on his computer, sorting through anonymous tips that came in on the website we established for Emma. He helped me carry in the groceries before we left for the press conference, but I never went upstairs.

I slowly slip my hand from his grasp, massaging my fingers. Staring at the wedding band that used to mean something. To Allen. I look up and meet his eyes. "So you had nothing to do with this at all?" I glance around the room, and he knows what I mean.

"Jesus, Sadie. *No.*" I wish I could fully believe him, that my mind wasn't plagued with doubt.

A lump forms in my throat and my eyes burn hot. "Allen," I say. "Look me in the eye and *swear to me* you don't know where Emma is."

He meets my gaze head on. "I swear."

ALLEN
THE DAD

Day Six

I sit at my desk at work staring at my computer screen. Investment port-folios are all a blur. Sadie doesn't know how I can come here, but I'm get-ting stir crazy being at home. She stays on her computer all morning long, connecting with missing-children's groups. In the afternoons, she drives around town, combing the streets for signs of Emma. I know it's futile.

The police have officers on constant patrol, but Emma's not going to be at some obscure playground with a group of kids she doesn't know, or riding a bike down an alley. She still has her training wheels on, for Christ's sake. She's too young to be out on her own.

I hope we get additional information on Cass soon. If Emma's at her house and safe, that would be an answer to prayers. I didn't tell Sadie the whole truth about Cass because I knew she'd take things wrong. Make mountains out of molehills. The Cass Curtis I knew never would have been deranged enough to abduct a child, but a lot of things have changed in these intervening years. She's had a tragic double loss. That would be enough to unnerve anybody. Send them into a horrible depression. But kidnap someone else's child? No. That seems like a lot, except when framed in the context of Emma's fake playdate with "Bobby."

Could Cass have broken into our house to take Emma's stuffed dog? That doesn't seem any more ludicrous than her taking Emma to begin with. I hope the police get in there quickly. Waiting sucks. Not knowing sucks. I want answers *yesterday*. I shoot Teri a text because we need to get on the same page. I don't think Sadie will reach out to her, but you can never be sure. Emotions are running high right now on all our parts.

I already texted Teri about the police. I let her know the very evening Mercer pressed me into a confession about us sleeping together. What I've yet to tell the police is where I was at eight fifteen the morning Emma disappeared. It's not like they don't know, though. I could read between the lines of Mercer's questioning. They assume I was with Teri.

But I haven't confirmed it and won't unless I'm charged and absolutely have to.

The problem with that fact is it doesn't give me and Teri mutual alibis. It makes us both look guilty.

I've got my own office on the third floor and lots of privacy here.

ALLEN
Hey. Want you to know.
Sadie suspects.

I expect a reply. It doesn't come.

Instead I get a text from Mercer. He seems to be communicating with me mostly and Claremont with Sadie. Maybe they've assigned it somehow.

MERCER
Forensics came back.
Only fingerprints on the scene were yours and Sadie's.
Plus some very small ones, likely from a child.

I groan with frustration Another dead end.

ALLEN
Has someone told Sadie?

Several dots on the screen.

MERCER
Yes.

I set my elbows on my desk and hang my head, reliving our conversation about me and Teri. How can she ever forgive me?
I hope she will.
My phone buzzes with a new text. I think it's Teri. It's not. It's Mercer again.

MERCER
Can you come down to the station?

I check my watch. It's nine fifteen in the morning. I've barely gotten in.

ALLEN
What? Now?

MERCER
Now would be best.
We've had a development.

My heart pounds.

ALLEN
Should I bring Sadie?

MERCER
No. Come alone.

O'REILLY
THE COP

Day Six

The chief calls me into her office and shuts the door with a shove. She's pissed. "Deputy Chief O'Reilly." She spits out my name. "Why didn't you tell me you're involved with a teacher at Stonefield Elementary?"

Holy fuck. I'm in deep shit now.

I stand at attention, chest out, hands behind my back. "I didn't see the relevance, ma'am."

"Didn't. See. The. Relevance?" She gawks at me like I'm from Mars. "Emma's in her class." The day's sunny beyond her window. I see the parking lot and a bright-blue sky over a stand of pines. A few patrols come and go. Rodriguez and Patel park. Get out of their car.

"Yes, Chief. I know that, Chief. The fact is she was cleared." I pause to peer down at her. She's glaring up at me, furious. "You cleared her yourself."

She fumes like a fire-breathing dragon. "What's the deal, O'Reilly? How long you been seeing her?" I hold myself steady, doing my best not to squirm.

"Just over two years." I clasp one hand behind me with the other, squeezing tight.

"Christ." She rubs her closed eyelids then looks at me. "Living together?"

I know I can't lie. She'll have my head. Then my badge. "Yes."

"Fuck."

Okay, this is bad. Claremont almost never curses. "When were you planning to tell me?" She gets all up in my face. Super close. Her big blue eyes are huge, her chin jutting toward me. "Never?"

"I haven't compromised anything," I rush to assure her. "Haven't uttered a word." My fingers pulse around my clenched fist, holding it against the small of my back. My uniform grows warm. My flak vest sweltering.

She starts pacing her office. She's got papers piled up everywhere. File folders too. I don't know how she keeps it all straight, but she does. She shoots me a glance. "But she's asked, hasn't she?" Claremont guesses correctly. "*Your girlfriend,* Kate Davis, has asked you about Emma's case?"

I'm in so much trouble and I know it. I hope I don't lose my job over this. I hope she doesn't pull me off the case. I need to be here. Have to solve it. I want to find that kid and bring her home.

"It's natural she's concerned." I clear my throat. "She's Emma's teacher."

She stops walking, breathing heavily. "Okay." She sounds resigned. "Truth time." She peers into my eyes, doing a deep dive. "What have you told her?"

"Nothing!" I hold up both hands. "I swear."

"Did you tell her who we've got our eyes on? Name our persons of interest?"

"Of course not. *No.*" I'm affronted she'd ask that. I thought she knew me better than that. "I'd never—"

"I want her brought in for questioning," she snaps decisively.

She drops down in the chair behind her desk, staring at me.

Ready for me to spring into action and order Kate to be brought in.

I swallow past the burn in my throat.

Her disappointed look says everything. *"Now."*

SADIE
THE MOM

Day Six

I'm driving around town searching for Emma. Going past the school makes me physically ill. The American flag on the flagpole whips mightily in the wind, but my only allegiance is to my child. I take a turn and then another, steering up and down the nearby streets. I even go by Caleb Walsh's home. His car's gone. He's at work.

Every time I see a group of kids, I slow down and pull over. They sometimes stare at me and scurry away like I'm some kind of lurky pervert. I don't blame them for skittering off. Their parents probably warned them about people like me. Strangers in cars slowing down and looking too closely.

I wish that Emma had run. That she'd been more like them. Maybe she was? Maybe she tried to get away but couldn't escape? My heart aches because I know that's not true. Emma always did what people told her. Everyone said, "What a good child." But her compliance scared me sometimes. I wanted her to be able to think for herself. Make judgments. Sense danger. But she couldn't. She was so small and innocent. Only five years old.

I clench my jaw when I realize what I'm doing.

Thinking of Emma in the past tense.

Like she's not here anymore.

Like we're never going to find her.

Tears prickle the backs of my eyes.

No. I am not giving up.

I drive down my own street and circle around in the cul-de-sac, noting the police cruiser parked there. A couple of officers sit inside holding coffee cups, watching my house. I snake through the other streets in my neighborhood and drive down Cass Thomas's street, slowing down in front of her house. I spy a police car in my rearview mirror. It's parked at the curb a few houses back. I went right by it but didn't see it. I was distracted, searching front yards and houses on the other side of the street. How many other things have I missed? Obvious things?

Cass's Jeep isn't in her driveway. She's not home yet. *Dammit. When will that warrant come through?* Why isn't what the police have already enough? I'm out of my mind with worry. I can't think or eat. I keep praying that Emma's unharmed, and that we can bring her home.

I turn around in the cul-de-sac and pass Cass's house again, viewing it from the driver's side. What if Emma's in there? Getting more frightened each day, while the police sit around watching and waiting but effectively doing nothing?

I'm so frustrated I could scream. I can't wait anymore. I have to know what Cass is hiding in that house. Did she find the key under our flowerpot and come in and steal Emma's toy dog? Did Emma tell her the key was there? Is that why the gate was open again after Allen said he'd fixed it?

I park my SUV in front of my garage and enter my house, walking into my office. I see the cop car in the cul-de-sac, but they're watching the front of my house. The other police car guards the front of Cass's. From the vantage points they have, none of the officers can see what lies between: our backyards.

I slip out my patio door and traipse across the springy summer grass, creeping through the gate. The sun beats down on my face. Bees buzz by the fence, and a butterfly flits above the honeysuckle. I try the latch, and it catches with a click. My heart pounds as I approach Cass's deck and climb its wooden steps.

I hold up my hands to shield my eyes against the glare and peer through a back window. It's the kitchen. Very bare. Only a card table with four chairs. I turn away from the window and my foot catches on something wedged under the picnic table. I peer under the table and my heart slams against my chest. There's an object beneath the bench.

My heartbeat races away from me as I bend down and pick it up.

A backpack. It's pink.

My Little Pony.

It's Emma's.

KATE
THE TEACHER

Day Six

Nerves gnaw at me when I get the call from Principal Rand's secretary. They wouldn't pull me out of class unless this is important. The secretary tells me to bring my purse with me. Shit. Am I being taken somewhere? Arrested? I approach Dotti as she works with a group cutting out shapes at a worktable. "Do you mind holding down the fort?"

"Sure thing, hon." She's got her apple earrings on today and a bulky red-and-green top. "What's going on?"

I confide in low tones, "Rand wants me." Dotti's pretty much unflappable. I can trust her with things. She never tells on me when I arrive late to school or sneak out midday for a chain store coffee. She didn't blab to the police about me not being in my classroom like I said I was at the time Emma disappeared.

I know my way in and out of this school, so no one ever sees me leave. So does Dotti. And we're not alone at Stonefield Elementary. Everyone knows where the indoor and outdoor cameras are. Which ones function, and which ones haven't worked in years.

Her face creases with worry. "Do you think it's about . . . ?" She intentionally doesn't say Emma's name around the other kids.

Sometimes you don't think they're listening, but they often are. And kids who overhear things tend to tell their parents. Unfortunately.

"I don't know." I straighten the belt on my dress and walk toward the door. I've got on bright red pumps that match my belt and a navy blue shirtwaist dress. My earrings are blue and red buttons, and I'm wearing my hair down.

Shane likes this outfit. He says it's cute, very patriotic. I'm not sure what he'd think about me being called to the principal's office. I doubt he'd be pleased. If this little chat with Rand concerns Emma, it can't be good news. Good news would have been broadcast on the airwaves and circulated immediately by faculty and staff throughout the school, with people celebrating Emma's safe return.

Rand's door is open when I get there, so I rap lightly. She looks up from the computer screen on her desk. "Have a seat." She's humorless as usual, but her extra-dismissive air chills me. I cross the threshold and the building temperature seems to drop by ten degrees. I think she's the fucking devil.

The door closes behind me and I turn to find two police officers standing there. Shit. Officers Patel and Rodriguez. I spin in my chair to address them. "Is, uh . . . something going on?"

"You're wanted at the police station for questioning," Rand says. Her expression's cold and hard. This entire investigation is clearly a burden to her.

Another black eye for Stonefield Elementary.

I'd like to give her a black eye, Katherine spouts, incensed.

I mentally shout *shut up.*

Rand's obviously not happy the police want to speak with me, Emma's teacher. An employee at her school. That can't look good, and it won't look good to the parents either. God forbid this gets out in the press.

Stonefield Elementary Teacher of Missing Child Held
for Questioning

I laugh nervously, glancing at the police officers. "I don't really need an escort, do I?"

Rodriguez answers. "We don't mind giving you a lift." She shrugs.

I'm not being arrested, no. I also very clearly get the sense I'm not being offered a choice. Still, I try to get out of it. I don't need Shane seeing me at the station or hearing that I've been brought in. He'll flip out, and that might be the end of us. Shit. I can't lose Shane. He's all I have besides this job, and at the moment that's not exactly looking secure.

"I'm starting a lesson soon," I tell them, putting on my best professional face. "Another class is joining ours." I grimace like this is a complication that can't be helped. "Really bad timing for me to be away." I adjust an earring that's slipped a bit. "Any chance I can answer here?"

Rodriguez glances at her watch and then says, "No ma'am. I'm sorry."

I don't think I've been called ma'am by anyone above elementary age *ever*. I'm barely thirty, for God's sake. How old is she? *Twelve?* Okay, okay. Maybe early twenties.

Ma'am. Wow.

I dart a look at Rand. She sits there, impassive. I know she's war-gaming this out in her head, deciding how to spin it with my fellow faculty members and my kids' parents. Or maybe she won't spin it at all? Maybe she'll turn on me like a rabid dog? Sinking her teeth in, the taste of blood only driving her harder.

Katherine entertains a brief fantasy of the K-9 dogs being set on Rand. There's blood on the pavement by the flagpole.

"Will this take long?" I ask Rodriguez and Patel.

Patel holds open the door and I stand, not ready to do this. I get the urge to break into a sprint and get the hell away from here. But I can't do that. I know how that would look. They'd slap me behind bars in a flash. I smooth out my dress, tweak my belt, and slide my purse strap over my shoulder.

"Hopefully not," Rodriguez says, motioning for me to follow Patel.

I raise my chin and leave without looking at Rand. No doubt she's gloating about this. I probably fit into her plan as an ultraconvenient scapegoat. I know about Walsh. Everybody at Stonefield Elementary does. He's like a fucking legend around here. I wouldn't be surprised if his fellow teachers built him a shrine.

If I were him, I would have done something to Rand in retribution. I wouldn't have been able to stand it, knowing she'd done what she had. It's odd how a wrongly convicted man is more despised in the general community than our despicable principal. I guess it's his fault for wearing his heart on his sleeve and being transparent.

Transparency doesn't pay in the school system.

Covering your own ass does.

Rodriguez walks behind me and I feel like a criminal leaving the school. A few teachers note our promenade through their open classroom doors, and we pass the janitor in the hall. The librarian sees us too but pretends not to notice. They all do.

I know they'll be gossiping about me later. Wondering why I was taken in by the police, and whether it had to do with Emma's kidnapping. I glimpse a few people taking out their phones and firing off texts. Snapping pics. It will be all over the school before I'm even downtown. Maybe on social media, going viral. Motherfuckers. Most people have no idea how hard it is being a teacher these days. Everybody's against you. The only person you can rely on is yourself.

The police car's parked at the curb right outside the front door to the school. Patel opens the back door and I climb inside. This was not supposed to happen. How can they know?

SADIE
THE MOM

Day Six

I unzip the pink backpack and go through it, resting it on the picnic table. My fingers tremble when they trace the lettering of the name written inside. My handwriting. "Emma Wilson" written in permanent marker. The backpack's main compartment still has the manila folder tucked inside. I pull it out and open its clasp to check it, finding the papers Allen and I completed to send to school the first day, emergency contact cards and doctor information.

I lay the manila folder on the picnic table and fish around in the front pocket.

It's empty.

No iPod.

My spirit shatters.

Where's my baby girl?

Did Cass take her? Hurt her? *Please God, no. Anything but that.*

I'll make a bargain. Let it be me. Punish me. Not Emma.

I stare into Cass's darkened house, and my eyes burn hot with tears.

I could run around to the front of the house to alert the police.
There are officers stationed right there. Close by.
But I want their top gun.
Someone I trust.
I call Claremont.

KATE
THE TEACHER

Day Six

Claremont asks me to have a seat in an interrogation room. My gut tenses as I glance at the cameras. "Is this really necessary?" I ask. Patel is with her. I don't like it that there are two of them here. It makes the interview seem less casual. I feel ganged up on, like maybe I should call in reinforcements. Katherine perks up, but I definitely don't need her here tipping her grimy hand. Who knows what sort of dirt she'd spill? I can't trust her and I don't. Only one thing unites us, our mutual love and mourning for Diane.

Claremont sits across from me and next to Patel. "I want to talk to you about your association with Deputy Chief Shane O'Reilly," Chief Claremont says.

Shane? What? That is so out of left field. "What—what do you mean?"

"You two are involved, I understand." He must have told her. So okay, no big deal. *Don't deny it, Kate. Act like you're cooperating. Be professional, respectful.*

Punch her fucking lights out, Katherine says. *Deck that little prick Patel too while you're at it.* She's scanning the room, assessing her prey. Fuming.

Shut the fuck up, Katherine. Shut. The. Fuck. Up!

I blink and stare at Claremont.

"Um, sure." I settle my purse on my lap and say, "He's my boyfriend."

Claremont rests her forearms on the table, her shoulders hunched forward. "I'm afraid that makes things problematic for us."

I lick my lips when they go dry. "Problematic how?"

Katherine's pacing about, striding back and forth in my brain.

Like a restless beast trudging through muck and mire.

"You're Emma's teacher," Patel explains. "That puts you very close to an investigation your boyfriend is actively working on."

"Yes, but. Shane hasn't told me anything, if that's what you're worried about. He's very professional." *Doesn't mean I don't overhear some of his phone calls, though. Like the one that came in from Rodriguez giving him Cass Thomas's address. I looked Cass Thomas up. She's a neighbor of Sadie and Allen's. A person of interest. Possibly a suspect.*

"Ms. Davis," Claremont says. "I need to ask you something very direct. Would you have any reason to harm Emma Wilson or her family?"

Maybe you should tell her the truth? Katherine advises. I want to throttle her. The truth won't set us free. It will land us in freaking prison!

I blanch and press a hand to my chest. Put on a face that says I'm floored she'd ask. "Chief Claremont," I say. "I take my responsibilities as a teacher very seriously. I *care* for my students. Of course I'd never hurt any of them."

Claremont narrows her eyes at me. I wonder if she's remembering that episode with the fly. Doubting me because of *her.*

"We found a past connection," Patel informs me. She squares her shoulders, hanging on to a narrow black book. It looks like a three-ring binder of some kind.

I tuck a lock of my hair behind one ear. "Oh yeah?" I ask casually, although my pulse races. Katherine's nerves hum too. "What kind of connection is that?" My forehead feels hot, my palms damp.

Chief Claremont clasps her hands together on the table. "One that, in our minds, could in fact give you a motive to harm Emma Wilson."

Our heart skips a beat. *Fuck.*

Patel lays the binder on the table and flips it open, revealing copies of photographs and newspaper clippings in plastic sleeves. One newspaper article is about the drowning of an area teen. "You had an older sister, Diane," Patel says. "We have a witness who says the night Diane died, she was with Allen."

We're stunned.

There were no other witnesses that night beyond us.

Wait.

We break a sweat.

And Allen.

ALLEN
THE DAD

Day Six
Earlier

Mercer writes something down. "Can you go over that story again?"

I do, even though it wrecks me. I hate thinking about what happened that night. The painful memories still plague me, even though I couldn't stop what happened. Even though it wasn't my fault.

"I was out with Diane swimming. Our parents had rented a beach house together, hers and mine. We used to do that every summer. I was good friends with Diane's big brother, Mark. Then, that year, Diane and I started dating. It was well after dark, probably eleven or eleven thirty in the evening. She went underwater and I couldn't find her. She got pulled in by a riptide. That was the conclusion later."

He nods. "I've read the reports."

I dart a gaze at the double-sided mirror. "I'm not in trouble for that now?"

"No sir. That's not the issue. Everyone ruled it as an accident then. Who am I to contest?"

"Then why bring it up here?"

Mercer straightens his tie. "We've been exploring every angle," he tells me. "Checking for any connection between your past and Sadie's, and what's happened to Emma."

I'm not following him at all. What does Diane's drowning have to do with anything? That was twenty-two years ago.

"One of our investigators found this." He drags over a three-ring binder that's been sitting on the table and opens it, exposing newspaper stories in plastic sleeves. They're about Diane. My stomach turns over. It was so very sad. Such a tragedy. It took me years to forgive myself. Years for me to understand I wasn't to blame. It was just a horrible accident.

"Yeah? So?"

He pulls the binder back toward him and picks it up, flipping through its pages.

"Your former girlfriend Diane had a kid sister?" he asks.

"Yeah." I search my brain. "Her name was Katherine, I think. Her family called her Kit-Kat."

He sets the binder back down and turns it to face me. There's a black-and-white photo from a news story. Looks like a shot of Diane's family at her funeral. Mark is there, and a little girl stands by his side. I remember that day. I was there with my parents.

Mercer points to the child in the photo. "This her, the younger sister?"

I study the photo again. "Yes."

He pulls a photo of an attractive blond woman from his suit pocket. It's a work photo. No, a school photo. *A teacher photo.*

Mercer places the teacher photo on top of the binder page next to the funeral photo.

My lungs seize up. The similarities are too strong to ignore.

He sets his palms on the table and studies me closely. "Were you aware that Emma's teacher, Kate Davis, was that little girl?"

"What the fuck?" I blurt out accidentally.

Mercer's eyebrows arch. "Apparently not."

I try to catch my breath. *What? What the actual what?* "No. There must be some mistake. Diane's last name was Martin. So was her sister's."

Mercer's eyes glimmer knowingly, and he flips to another page in the binder. It's a Social Security card name-change application. "She legally changed it."

"Christ. But why?"

Mercer shrugs. "Maybe she was tired of her family?"

KATE
THE TEACHER

Day Six

I get home from work in the afternoon and Shane's squad car is parked outside our apartment building. My stomach flutters with nerves. He's never home this time of day. I walk into the bedroom when I hear him in there. "Hey, hon." Crap. He's packing. I search his eyes. "What's going on?"

He takes folded shirts out of his dresser, laying them in a suitcase one on top of the other. "You should have told me, Kate. Told me about Allen." His tone is angry, harsh.

Fuck. Nooo.

I knew it would come to this. It's been like waiting for the other shoe to drop but praying that it wouldn't. I stare up at him, pleading softly. "Shane, please. That was a long time ago. It has nothing to do with now."

He turns to face me. "It has everything to do with now. Christ." He rolls back his shoulders. "How could you not have seen that?" He's still in his uniform, fully suited out and armed. He's come home from the station to do this in the middle of his workday. He got in trouble somehow. Maybe with Chief Claremont.

"Why are you leaving?" My voice trembles. "Am I a suspect?"

He shakes his head. "A person of interest now." He stands up straighter to glare at me. "I could lose my badge over this. Did you ever think of that? Do you even care about Emma Wilson? That helpless missing child? Or are you secretly glad she's gone?" I can't bear the way he's looking at me. So disillusioned. Like I'm despicable. Like he's been sleeping with the enemy. An enemy he hates. "*Oh my God,*" he groans and turns away.

The wound's so deep, my heart stops beating. Then *there*, a painful gush, blood pushing through arteries. Afterward, a dull ache. It happens again. A third time, a fourth. *Fuck me.* "Shane." I walk between him and his dresser. An open drawer hits the backs of my knees. "You've got to believe me," I beg him. "I had nothing to do with taking Emma."

"Do you know who did?" His stare penetrates my soul and I freeze, paralyzed by doubt and fear. I so badly want to confide in him. Tell him about Emma's backpack and the teacher note. Explain what really happened, and my reasons for hiding them. But no. No matter how much I wish it were otherwise, he's a cop first. He'll turn me in.

I push back my hair, my hand shaking. "No."

"Dammit, Kate. You're not even who you said you were. For fuck's sake, you're not even an orphan. You've got a mom and a dad. *A brother.* You changed your name from Martin to Davis. Maybe you had your reasons for that. I don't know. What I *do know* is you didn't trust me. Didn't tell me the truth about a lot of things, apparently. Your big sister, Diane, was with Allen the night she died. Did you think it was his fault? Have you been harboring a grudge against Allen Wilson? Against his family?"

When I don't answer, he waves me aside and I step out of his way. He shuts the empty dresser drawer with a bang, and yanks open another drawer. He's pissed. Fuming. Going through the motions as fast as he can but with precision tactics. Carefully, methodically, ridding himself of me. Through the open bathroom door, I see an athletic bag on the vanity. He's dumped his personal toiletries into it. "Where are you going?"

"I'm bunking with Rodriguez for a while."

"Rodriguez?" Fuck. "The pretty woman cop?" He's always talking about her and how great she is. Smart. Savvy. Bound to be the boss someday. If I hadn't been so secure about him loving me, I might have been jealous of Rodriguez. Now, I'm out of my head *sick* that he's going to be staying with her.

"I don't see pretty," he lies, because he's all about complimenting me. Or was. "I see integrity." The verbal slap stings. He turns his back on me and zips up his suitcase. "She's got a spare room." He strides into the bathroom and zips that bag too, slinging its strap over his shoulder. I can't believe he's leaving, walking out on me, but I don't know how to stop him. Even if I beg, I know he won't stay.

I ask a question. "How long will this last?"

"I don't know," he says coolly. "As long as it takes."

He walks out and shuts the door.

O'REILLY
THE COP

Day Seven

We finally get a warrant to go into Cass Thomas's house. We bring the dogs. We've got maybe a dozen officers on the job, all wearing blue gloves. Cass is at work, but all the better. She won't be here to interfere. The K-9 unit brings two dogs onto the porch. They sniff around, vigorously checking the floorboards and railing. The threshold of the house too. In a flash, one goes up the stairs, tugging at its lead. The other dog follows with both officers in tow.

I search the downstairs. It doesn't reveal much beyond what I noticed the other day. I'm heading upstairs when the two dogs come racing back down the steps, and out the front door into the yard. They lie down on the grass, heads between their front paws. They've found nothing.

Claremont's upstairs. She hollers for me, and I take the steps briskly. She points to a bedroom. There's nothing but a camp cot covered with a blanket inside. A teddy bear's propped against the pillow. "What do you make of that?"

I back into the hall and check the other bedrooms. One is empty. The other has a double bed and a dresser. One nightstand. Not much. "Kid's room?" I say to Claremont.

"Yeah, but." She removes her hat and runs a hand through her hair. "What kid?"

SADIE
THE MOM

Day Seven

Deputy Chief O'Reilly comes to our door to tell us the search at Cass's house has been completed. They unfortunately found nothing to indicate she's involved. There was no sign of Emma in her house. The dogs alerted briefly in the front hall, but that could have been from when I went over there with Emma for that fake playdate. Thank goodness I heeded my instincts and didn't leave Emma there. Even if Cass didn't take her, she's clearly an unbalanced individual. Who makes up stories about having a son when that child's deceased? How sad.

"What about Emma's backpack?" I ask. "That was in her backyard, right by the house."

"Yes, but not inside her house," O'Reilly says. "Anybody could have put it there."

"It was enough for a search warrant," Allen points out. He's seated beside me on the sofa. I don't want to believe he has anything to do with Emma's disappearance, I don't. But if it wasn't Cass, and since it couldn't have been Caleb Walsh, that only leaves Teresa in my mind.

"Yes, lucky break," O'Reilly says. "We're sending the backpack to the lab for analysis. Maybe we'll get some clues."

My stomach churns. Why can't somebody do something? Why is this taking so long?

O'Reilly stares at Allen. "When's the last time you spoke with your ex-wife?"

"Teri?" Allen blinks. "It was that first day when Emma disappeared, at the station."

"She hasn't been in touch with you since? To check on the two of you? Say how your son is doing?"

Allen snaps his fingers. "Sorry, yes. She texted to say she was sending Forrest to her mom's place in Virginia for a few weeks. I agreed that was a good idea."

"Sending or taking?" O'Reilly asks him.

"Sorry?" Allen's forehead creases.

"Did she say she was taking her son to Virginia, or that her mom was coming to North Carolina to pick him up?"

Allen shifts in his seat, thinking. "I'm pretty sure she said her mom was coming here to pick him up. Why?"

O'Reilly sets his hands on his duty belt. "It now appears she's left town herself."

I feel like the wind's been knocked out of me. "Gone?" I ask. "Teresa's missing?"

O'Reilly nods. "Took a leave of absence from work, apparently. Officer Patel stopped by the observatory with a few follow-up questions and spoke to her boss."

The blood drains from Allen's face. "Maybe she's gone to stay at her mom's place with Forrest?" he offers up as an excuse. Why is he defending her? What does he know?

"I suppose you have her mother's contact information?" O'Reilly asks.

Allen sits back on the sofa. "I'm not sure. I think she's moved since Teri and I divorced."

O'Reilly narrows his eyes at Allen. "That's okay. We'll run her down."

"Why do you need Teresa?" Allen asks. "She's clearly not a suspect." I don't know how he can be so sure unless he was with Teresa at the time of Emma's disappearance. My heart aches. That must be the case. Of course. How stupid of me not to see it. That's probably what he told the police. He and Teresa are each other's alibis. A wave of nausea roils through me. They were together—maybe even having sex at the very hour Emma went missing, the exact minute.

"We received an anonymous note mailed to the station," O'Reilly says. "It was supposedly in Sadie's hand." He stares at me. "But I'm guessing you didn't write it?"

The lights in the room seem to glow brighter and blur. "What note?"

"The one addressed to Emma's teacher, saying a family friend was picking Emma up from school early that day for an appointment."

"Friend?" I scoot to the edge of the sofa. "What friend?"

Allen pulls out a handkerchief and wipes his forehead. His neck and face glisten. "No, she wouldn't have."

"Teresa Wilson," O'Reilly says.

Reality hits. *There was no iPod.*

KATE
THE TEACHER

Day Seven

I fill a banker's box with a few things from my desk. The special coffee mug a student gave me for Teacher Appreciation Day a few years ago. My personal pair of sharp cutting shears, pens and permanent markers. The framed photo of me and Shane in the mountains that I keep in a desk drawer. My heart thuds with a dull ache. I don't know where things will wind up with Shane, or if he'll ever forgive me. He still doesn't know the whole truth.

Dotti walks over and hands me the sweater I usually leave draped over the back of the rolling chair that sits at my desk. "Don't want to forget this, doll."

My chin trembles and I set my jaw. "Thanks, Dotti." I fold the sweater and lay it in the box. I believe I have almost everything, but it's hard to think clearly. The students will be here in another fifteen minutes and a substitute teacher is on their way. Principal Rand gave me less than thirty minutes to clear out my personal effects.

Although I'm not technically a suspect, I'm on administrative leave until further notice. Additional questioning by Principal Rand poked holes in my fellow teachers' stories, and she shared this new information with the police, who conducted a fresh wave of interrogations.

The art teacher admitted she'd told me to go ahead and grab whatever I needed from her classroom, but she was working on setting up a new display in the main hall and didn't witness my going into her room or note how long I was there. She keeps several rolls of masking tape on hand, so it's impossible for her to say how many were there to begin with versus after when I supposedly borrowed one.

Even Dotti shared I'd been away from my classroom around the time of the bus's arrival. When she came back with the kids, I wasn't there. I came hurrying in, looking disheveled and saying that I'd gone to retrieve my cell phone from my car. We later found it on a bookshelf. I know Dotti didn't throw me under the bus intentionally. Principal Rand has that intimidating way about her that sets others on edge.

I consider asking Dotti about the backpack. I'm wondering if she saw it. If she did, then she's covering for me by pretending she didn't. If she didn't see it, on the other hand, I don't need to call her attention to it now. Why give her one more thing to squeal about later to Principal Rand?

I wouldn't be surprised to learn Rand had something to do with the backpack landing where it did herself. I'm less sure about her motivation in taking Emma. That doesn't seem like Rand. Risky to have a child go missing on her watch, and have things reflect poorly on the school. No, she wouldn't do it. But she might cover up for someone else who did.

Still, Teresa seems the most likely suspect in my mind. It was her name, after all, on the note about Emma leaving school early. She'd certainly have her reasons for wanting Emma out of the way. An attractive divorcee with a nice job who hasn't dated at all? At least not that's been obvious at school events she's attended for Forrest. So, if she has gone out, it hasn't been serious. Seems to me like she was waiting on someone.

TERESA
THE EX-WIFE

Day Seven

I take public transportation to another train station and buy a ticket using one of the preloaded debit cards I purchased from a big box store teller machine.

I board the train and set the suitcase with Emma's belongings on the rack above my seat. I brought nothing for myself but what's in my purse. My cell phone and its charger, my wallet loaded with cash. I'm going to ride this train to the end of the line and then purchase another ticket at a kiosk at that station, taking a zigzag course across the country.

They won't check my ID on the train. They never do. Especially in first class. I've got Emma's suitcase with me, with everything I bought her. After Allen and I made love on my sofa, it didn't take a second to decide. He left me bleeding on the side of the road, but I came back. Climbing out of the wreckage with a beating heart.

Allen leaves and I stand there staring at the door. Part of my brain accepts what he said about Sadie, but the other part rebels. I sit down on the sofa and swaddle myself in the blanket that smells of us. Me and Allen together.

How is it fair that Sadie has everything? I love my cabin in the woods, but her house cost three times as much. I'm no pauper, but I'm essentially an academic so have to watch my bankbook. But it's not Sadie's comfortable financial life I'm after. It's Allen.

I spot the iPod on the coffee table. Allen's left without it. What he took with him was a piece of my heart. Every time I see him, he takes a little more. Chipping and chipping away at me, as I wither and wilt like a rose on a vine. Nothing blooms without him.

I fall into the black hole of my loneliness. Though I've tried to downplay it, it's been almost unbearable these past nine years. Allen left when Forrest was only a baby. He's missed so much, and I've missed having a full-time husband and partner to help with Forrest's care. Sadie has had that with Emma, and I resent her for it. The truth is I hate her. Hate Sadie for taking away what I had. For robbing me of my life with Allen.

If she hadn't been in the way, he might have come back. Could have been lured into reconstructing our family. Now there's no way. Unless. The iPod shimmers on the coffee table, catching waning light through the window. Unless I were more like Sadie.

If I were Emma's mom.

KATE
THE TEACHER

Day Eight

I sit on my bed streaming cop shows and missing Shane. It's early afternoon and I should be teaching, but I have a feeling my teaching days are done, at least for a while. Nobody's put me under arrest, but I know it's coming. Most normal people would be plagued with remorse after covering up a kidnapping. That's not me. Basically, I don't suffer a lot of guilt.

I feel two emotions: anger and sorrow. I don't know why I get angry, I just do. My sorrow began over losing Diane, the one person during my childhood who was genuinely nice to me. She fixed my hair and took me out for smoothies, did big-sisterly stuff. Nobody had to ask her—she wanted to. Diane was good with kids and would have made a great teacher, probably a lot better than I am. Or *was*, anyway.

I hate remembering the look on Shane's face when he walked out, and I'm really sad to think he's not coming back. I wish I could say I love him, because I believe he loves me. I guess I care about him to the extent I'm capable. I kept waiting for those romantic feelings to develop, but they didn't. I'm not saying it's impossible. Anything is possible. For a lot of individuals, I suppose. Some things are just harder than others for *her*.

I met Shane not long after I started teaching, and he didn't expect me to be anyone but whoever I wanted to be. The first time I smiled at him naturally, it came as a shock. Then he made me laugh and I worried he'd never make me angry. I could get stuck with him forever. After a while, being stuck with Shane seemed okay.

Shane paid way more attention to me than my family ever did. It was very, very clear to Katherine from the time she could comprehend it that she was a mistake. Her parents never did any of the normal parent things. Didn't teach her to brush her teeth or tuck her in at night. If they saw her lurking about too late, they'd ask, "What are you doing out of bed?" It was like they couldn't remember they'd failed to put her there in the first place.

They teased her and called her Kit-Kat, which they knew she hated. They even put it on her enrollment papers all through elementary school. Talk about humiliating. Katherine abhorred school, but it had its good points for her. Those mostly involved being away from her family. There was no laughter in that house. The few times Katherine smiled, her mom called it a smirk and slapped her hard across the face.

She used to fantasize about running away. Or living at a fancy boarding school like those in kids' literature. When that reality failed to develop, she went into teaching. She wasn't overlooked as a teacher, and no one ever hit her when she smiled. People liked Kate and she liked herself as Kate more too. So Katherine agreed to back down and let Kate have the first and final say.

Wherever I go, people are kind to me. *They pay attention.* Which is what makes Emma's case so weird. Everybody pays attention to everything at school. There are so many security protocols in place it's dizzying to read through the manual on the first day. Then there are the multiple drills. For fires. Tornados. Active shooters. My God. They never end. And yet, a little girl goes missing at Stonefield Elementary. *Completely disappears*, and no one notices.

Which is why I know that is a falsehood.

Somebody noticed and *someone* knows.

SADIE
THE MOM

Day Eight

The doorbell rings and I jump. Allen's gone in to his office and I'm here by myself. Claremont says it's good for us to keep working. Stick as much to our regular routines as we can. I don't know fucking how. I spend *every single minute* thinking about Emma. Seeing her face, hearing her voice, smelling her sweet little-girl smell, feeling her in my arms.

I open the door and someone stands there with a plant.

It takes my brain a second to register the impossible.

Cass.

She hands me the leafy fern in a heavy planter pot. "Sadie," she says gently. "Please accept this. I wanted to do something." Lines form around her mouth and eyes. She has the nerve to look concerned.

I take her gift and the weight of it sinks in my arms.

I'm speechless.

Is she hiding Emma somewhere?

Or, heaven forbid, has she done something to her?

My mind shouts me back down.

Don't be ridiculous. Why would she be here?

"Uh, thanks." I retreat into the foyer, letting her in. I'm stunned she's not livid about the search warrant on her house. But then, why would she hold *me* accountable? That was clearly the police's doing and not mine. She has no idea who found the backpack and who alerted the police.

"I've been watching the news," she says. "It's terrible. Then yesterday, the police searched my house. Emma's backpack was found in my yard. I'm sure you've heard. I was as stunned as you all were, I promise, and cooperated fully with the police." She scans my face and I balk internally. "Are you *okay*?" I don't like her frown, or her false sympathy.

How on earth can she ask me that? What business is it of hers? She might be guilty of taking Emma. The hell that Allen and I are living through could be all because of her. I set down the plant in the foyer to the left of the front door. "Cass," I say flatly. "Did you have something to do with what happened to Emma?"

She blinks, astounded. "What a question, Sadie. *No.*"

I call her bluff. "I know you were lying about Bobby."

"Lying?" I'm stunned by her guileless face. She's an amazingly good actress. A real sicko. She shuts the front door behind her and the latch clicks. "I'm afraid I don't know what you're talking about, Sadie." The poor woman really is very far gone. But no. I won't feel sorry for her. Not if she's taken Emma. I cross my arms and stare at her.

"You said you had a kid, invited Emma over for a playdate."

She fiddles with her watchband. "I'm so sorry about that. Really I am." What's she fucking sorry about? The fact that she lied she had a kid? The idea that she wanted to be left alone with Emma? The terrifying possibility that she kidnapped my little girl and might be hiding her somewhere? Or that she did something worse?

"I know the truth, Cass." My face grows hot. "Your former husband Richard and your son died in a car crash years ago." The blood drains from her face but she doesn't deny it.

"Yes," she says weakly. "That's so."

A human emotion washes over me. Pity. "Is that why you've left your house . . . the way you have?" I struggle for a kind way to say it. "So—undone?"

"I haven't had the heart." Her voice shakes. "The energy." My pity flees like a field mouse chased in angry swoops by my hawkish ire. *No, but maybe she had the energy for something else. Stealing someone else's child.*

"Then why the playdate, Cass? Hmm? Why? Was it because you wanted Emma for yourself?" My eyes bore into hers like daggers. I hope she feels. Every. Pounding. Jab.

"Wanted her? What? No." She flinches, stepping back. "It's not about that, was never about that. I saw you and her together in the yard, and it reminded me. Made me want to men—mend things. Make them whole."

"*Whole* by breaking my world apart?" I charge toward her. "By shattering *us*, our family?"

"Sadie, wait!" She holds up her hands and they're trembling. "I know how upset you are, but you're getting this all wrong. I would never have harmed Emma."

"What about your history with Allen?" I charge.

She pales further, then says, "Hold on. Are you talking about high school?" Her mouth hangs open. "Sadie, listen to me. Allen was very cute. Of course I was infatuated. Half of Braxton High was infatuated."

"Maybe you still are?" My heart hardens. "Maybe you still want Allen?"

"What? No." She blinks and backs up a few steps.

"But Allen's not enough, is he? You want Emma too. Just like Teresa."

"Teresa?" She starts inching toward the door. "Allen's ex-wife?"

I lunge at her, and she shrieks.

"Sadie! Stop!" Her eyes are huge and terrified.

She claws at my arms. I see my hands around her throat and freeze.

The Last Morning

Crap! What am I doing?
I let her go and she backs off, breathing hard.
"You. Need. Help," she says, wheezing.
Talk about the pot calling the kettle black.
She opens the front door and bolts through it.

ALLEN
THE DAD

Day Eight

I'm growing very concerned about Sadie. She's not handling Emma's disappearance well. Neither of us is, that's natural. This is life-altering stuff. Abysmally hard. But she's started acting unpredictably. I received a call from Mercer about her attacking Cass Thomas. He said it was off the record and that he'd heard it from Claremont. No charges will be filed, but maybe it's time we thought about counseling, or Sadie seeing a doctor. Like there's time. We need to find our daughter first.

Sadie's in Emma's room when I get home at slightly past six p.m. She's almost catatonic, sitting there on the bed. "Sadie?" I ask. "Have you been here all day?"

"No, just since Cass left."

I sigh heavily and sit beside her. I can't believe she lunged out at Cass Thomas. She did virtually the same thing to Caleb Walsh by invading his home. "We need to remember what the police said about not disrupting their investigation."

"Disrupting?" She goggles at me incredulously. "They keep clearing suspects, Allen."

"Persons of interest," I correct gently. "And Sadie. A process of elimination is good and to be expected."

"Yes. But." She stubbornly sets her chin, and I suddenly see Emma. My heart weeps. "How do we know they haven't cleared the wrong people?"

"We don't." I take her hand. "We just have to have faith." She gives me the side-eye in a way that unnerves me.

"How do I know you're not involved?"

"For God's sake, Sadie."

"Claremont said you might be."

"Claremont?" I'm gobsmacked that she would turn on me. "I don't understand."

"It's often a parent when a child goes missing."

"Christ, Sadie. You can't honestly believe it's me?"

"What about you and Teresa?"

Now she's wading into the deep end. I need to pull her back to safer ground. "Sadie, look at me." She does, but her eyes are vacant. Almost like she can't see me sitting here. Oh my God, Mercer's right. This is too much. It's breaking her, but I've got to stay strong. Strong for the two of us. I'll carry the load until we get through this. "There is no me and Teresa," I say.

"You're lying."

"Sadie, no."

"Allen, I know." She stares straight into my eyes. "You slept with her."

My pulse pounds. "Who told you that?"

"O'Reilly," she says without flinching.

SADIE
THE MOM

Day Eight
Earlier

Deputy Chief O'Reilly arrives not long after Cass leaves. She must have phoned the police as soon as she got home. Maybe I should have called the police on her? She's trying to play mind games on me. Acting like she cares about what Allen and I are going through when she herself might be responsible for kidnapping our little girl. That's what she was doing by bringing that plant by, trying to paint herself as innocent. A concerned neighbor. Sure.

His expression's haggard when he says, "Can we have a word?"

I nod and we sit in my living room.

"Sadie," he says and catches himself. "All right if I call you that?"

Of everyone, I like O'Reilly best. "Yes, please."

"Sadie," he reiterates, rubbing his hands together. "We can't keep doing this. Having you go off half-cocked on people you suspect of taking Emma. It's not good for them, or you. It makes you look—irrational." The weight of his disappointment hangs heavy in the air.

"But Deputy Chief O'Reilly—"

He smiles softly. "You can call me Shane." It feels like we're old friends now. Bonded through trauma.

"What if I'm right?" I ask him. "What if one of them did it?"

"We're working on several angles. You'll have to trust us." My trust has been solid, but my patience is running out. I'm trying not to get discouraged, but it's so, so hard. Every morning when I wake up and Emma's not here, I'm filled with such unbearable grief.

"It's been a week now, Shane," I say, wringing my hands together. "I want my child brought home."

"I know you do." He heaves a sigh. "But here's the thing. Cass Thomas being involved now seems unlikely. Some witnesses have stepped forward from her school, Our Lady of Our Savior. They saw her carrying equipment from a storage room into the gym at the time of Emma's disappearance."

What? No. "Maybe they're lying."

He shakes his head. "They're nuns, Sadie."

"So?" I say brashly. "Nuns lie. I mean, I suppose they can. For the right reason."

He sits back in his chair. "But there are no reasons here. Why would they invent that story? Why would they protect Cass? What's their incentive?"

My soul burns so raw it stings. "Cass knew my husband in high school, Deputy Chief O'Reilly. She had a thing for him, did you know that? A major obsession."

"Yes, she told me." His eyebrows arch. "Although she says it was more of a minor crush."

"What about Bobby?"

"Cass's fabrication may be sad, but we don't believe that's relevant anymore. We had Cass come down to the station for questioning, and our team psychiatrist spoke with her. The gist is she wanted to pretend she was someone's mom again, if only briefly, not that she intended Emma any harm. The nuns at her school all vouch for her. They say she's kindhearted but that—since losing her ex-husband and son so tragically—she's suffered from periodic bouts of depression. Plus, she's got her alibi at the time Emma disappeared. Rock solid now."

"Oh my God." I feel so alone. Like I'm fighting this battle by myself. At first, I thought I had Allen with me. That was before I started to doubt him. "Emma's backpack was in her yard."

"We're under the impression someone planted that."

"Intentionally? Why?" I gasp, knowing the answer. To throw suspicion on Cass, which means maybe she's not connected after all. I hold my head when it spins.

O'Reilly knows I'm dying for reassurance. He gives me some. "We've narrowed the field and are looking at three persons of interest, one at the school."

"At Stonefield? Who?"

"A teacher, but that's all I can say."

"Emma's teacher?"

He's silent.

The instant Allen told me about Kate Davis being Diane's kid sister, I guessed she might be involved. My gut wrenches. How horrible. If it's her, Allen and I unknowingly sent our baby into the mouth of a wolf. But Shane said *three persons of interest.*

"And the second?" I ask.

"Maybe you should talk to your husband about his ex-wife."

Shit. Teresa. I knew it.

My stomach roils. "Deputy Chief O'Reilly," I say. "What's going on here?"

"I'm going to tell you something, but only if you promise me you won't take matters into your own hands again and do something rash."

My heart pounds in my throat. "I don't know if I can make that promise."

"Sadie." He dives into my eyes. "Think of Emma. Let's do this carefully. For her sake."

"I'll do anything for Emma," I say hoarsely.

"Good. Then keep this in confidence, please. We need to keep this circle very tight."

I nod. "The police, me, and Allen?"

He shakes his head. "The police and you."

I know then and there who their third person of interest is.

It's Allen.

SADIE
THE MOM

Day Eight

"What do you mean O'Reilly told you?" Allen stares at me blankly, but I can tell it's an act. It's getting so I hardly trust anything he says anymore. I stare at Emma's dresser and the vacant place where her carousel lamp stood.

Is Allen the one who trashed this room, like I suspected earlier? Or was it Teresa, using Forrest's key, when she knew we were giving the press conference? Did one of them rip everything apart to cover their tracks in sneaking Emma's stuffed dog out of the house to make it look like a home invasion and throw off the police?

Are Emma and Night Doggie with Teresa now, with Teresa waiting to rendezvous with Allen? Somewhere else in the country? Maybe in another state? I don't think it could be overseas. Emma would never get across the border without a passport, and we haven't applied for one for her yet. Besides, crossing a border would create more chances to alert the police.

"I want you to tell me the truth, Allen," I say. "About you and Teresa."

His neck and face are flushed. "The police have it wrong. I don't know why Deputy Chief O'Reilly would have said that. They've got no evidence of anything."

"*Allen,*" I say dramatically. "They've got a note from Teresa saying she was picking Emma up early at school. She was planning to take her. My God, Allen. Were you in on it?"

He sets his jaw. "How do we know Teri wrote the note?" I hate it when he calls her Teri. It's too familiar. Cozy. A pet name. They're divorced now, for goodness' sake, but maybe their relationship isn't over. Shane says the police believe it's not, but he wouldn't share the details. He said it was best if I got them from Allen, who is clamming up. That only makes me think the police are right. Allen's gotten himself roped into this somehow. How could he do that? How could he endanger Emma?

Anger boils up inside me, but I tamp it back down, remembering Shane's caution. Teresa's already fled the scene. The police don't want Allen to do the same. He's their only tie to Teresa now. If Allen goes missing too, it might be impossible to find them. *To find Emma.*

"O'Reilly says they're getting a handwriting expert," I tell him. "They'll subpoena Teresa's bosses and get samples from her work."

He rakes both hands through his hair. "Oh my God."

"There's something going on between you and Teresa, isn't there?"

"Sadie, for goodness' sake. Our child's missing."

"You keep saying that, Allen. And that's *precisely why* the police are interested in your relationship with her."

"We have no relationship other than to coparent Forrest." He keeps lying and lying. Is it a knee-jerk reaction for him now?

I decide to hit him with the truth, but not all of it. I'm guarding the part Shane shared in confidence. "You told Mercer you slept with her."

"Shit. He wasn't supposed to—"

"What? Say anything?" I gape at him, stunned.

"It was only one time," he says like that excuses it. I clutch my stomach, feeling ill.

"When, Allen?" My cheeks burn hot. "When was this?"

"I don't know." I'm sure he does. He sighs and hangs his head. "Sometime last week. No, the week before. It was the week before Emma disappeared."

"So you and Teresa could have arranged something, couldn't you have? Might have decided together to have a fresh start, the two of you with Forrest and Emma?"

"That's nonsense, Sadie. Just hear yourself."

"Is that why Teresa wrote that note and slipped it in Emma's backpack? Had the two of you planned to run away?"

"From our lives, our jobs? That's ludicrous."

I sit back on Emma's bed and cross my arms and legs. "The police don't think it's so far fetched. And now that Teresa's disappeared herself, things look even more suspicious. Maybe something went wrong? You got cold feet? Stood her up?"

"For God's sake, Sadie, *stop*."

"And then there's the teacher." I swing the foot of my crossed leg. "Kate Davis. The baby sister of your old girlfriend. It stretches my imagination that you didn't recognize her at the open house. That you didn't know who she was."

Allen goes positively white. "Christ." He stands and starts pacing around Emma's room, circling past her dollhouse and stables, walking by the window seat crowded with stuffed animals. "Don't you see what this is, Sadie? The police are trying to turn us against each other, to see if one of us will crack."

"I'm not the one who's going to crack, Allen!" I stand angrily to face him. "You are! You've been lying to me this whole time, haven't you? About God knows what!"

Teresa's alibi is weak, and Allen's fell through. The police suspect very heavily that Allen and Teresa were together at eight fifteen on the morning Emma disappeared. The only thing they haven't been able to pinpoint is *where* they were. If one or both of them were at Stonefield Elementary, they took Emma. Allen abducted his own child.

My soul's a piece of paper torn slowly down the middle.

I'm left in tattered halves.

I can't trust my husband.

TERESA
THE EX-WIFE

Day Ten

I stare out the train window as flatlands open to a magenta sky. We're crossing a desert with tall buttes and canyons. The landscape's orangey brown. They'll hold my job at the campus telescope for six months or so, maybe more. I requested a leave of absence, saying I was going on a wellness retreat. I don't know if I'll ever return to North Carolina.

I pull out my phone and check for breaking news stories about Emma's disappearance. It's been more than a week now, and the excitement has died down. Allen and Sadie have slacked off on giving daily press conferences, or maybe they had no choice. I tap into the videos shared on the local news, wondering how long Emma's story will receive any coverage at all.

It can't possibly go on forever. People are bound to forget.

It breaks my heart to leave Forrest behind. But he's in a safe place until everything dies down. I know Allen will keep looking for Emma. I also know he won't find her. When I saw him and Sadie at the police station, I understood I'd made a devastating miscalculation. Allen desperately loves Sadie.

He was just using me.

Allen shows up at my office. I left a back door to the building propped open so he could get in without a pass card. We used to do this all the time when we were married. He knows the drill and shuts the door behind him, taking the stairs to the third floor. My office door is slightly open. He walks in without knocking. "Teri? What's this about?" He sees Sadie's iPod on my desk, but I think he knows. This isn't about my giving back the iPod. It's about me taking what I want. What I've dreamt about forever.

"Allen, I needed to see you—alone."

He closes the door at his back. It's got an opaque window that light shines through. Someone might see our blurred images but not what we're doing. "Did Forrest get off to school okay?"

I nod and walk toward him. "Emma?"

"Yeah, Sadie texted to say she made it on the bus." He rubs his cheek. "She's growing up so fast. I didn't expect kindergarten to come this soon."

"Time flies."

"Yeah, it does."

He shifts on his feet, noting we're very close. Close enough for him to hold me. "I'm sorry about the other night," he says.

I stare into his gorgeous blue eyes. "I'm not."

"Teri." He draws in a breath and holds it. "I don't think—"

My fingers find his face, tracing the rugged outline of his jaw. "Why not?"

"Sadie."

"Maybe Sadie was the mistake?" I undo his necktie and slowly pull it off. I toss it onto the desk, where he's left his keys.

My blouse is unbuttoned lower than it should be. I catch his eyes on my bra. "Teri." His tone's labored, resistant. "No."

My hand slides from his face down his neck, across his broad shoulder and down his arm. I link my hand in his and press his hand to my heart. "We were good once," I say. "You know it."

His Adam's apple rises and falls. "We were."

223

I pull him toward me. "It's not too late."

His eyes flicker with emotion. "For what?"

"For us." I move closer. "For this." I plant a kiss on his lips.

"Oh God," he whimpers, and I kiss him again. "We shouldn't."

His hands massage my upper arms, my shoulders, and lace up into my hair. My heart pounds in a sexy rhythm as I reach down and tug his shirt out of his slacks. Nothing seems impossible anymore. He goes hard against me, and I unbutton his shirt, peeling it back.

"What if we did?" I whisper. I kiss his naked chest and peer up at him, stripping off his shirt. "What if we made a go of it, you, me, Forrest and Emma?"

"How?" His mouth hovers over mine, so near I'm desperate to taste him. Dizzy for his kiss. His erection thickens, jamming against his fly.

"We could take a little trip," I say. "I've already arranged it." I kiss him smoothly, deeply. "You, me, and the kids, a mountain getaway."

"I don't think that's a good idea." He kisses the side of my neck. Nibbles on my earlobe. I guide his hands to my boobs, and he molds them, squeezing and releasing, each pulse getting firmer. I grow warm between my legs, wet.

"We could go this weekend?" I've gone breathy, antsy with need.

"Too soon." His hands move to my hips, hiking up my skirt. "Did you lock the door?" His tone's gravelly, low, sending a thrill right through me.

I reach behind us, and the lock clicks.

"Shit, Teri." He squeezes my bare ass. "You're not wearing any panties." He lightly bites my breast above my nipple. My breath hitches. He takes my nipple in his mouth, giving it attention before pleasuring the other side. Ecstasy sparks through me in electric waves. Every inch of me burns, begs for more.

I fumble for his belt buckle and unzip his fly. "I know," I say against his lips.

He holds my face in his hands, delivering hot, wet kisses, exploring my tongue with his. "We shouldn't," he says, but it's clear that we're going to. He kisses me some more, then spins me toward the wall and out of view of the door and its window. I can't wait to get out of my clothes and for us to start.

224

I unbutton my blouse and unhook my bra, dropping both things on the carpet. He groans and brings his mouth down on mine. I melt into his kisses, and he shoves down his slacks and boxers, hoisting me up in his arms and pinning me to the wall. He's strong. Sexy. I can't believe this is happening. I'm delirious with happiness. Desire. Need.

His blue eyes penetrate mine. "Teri," he says. "I love you. I never stopped." His dick hammers into me, so full, so good.

"Oh!" I cry out and he muffles my cries with his kisses. Deep. Sweet. Sweeping. He holds my ass and fucks me against the wall, my bare tits pressed to his chest. My nipples harden, my insides explode. My heart breaks with joy. The lamp beside us rocks on its base. Volcanic eruptions rocket me to the stars.

"I love you too," I whisper again and again. "Oh God, Allen. I've missed you."

He devours my mouth, my body, ravages my soul.

A phone rings. We ignore it until the call ends.

It rings again.

Allen pulls away. "I'd better check that. It's Sadie's ringtone."

Sadie. Of course.

I find my footing and he lets me go, all throbbing heat, unsteady knees. I tug down my skirt, and he grabs the pants that have pooled around his ankles, pulling his phone from a pocket. "Christ, there's a text." He stares at me, panicked. "Something about Emma? Urgent!"

He punches in Sadie's autodial number, holding his pants by the waistband and belt. "Sadie?" A pause. "What?" The blood drains from his face. "Did you call the police?"

Crap. Something's gone horribly wrong. I pick my blouse and bra up off the floor as he scrambles for his shirt. His tie. "What happened to Emma?" I gasp. "Is she all right?"

"No." He just grabs his keys off my desk. "She's missing."

The earth gets yanked out from under me.

My world goes dark.

O'REILLY
THE COP

Day Fourteen

The investigative team is trying hard not to get discouraged, but the fact is we are. I'm at Rodriguez's townhouse and we sit across from one another at her kitchen table on our laptops, both of us glued to the case. The media's lost interest in doing daily press conferences, and every new lead we follow turns up dry. Christ.

"Any thoughts?" I ask, biting into my sub. I picked up sandwiches at a deli on the way here. Rodriguez made coffee.

"Just running down more rabbit holes," she says without looking at me. "Hoping to hit pay dirt."

I'm hoping for that too. I'm also really hoping that Kate's not involved because that would majorly suck. I stretched the truth a bit when I told her I'd be sleeping in Rodriguez's spare room. She hasn't got one. I'm on the sofa. Rodriguez says it's not an imposition, but I feel like it is. Still, she's been gracious about it and everything's been aboveboard between us, our minds all on business. I like her even more than I did before.

She's getting me to clean up my habits too.

Rodriguez descends the stairs wearing gray sweatpants and a black cop T-shirt. I barely see her because I'm half-asleep. It's early. Rodriguez is an early riser.

Thank God she makes the coffee.

She walks beside the sofa and trips over her feet. "What's this?" She bends down to pick up the socks I dropped by the coffee table. She scrunches up her face, wrinkling her nose. "Disgusting." Her dark-brown hair is long and curly, her eyebrows lowered.

I'm not fully awake, stretched out on the sofa. I've got a pillow under my head and a blanket over me, and that's all I need. "Sorry?" I rub my eyes and the living room comes into focus. Light filters in through the window with the shade slightly raised.

"Socks," she proclaims, dropping one on my chest, "don't go on the floor." She drops the other one on top of me next. "They go in the hamper!"

I stare down at the socks on my undershirt and raise my head to look at her. "I don't have a hamper." Which is true. I've not exactly moved in here. I'm only staying temporarily.

Still. Evidently there are rules.

"Right." She sets her pretty dimpled chin. "We'll fix that."

She's like my freaking mother.

Except. A whole lot hotter.

I never leave my socks on the floor again.

Rodriguez shakes her head and stares at her computer. "I don't buy this guy, Walsh."

It sounds more like she's talking to herself, but I comment anyway. "He was unfairly convicted, if his story's to be believed."

"True." She looks up. "*Which means* he's got an axe to grind with Principal Rand and Stonefield Elementary."

"But why take a kid when he's maintained his innocence in harming children?"

She sighs heavily and flips shut her laptop. "Dammit, you're right. But I can't help feeling we're missing a connection," she says. "You know what I'm saying?"

She stares into my eyes and electric current buzzes through me. Holy cow. What the fuck?

Shit, yeah. I face it. I'm attracted to Rodriguez. Very attracted. I've been fighting it like hell, but she's worn me down with her dark-brown eyes and dimpled chin. But it's her mind that I find the most enticing. I rein myself in. Now is *definitely not* the time.

Her face reddens but she doesn't look away. Maybe she's attracted to me too? She deflects the tension by running a hand through her hair. At work she keeps her long dark curls pinned up, and they're undeniably sexy. "Anyway," she goes on. "I say we keep looking."

"Be nice if we could locate Teresa," I muse.

Rodriguez laughs, but it's a sad laugh. "Be nice if we could find that kid."

"Yeah." My heart breaks because I'm losing hope. "It would."

O'REILLY
THE COP

Day Twenty-One

Rodriguez goggles at her computer screen. "Holy fuck. How did we miss this?"

I stare across the station from where I sit at my desk. "What's up?" We're short on space. Only the chief's got an office.

She motions for me to come over, so I do. I stare at her computer when she points at the screen. "Look at this shot from Walsh's trial." It's a photo that appeared in the local paper, under the headline "Stonefield Teacher Sentenced to Eight Months."

A crowd gathers outside the courthouse. I'm guessing of angry parents. Walsh has his head bowed and is being led away. An older man walks beside him. He's barrel chested and heavyset, with gray hair and a beard. Maybe Walsh's dad?

I'm clearly not seeing what Rodriguez is seeing. I raise my eyebrows at her, and she taps an image on the screen with her finger. "Here."

I peer closer at a woman on Walsh's other side wearing a long gray braid. She's got her hand on his arm in a sympathetic fashion, and his hands are cuffed.

Jesus Christ.

That's Dot Gilmore, the teaching assistant for Emma's class. "What's she doing escorting Walsh at his trial?" I ask Rodriguez.

"Don't know."

She stands and gathers papers on her desk.

She closes her laptop and tucks it under her arm.

"But I'm going to find out."

O'REILLY
THE COP

Day Twenty-Two

We learn Dotti Gilmore is Caleb Walsh's mom. Gilmore was the name she took when she married Caleb's late stepfather, Jack. She and Walsh now top our list as persons of interest. Dotti could be an accomplice to Walsh. His house is near the school. While Caleb was at work, Dotti could have taken Emma to Walsh's house and left her there. Possibly restrained her, or worse. We've got motive. Revenge against Allen Wilson, the jury foreman who convicted her son, and Principal Rand for not standing by him.

My stomach sours. I hope they didn't go to extremes and murder an innocent child in retribution. I hate that I even have to entertain that thought. Jesus. What a fucked-up world.

I'm outside Walsh's house when they bring in the dogs, our best K-9 unit. Claremont's in the front yard with Mercer. Mercer's brought in the feds.

I'm scared of what they'll find inside, and afraid of what they won't.

An officer calls out, "Police!"

No one answers.

Either Walsh isn't home or he's hiding.

The dogs are chomping at the bit, tugging to get in. An officer kicks in the door and the dogs dart into the house, their handlers following close behind them. Claremont and I go in too, and the dogs go nuts, alerting everywhere, sitting at attention and barking in various spots. By the living room sofa. At a table in the kitchen.

Fuck.

Cops whip around corners with their arms and weapons extended. But the house is empty, except for one bedroom closet—in which they find Walsh cowering in a corner.

Tears streak his cheeks when they haul him outdoors and toward a squad car. "I didn't do anything! I swear! What the hell's going on?"

My heart sinks like a stone.

Something's happened to Emma.

SADIE
THE MOM

Day Twenty-Two

Allen and I sit numbly on the sofa while Claremont talks to us. O'Reilly's with her. A connection's been found between Caleb Walsh and Dotti Gilmore. Dotti's Caleb's mom, and they're both now suspects in Emma's disappearance. Suspected accomplices. Both are in police custody.

I grip the arm of the sofa when the room somersaults around me. "So then, Emma?" I ask hopefully, even though my heart clenches with dread. "She's all right?"

Claremont swallows hard. "I'm afraid we don't have further information on Emma yet, although her DNA was found at the house."

DNA could mean body fluids and that she's been injured.

My stomach roils.

"Blood?" Allen asks, horrified.

O'Reilly shakes his head. "A few strands of hair."

Allen firmly grips my hand. "Doesn't mean she's dead."

My soul twists like a sheet in the wind.

Doesn't mean she's alive either.

Hot tears spring to my eyes and I scrub them back. How could they have hurt her? How? She was an innocent. A baby. *My baby.* My shoulders shake with my sobs. I think of Night Doggie holding her spot. "Did they break into this house? Take her stuffed dog?"

O'Reilly shakes his head. "We can't be sure. We didn't find anything like that at Walsh's house, nor any of Emma's personal belongings." Her clothing, he means. Oh my God. That could mean anything. None of it good. My mind starts spiraling.

Stop it, Sadie.

I need to stay positive. For my own sake. For Emma's.

The tiniest glimmer of hope blooms in my heart. Wait. Maybe they took her somewhere else and she's okay? The fact that they took Night Doggie has to mean they weren't intending to harm her. If it was in fact them who broke into our house, and not Teresa. Maybe they wanted Emma to have the special lovey she needed to sleep. Maybe Emma told them where we keep the spare key?

"When will we know more about Emma?" Allen asks. He's sitting near the edge of the sofa and gripping his hands.

"Soon," Claremont says. She and O'Reilly stand. "We're headed back to the station to interrogate Walsh and his mom now."

KATE
THE TEACHER

Day Twenty-Two

My phone buzzes in my pocket and I pull it from my jeans as I wait for my latte at the coffee shop. I had to get out of my apartment. I was going stir crazy in there.

The open-air place used to be a mechanic's garage. The garage door's raised and there's a coffee bar inside. Metal tables with funky chairs stand on the patio outside.

I check my phone for the news alerts I set up.

Two Suspects Detained in Stonefield Elementary Kidnapping

The article photo shows two people getting led out of a cop car in cuffs.

A lump wells in my throat.

Fuck.

One of them is Dotti.

Memories crash over me like rolling ocean waves, and I'm back at that first day of school.

It's been a shit day. A child in my class got kidnapped. A child that I hated through no fault of her own and thought horrible things about. A child I dreamed about getting rid of. Then school closed early, and I was questioned by the police.

While Chief Claremont's inquiries were probably routine, I didn't enjoy her probing questions. They made me incredibly anxious, though I covered it well with my poise.

Until Katherine lost her shit over that fly.

Fuck.

I'm more on edge than I realize. Claremont unnerved me. It was almost like she knew something. Like she suspected I held a grudge against the Wilsons. But how could she possibly figure that out? No one can draw a connection between me and Allen all those years ago.

I'm not Katherine Martin anymore. I emancipated myself from my family when I went off to college. I was so sick to death of the name and people taking pity on me. Judging me. Sometimes harshly.

All through school I was known as the kid sister of the girl who drowned. I heard kids and adults whispering about me behind my back. Gossiping about my family and how screwed up everyone became after we lost Diane. My brother was a junkie. My parents divorced. Some called me the twisted devil sister because they thought I was weird.

In middle school, a mean girl clique speculated that I was a witch, and that I could curse people into dying. Saying that maybe Diane's death was a suicide due to a spell I'd cast. I got them to shut the fuck up by indicating I might put a hex on them, causing them to be dismembered by bloodthirsty crows. It was not any great shakes being a Martin.

So I moved up the alphabet to Davis and reinvented myself as an orphan. That suited me better and felt truer to form. I severed contact with my family and paid my own way through college after working for a few years at a day care to save up money for incidentals. I got one of those teacher scholarships that funds almost everything so long as you work for the system when you get out. That's what landed me at Stonefield.

I set my lunch bag on my desk and slide my chair forward, opening my laptop. Maybe there's some news on Emma? My foots hit something under my desk. It gives on impact, like a soft piece of luggage. What the heck?

I push back in my seat and peer at the floor. I think I might vomit. It's a pink backpack like the one Emma was wearing when she disappeared. It has a My Little Pony design on its front like the one that was described in Emma's Amber Alert, the one that flashed across my phone twenty minutes after I turned our classroom attendance report in.

How in the hell did that get here?

"Kate!" a loud voice calls.

I blink and numbly lower my phone. Fuck. Where am I? I view the packed tables on the patio, crowded with student types and university professors.

Right.

O'REILLY
THE COP

Day Twenty-Two

Walsh is no help during questioning. He claims to know nothing and to have only seen Emma once at the grocery store with her mom, Sadie, before Emma's face was splashed all over the news due to her abduction. He doesn't know how her DNA got in his house. He has no clue why the dogs alerted to Emma's presence there.

He's very convincing.

He wears jeans and a black T-shirt. Has sinewy tattooed arms, longish blond hair and a dark bushy beard. "Maybe it was Sadie?" he speculates desperately. "Maybe some of Emma's hair was on her clothing? She came to my house! Accused me of hurting Emma. I didn't!" He stares at me like a wild man. "Deputy Chief O'Reilly knows," he says. "He was there."

Claremont's beside me. A court-appointed attorney is with Walsh. His attorney leans toward him. "You don't have to answer these questions. You'd do better to plead the Fifth right now."

"But I've got nothing to hide!" Walsh insists. "Why won't anyone believe me? *Please*. Give me a lie detector test," he challenges me and Claremont. "Are those a real thing? I'll take one!"

Claremont and I look at each other.

We're both thinking the same thing.

He's telling the truth.

Maybe we'll have better luck with Dotti.

KATE
THE TEACHER

Day Twenty-Two

I turn and walk toward the coffee bar.

"Half-caf nondairy latte?" the barista asks. They've got a nose stud and tattoos.

"Yeah, uh, that's me." I take the ceramic cup, still dazed. "Thanks."

The tables out front are full, so I find a vacant spot at the end of a picnic table around the corner. A couple's already sitting there, drinking their coffee and reading their phones. "Okay to share?" I ask.

One guy looks up. "Yeah, cool. No problem."

I slide onto the bench and settle my cup on the table.

I go back to my phone and scan the news story.

You've got to be fucking kidding me. My mind reels.

Caleb Walsh is Dotti's son?

I'm back in the moment on that very first day, staring down at the floor.

The backpack was apparently sitting under my desk the whole time I was talking with Chief Claremont. Oh my God. The dogs might have found it while they were searching through the school. Why didn't they? They gave a cursory sweep of the hall, then went back outdoors and around the side of the building.

Dotti attested that Emma was not in the line of children she brought inside, and none of the other teachers were completely sure about whether they'd seen Emma getting off the bus. The cameras at the front of the school show the main entrance and the flagpole. The bus that Emma rode parks farther down, in front of the art teacher's room and closer to the woods.

I peek at the hall and see it's empty. Then I carefully reach for the backpack and set it in my lap. It's coated in something very fine—a powder, maybe?—that glitters and sparkles in the light pouring in from the windows. A strong whiff of perfume wafts toward me, and it's vaguely familiar. Dotti. No, wait. That's the perfume she spilled earlier when she was standing by my desk. The bottom of the backpack is damp where the spilled perfume leaked through.

I unzip it and see Emma's name written on the inside in permanent marker. There are papers in a manila envelope stuck down in its hollow. I don't touch them. They look like the opening day forms completed by her parents.

Why is her backpack here? Under my desk when Emma's gone missing?

Crap. Does someone know about Allen and Diane? My forehead burns hot. Is someone trying to frame me? I check the front pocket of the backpack next. There's a teacher note inside it, addressed to me. I reach for it and freeze, staring down at my hands like they're covered in blood. They might as well be.

I've been rifling through Emma's backpack. An item belonging to a kidnapped child. I should call the police. Turn this in.

A painful knot forms in my throat.

I might as well let them handcuff me at that point.

They'll want to know how I got the backpack. When I say I don't know, they'll think I'm lying. They'll start digging into connections between Emma's family and me. They'll learn about Diane. That will give them a motive. Revenge.

I'm Emma's teacher, in a position of authority. She would have done what I told her and gone where I said. They'll assume means.

Emma's a student in my class. She's new and unsure about her environment. Meanwhile, I know Stonefield Elementary inside out. I could have hidden her somewhere temporarily. A clear opportunity—even though others here vouched for me.

When people are pressed, their stories might start crumbling. They'll begin doubting what they recalled under pressure, silently pointing their fingers at me. Dotti will say she saw me rushing back into the classroom minutes before the start of school, and that I was out of breath, claiming to have run out to my car for my phone. She'll also testify she saw my phone was already in the classroom at the time.

When asked to think again, Mitra Parikh will say she did in fact tell me I could borrow masking tape from her when I asked. In truth, she was fixing an art display in the hall near the cafeteria at eight fifteen. She told me to go ahead and grab what I needed, no problem, but she was not personally there to serve as a witness.

Essentially, no alibi. Not one that holds up.

I stare down at Emma's pink backpack knowing I'm fucked.

Principal Rand doesn't like me. She never has. I don't know if it's because I'm pretty or because I'm well liked. She's neither. Most of the faculty hate her. I'd say like ninety-five percent, and she treats the staff even worse.

She's a suck-up to the parents when she wants to be, but everyone at Stonefield knows Principal Rand basically looks after herself. She's like a self-important queen on her throne at this elementary school. If anyone crosses her or threatens to make her look bad, it's off with their heads.

Panic spikes through me.

I'll be fired. Get put on administrative leave at best.

Then, after an investigation—no matter what is found—I'll lose my job like Caleb Walsh did. Yes, I've heard the stories. Everyone here loved him. That was the nail in his coffin. At the first sign of trouble, Principal Rand was all too eager to hammer it in.

MISS DOTTI
THE GRANDMA

Day Twenty-Two

The instant I saw Emma Wilson, I knew she was my lost child. The granddaughter Principal Rand so selfishly robbed me of and the babe I barely got to hold in my arms. If Principal Rand had stood up for my son, Caleb, seven years ago instead of fretting over her supposed sterling reputation and her job, Chelsea never would have left him. Wouldn't have walked away with their infant daughter, Nellie, and moved out of state.

Every time I'm introduced to someone new who's around my age, they note my gray hair and ask, "Do you have grandchildren?" That's such a common topic of conversation, though it's honestly insensitive. It's like asking someone, "Are you rich or just struggling to get by?" More than a bit rude and nobody's fucking business. After I was denied contact with Nellie out of her mom's efforts to shield her, it felt like a lie to say yes, the knife plunging deeper into my heart.

And then I met Emma in person at our school open house, and she instantly melted my heart. She didn't take to many of the others in the room, not even her teacher, Kate Davis, though I can't blame Emma for that. I've never liked Kate myself. She's always looked down her nose at me, as if I'm not as smart or talented as she is. But I am twice as brilliant and far more sly. She doesn't know it, but I also went to college, undoubtedly a better one than she did. I'll bet my GPA was higher than hers, too. But she's got good looks in her favor. I don't.

My husband Jack had a bad heart and Caleb's trial was rough on him. Not long after the verdict was called, Jack was out shoveling snow and he keeled over with a heart attack. Dead. Yes, we get snow in this part of the state. Though it's rare, when it hits, it sometimes hits big, complete with a good solid icing. It was probably the heavy ice part that did Jack in. That, and Caleb's unfortunate circumstances.

I've been watching the Wilson family ever since Forrest started at Stonefield Elementary and I recognized his father as the man who'd locked my boy, Caleb, away. Mr. Wilson is a despicable man, the jury foreman whose pronouncement of "guilty" changed Caleb's life, and so many other lives in turn.

People assume Allen Wilson is a respectable, upstanding citizen who does no wrong. But there's no greater sin than convicting an innocent person. Allen's also someone who doesn't honor his commitments. He divorced his first wife and married a younger and prettier one, who arrived at Forrest's school events with a cute bundle in her arms. Emma had to be around a year old the first time I saw her. Maybe a year or so younger than Caleb's daughter, Nellie.

Each year, Emma only got cuter, and the anguish inside me grew like a firestorm. Nellie had been taken away from us, and Caleb had served several months in jail for a crime he didn't commit. I never got to hold Nellie in my lap, fix her hair, or read her stories. Thanks to two people, Allen Wilson and Principal Rand.

Hatred burned holes inside me. My rage was so deep I found it hard to function at school, until—one day—I saw my new class list. Emma Wilson was on it. Joy welled in my heart. It would be almost like seeing Nellie day after day. Resentment set in within hours after that. Why should one year be enough? Why couldn't I reclaim Nellie for always?

It infuriated me that Principal Rand had remained unscathed after her role in railroading Caleb. I wanted to knock her off her high horse and make her pay. She didn't deserve her leadership position, and she'd lose it, I was sure, if something else scandalous happened at her school. I was equally mad about Allen Wilson getting to live his perfect life, with his perfect wife and child. Why should he have it all, while I had nothing?

The day of Emma's open house, she seemed to be having a bad time at school. I worked hard to bring her around by telling her a secret. Do you know what I said? I asked her in an impish way if she likes playing hide-and-seek. Her grin was so huge, it was clear that she did. "Don't worry," I promised. "We'll play that on your very first day."

I guess she didn't tell her parents, because they might have become suspicious of me then. But nobody ever guessed it was me. Not the parents, not Rand, not the police. Not even Kate, ice bitch that she is. Kate's got one of those faces everyone loves.

She's pretty and outgoing, but her effervescence is entirely for show. She might fool others at the school, but she's never fooled me. I can't stand people like her. Talk about corruption of minors. Sweet Emma didn't need to be in her class.

Didn't need to be exposed to *her*.

Role model. *Right.*

The first day of school comes back to me crystal clear.

I get Emma off the bus while classes line up on the sidewalk to go inside. It's a gloomy day with high humidity. Some mugginess is to be expected. It's August. Emma's so cute in her pale-pink backpack, with her big trusting eyes. I lean toward her and whisper, asking if she wants to play that game we talked about at the open house. If she hides well enough so no one can find her, she'll get a special ice cream treat.

She nods and her grin is huge. I instruct her to wait while I speak to another teaching assistant, Betsy Reynolds, asking her to watch my line. I say a kid is sick and I need to rush him to the bathroom—will she watch my group and bring them inside when it's time? I'll meet her in the hall.

Betsy's new and looking flustered by all the noise of buses arriving, kids chatting, teachers shouting, and the stench of diesel fuel filling the air. She says of course, and I take Emma by the hand and lead her around the corner of the building near the woods. There's so much commotion out front with the new kids getting mixed up about where they're supposed to stand and teachers reshuffling lines, nobody sees us slip away. I'm very careful to check that no one is watching before we do.

We scurry off at a fast clip and Emma giggles. "Miss Dotti?" she asks. "Why are we running so fast?" Her small legs barely keep up with my short stubby ones.

"So nobody finds us." I wink and hold my finger to my lips. "You'll have to be as quiet as a church mouse now."

She wrinkles up her precious nose as we approach the door I've left propped open to the media room with a wood block. It's a fire exit but has no alarm on the door. The AC is crap in the school, and teachers are always propping open these types of doors, even though they're not technically supposed to. There are no cameras outside on this part of the building either. "What's a church mouse?" she asks a bit too loudly.

"It's a very quiet critter," I say in hushed tones. I smile at her. "And very quiet critters who hide well get ice cream."

Her eyes twinkle merrily. "Yay!"

"Shhh," I caution, leading her toward the door. "We don't want anyone to find you. Which is why I've brought my special magic fairy dust." Before we go inside, I unzip the fanny pack I have strapped around my waist. I keep a myriad of supplies in there, including first aid items for needy children. Today, I've mostly emptied it out to hide my special stash. I withdraw the flat tin can with a screw lid and a big plush powder puff.

Emma's eyebrows knit together, but she looks happily intrigued. "Fairy dust?" she whispers like the good church mouse that she is. My late husband Jack was a hunter. That's how I learned about camouflaging human scent. I take one of Emma's small arms and dust it till it's sparkly. She giggles as I dust up her front and back, little legs, backpack, and all. I added glitter to the camodust to make it fun. It may leave a slight trail inside, but I've got a micro pack of cleaning wipes so I can mop that up. I'm not stupid.

I've also brought along a spray vial of my signature perfume. "And now for our garden gnome scent!" When I'm done with the powder, I give myself a spritz, then spray-spray-spray Emma's little form—backpack and all—until she coughs and giggles some more.

I've got a nice spot prepared for her in the media room under a built-in counter holding computers. A long window above it has a view of the library's main room, letting in plenty of light. The library kids get cushy mats to sit on when the librarian's reading them stories. I brought one in here from the stack that nobody ever tallies. I've selected some fun books for her to browse through too.

"Why don't you sit here and look at these?" I say. "The one about the baby elephant and its mother is really fun."

Her eyes grow large when she sees the huge pile of books I've selected. "Do I have to read them all?" I know she can't read, at least not more than a few words, but she can certainly enjoy the pictures. I want to be sure she has enough to keep her busy until I return, which should be in less than fifteen minutes. Though fifteen minutes can seem like an eternity to a child.

"Oh yes," I say. "Please do. I'll want to ask you questions about them later."

Her eyebrows knit together. "Like a test?"

I thumb her adorable nose. "Not a very hard one, I promise."

She nods when I point to the place where she's going to sit. Then she scrambles down to get under the counter, but her backpack bumps underneath it. "Oh dear," I say lightly. "You're stuck like a little turtle who's hit his shell."

She giggles and I remove her backpack, setting it on the floor beside her. "Now remember." I hold my finger to my lips.

"Church mouse," she whispers softly.

KATE
THE TEACHER

Day Twenty-Two

I finish my coffee, my lips quaking against the rim of the cup. Now that Dotti and Caleb are under arrest, am I next? Will the police come for me? *Fuck.* I found the backpack. I thought someone was possibly trying to frame me. All this time, it was Dotti who took Emma?

Dotti?

Was she trying to make me look like the culprit? Implicate me? Or was she simply stashing Emma's backpack there until later? What the hell happened? *What the hell* did *Dotti* do to Emma?

The day is so real in my mind, I can still feel it happening. The panic, the absolute fear. I've found Emma's backpack under my desk. The police will poke holes in my alibi. And if they find out about Diane

. . .

Terror runs like ice through my veins. I might get convicted. Go to fucking jail. Walsh was convicted and everyone here says he was innocent. That was of a minor sex crime, not kidnapping.

Fuck me.

My heart breaks into tiny pieces. I'll lose Shane. He's the one good thing I have. The only person who believes in me, loves me for who I am. I grew disgusted with my dysfunctional family. My parents became so self-focused they couldn't see their two remaining children anymore. Mark didn't care about me, either. He had his own demons to face.

I wanted to build my own life. Start fresh, and I was doing okay until I first passed Allen Wilson in the hall. Seeing him again was like ripping a bandage off my bleeding heart. It brought back all the awful memories. Made the loss so present.

Allen and Diane were underage drinking, and I know it was Allen who supplied the booze. He had an athlete's body and looked older than he was. They never carded at that one convenience store at the beach anyway. I'm not sure who bought the marijuana. Maybe Allen or maybe Mark. Either way, it was Allen's fault for exposing Diane to drugs and alcohol.

She was never a party girl before she started dating Allen. If she hadn't been doped up, she might not have been carried away by that riptide. Might have been mentally sharp enough to guess what was happening and physically strong enough to swim parallel to the shore so she could break out of the current. Allen contributed to Diane's death in a way I read as murder, though I'd take a manslaughter charge as a consolation prize. Now, I can't pursue either.

With Emma disappeared, Allen's living in his own kind of hell.

Good. At least that's something.

I zip up Emma's backpack without touching anything inside and drop it down on the floor, pushing it under my desk. It's not like this backpack will help anyone find Emma at this point. She's clearly long gone by now. Maybe she's okay? Being looked after somewhere, and not in danger?

One thing I know.

I can't endanger myself.

Dotti's gone home and I'm alone in my room. But Mitra Parikh's lights are still on in her room across the hall. I could have gone home after Chief Claremont cleared me, but I stayed to revise my lesson plans for tomorrow. Seeing as how today was scrapped and tomorrow will be a short day, they needed tweaking. Maybe that's what the art teacher's doing too?

I finally see her come out of her room and lock her door. She spots me at my desk and waves. "Let's hope they find that girl," she says.

"Yeah," I answer. "Hope so."

After she leaves, I check the hall. All the other rooms are empty. Doors locked and closed. Lights out. I go back to my room and shut the door. I put on plastic gloves from my first aid kit and grab Emma's backpack from under my desk. I take out the note addressed to me and read it. Her mom, Sadie, says a family friend is picking Emma up early from school today. The note doesn't sit right with me. Doesn't seem real.

Fuck. What does all this mean?

I decide to keep the teacher note until I can decide what to do with it. Maybe mail it anonymously to the police? In the meantime, I hide it in my desk drawer beneath a divided tray holding paper clips and such. But there's no place to conceal this backpack where it won't be found. I can't leave it at the school, where it will implicate me.

I take the backpack and wipe it down front and back with chlorine wipes to erase my fingerprints from the outside, its front pocket, and zippers. Then I place Emma's backpack in a large paper sack and carry it out the side door of the gym, where there are no cameras, hiding it in the trunk of my car.

O'REILLY
THE COP

Day Twenty-Two

Dotti's a lot cagier than her son. She wants to bargain with us in exchange for her story. It's very clear she believes she's holding the winning hand. "I can tell you things," she says shrewdly, surveying the interrogation room like she owns it. "But I want assurances first." She's got a long gray braid slung forward over one shoulder and wears earrings that look like giant crayons. I'd say she's in her mid-to-late sixties.

"I'd caution you against cutting deals at this juncture," her counsel advises.

She ignores her well-meaning attorney with a haughty snort. "First, I want my son, Caleb Walsh, set free," she tells me and Claremont, feeling free to make her demands.

Claremont sits up straighter in her chair. She steals a peek at the surveillance camera. "I'm afraid we can't do that. He's a suspect in the kidnapping of a minor."

Dotti clicks her tongue. "He had nothing to do with it."

"Ma'am," her attorney says.

Dotti shushes her and continues talking. "Caleb never knew we were in his house. He was at work. I've got a key."

Claremont's ears perk up and so do mine. "We?" I ask.

Dotti stares smugly around the room, preening for the cameras. She's not intimidated at all about being here. I have the very weird sense she's enjoying the attention. "I've got news for you folks. Quite interesting news that I'm sure you'll want to hear. But first, before you get the details, I want my deal."

She crosses her arms and sits back, waiting like she's got all the time in the world.

"Details?" Claremont questions carefully. "About what?"

Dotti's attorney leans forward, but Dotti waves her aside like she's being a pest.

She raises her chin and says leadingly, "Emma Wilson—is alive."

MISS DOTTI
THE GRANDMA

Day One

After situating Emma in her hiding place in the media room, I sneak through the library and dash down the hall, ducking into a bathroom near where the classroom lines form. I come out almost immediately and grab a boy's elbow, pulling him quickly toward me and then pushing him back in line. He's young, confused, a kindergartner, not sure what he's done. Maybe wondering if he's in trouble. "Hope you feel better," I say before walking away.

The kid stares at me with his face scrunched up, and Principal Rand catches my eye. She stands inside the main entrance directing children this way and that like a traffic cop, although she effectively has no function. The kids' teachers and teaching assistants are getting them where they need to go. "Is something going on?" she asks, standing pertly in high heels and a slacks-and-jacket suit.

"Oh no. Just stomach flutters," I report. "You know kids." I shrug. "First day."

I find my group and thank Betsy for spelling me during my "emergency," leading my kids to our classroom. When we get there, Kate is just rushing in the door like she's been out somewhere at the very last minute. I shoot her a questioning look. She seems out of breath. "My phone," she tells me. "I thought I left in the car."

I see her phone on top of a bookshelf close to her rocker. "It's over there."

"Oh gosh! Thanks, Miss Dotti."

We take attendance and one child is absent, Emma Wilson.

Kate submits the attendance report electronically, and we gather the kids, getting them in line. Principal Rand's holding an opening day assembly. I've suffered through these for many years. This morning, though, I have other plans.

These assemblies are held in the auditorium, where children take their seats and teachers huddle in groups near the back of the room or alongside the walls, in the aisles. Overseeing the students at these events is more of a village effort, so it's simple for an individual to step out with no one noticing them, especially with most of the room darkened except for the stage.

Principal Rand stands at the podium making humorless jokes and running a goofy slide show about the wonderful world of Stonefield Elementary. Droning on *and on* about the joys and responsibilities of attending school here. She never changes her script, even though most of us have heard her speech *so many* times we could essentially recite it ourselves.

When I return to Emma, I check my watch. I've only been gone seventeen minutes, but I'm sure it seemed like a lifetime for her. She hears me come in and creeps out from under the counter, holding her books and dragging the cushion out with her. The entire school is forced to be in the auditorium at Rand's mandatory assembly, so I don't have to worry about observers. I say she's done a great job and stayed hidden very well.

"Nobody found me." She seems very proud.

"Yay, you!" I give her a thumbs-up, and she mimics me. Precious.

I roll up my pants legs to prepare for our adventure and take her hand, aware of the time. I've got to get her to her next spot and sneak back into the auditorium before Rand's annoying address ends. I've got twenty minutes. That should be more than enough. "Come along," I say and lead her toward the exit. I scoop up the books she was reading and her seat cushion too, hoisting them along with her little frame into my arms. I don't want her leaving any ground scent, and from the dark clouds gathering on the horizon, a heavy rain's coming. Sooner rather than later would be good. I'm grateful for the creek we're going to cross and the precautions I've taken in case of the dogs, and I'm betting there will be dogs.

"We're not having ice cream at school?" she asks, perplexed.

"Oh, no! Not here. Someplace much more cozy. There will be plenty of time for school later," I say.

Caleb's house is only two blocks away, but the shortcut through the woods gets us there in no time. My mom is waiting to take care of Emma, with all the makings for a hot fudge sundae. She's got my fresh pair of shoes and socks for me to change into as well, as wading through the creek left my feet soaked.

I hurry back to the school, hopping across stones while forging the creek, then wait with the group of teaching assistants at the back of the auditorium as Principal Rand's boring morning address winds down. That's when I remember Emma's backpack. Crap. She didn't have it on when I took her to Caleb's house. We must have left it in the media room.

I need to get it before it's found and hide it until I can sneak it away. Emma's scent might be cloaked enough on it to fool the dogs, but I'll add some extra camodust just to be sure, then shake any excess off outside the media room's exterior door.

I check the auditorium clock against my watch. I have just enough time to grab the backpack and hurry it into my classroom, hiding it under Kate's desk before the assembly's over.

Kate sees me dashing back toward the auditorium when the assembly gets dismissed. "Dotti? Are you all right?"

I hold my stomach and grimace. "Just a touch of something. Must have been my breakfast biscuit."

Kate almost never sits at her desk, preferring to take her lunches in the teachers' lounge. I'll grab the backpack when she's at lunch and sprint it over to Caleb's house. I'm not on lunch duty today. Thank goodness. That helps.

But then Emma's Amber Alert hits my phone, and all hell breaks loose, with the police and her parents showing up at Stonefield and school getting dismissed early. Between the police presence here with dogs circling around and around the school, and Kate being in her room, getting that backpack's impossible.

I'm scared to death she's going to find it—that *someone's* going to find it and implicate me. It's got my perfume on it, dammit. A light bulb goes on in my head. The best way to hide my scent is by adding some more. So in Kate's plain view and during the chaos of the Amber Alert upheaval, I unscrew the spray cap on my perfume bottle and "accidentally" drop it right in front of her desk with a big surprised cry.

I catch a flash of annoyance in Kate's eyes. "Dot," she sighs heavily. "Now?" Kate acts like she's as cool as cucumber, but she's secretly very hot under the collar, if you ask me. I'd hate to see what she's really like at home when she takes her fake smiling face off.

"I'm sorry! So sorry!" I feign being clumsy and scurry for some paper towels. But instead of mopping up, I'm pushing the puddle forward, silently sloshing it under her desk as Emma's backpack soaks up the cloying scent like a stealthy sponge.

I decide to go back to Stonefield later, when everyone's left for the day, to retrieve Emma's backpack. But when I return, the backpack's not under Kate's desk. It's gone.

I freeze with fear, wondering who's found it and whether they've turned it in to the police. Whether or not my perfume cover-up worked at throwing off the dogs, my fingerprints are still there. I hide at my house on the outskirts of town, waiting for police sirens to blare, with officers storming in to lead me away in handcuffs. That never happens. Once I'm sure the coast is clear, I drive back to Caleb's place to pick up Emma and Mom.

MEEMAW
NANA'S MAMA

Day One

The child and I walk down the gravel drive after being dropped off by her nana. I hope she'll feel at home here. I know I'll do my best. It's devastating that things had to go this way, but life is harsh. You make accommodations. We're making the best of what we've got. The hand that life dealt us. My daughter, Dot, says the poor child's mother has passed, and if not left to us, the girl might become a ward of the state, since Caleb's ex insisted on sole custody.

Of course, Caleb might step in himself, kind soul that he is. But he'd be in over his head with a little girl he hasn't seen in years, and his overt involvement could trigger legal issues besides. He'll have no difficulties visiting his daughter here. Dot and I will make sure of it. Poor child has lost so much already. Heartbreaking.

"All right, darling," I say to the child. "Come with me." We're on a country road and miles from any highway. Miles from most places really. All day long it's chirping birds and buzzing bees. The scent of fresh-cut grass and honeysuckle. The only commercial place nearby is a gas station that doubles as a convenience store. They also sell delicious deli sandwiches.

Hayfields spread out around us. The farm next door grows tobacco and corn. The people behind me keep horses. Maybe the girl and I can visit so she can feed them carrots and apples.

I take her hand and lead her toward my house. It's a nice house and very homey, with cheery lights glowing inside its front windows.

Dark clouds roll across the sky. A storm is coming. Probably later tonight or this evening. I feel it in the bursitis in my shoulder. A sure telltale sign of changing weather. Getting older is a pain, but then small bursts of sunshine surprise you, like this sweet child here.

She looks up at me as we walk along. "Who are you?"

I'm surprised she doesn't know, although I shouldn't be.

I smile at her sweetly. "Why, I'm your meemaw!"

She wrinkles up her adorable face. She's in red shorts, and her shirt has lots of different-colored balloons on it. She really is the cutest nugget. Maybe that's what I'll call her? Nugget. I like it. It suits her. "I haven't got one of those."

"Of course you do," I assure her. I nod as we approach the pretty covered porch with potted plants all around. Several hold blooming flowers. The hibiscus draws butterflies and hummingbirds. I bet the child will delight in that. "I'm your nana's mama."

Two rockers perched on either side of the front door sway in the breeze. I've owned this house for sixty-five years. My Dot grew up here along with her brother, Harry. Harry sadly passed last year.

She shakes her head, and honey-gold hair swings past her shoulders. "Haven't got a nana either." *What in heaven's name have they told her about her family?*

"You probably just haven't spent a lot of time around her, that's all. Otherwise, you'd remember. Kids call her Miss Dotti. Maybe you know her from kindergarten?"

Her brown eyes twinkle. "Oh yeah! We played hide-and-seek."

"You see," I say, and she grins. "You'll only have friends here."

We reach the front of the house and I drop her hand. "Now," I say warmly, "turn around and let me look at you."

She does what I tell her. Such an obedient child. "My, how you have grown!" Before today, I hadn't seen her since she was a babe in arms. Everyone called her Nellie then. I crouch down to look in her eyes, deciding she favors her mother. "Do you mind if I call you Nugget?"

She shrugs. "When can I go home?" Her distressed expression pains me.

"After a bit," I say noncommittally. "But first, how about some supper?" It's been hours since the ice cream and that wasn't exactly a healthy lunch. I'm sure she's hungry. I bought hot dogs because I couldn't for the life of me remember what kids that age eat. It's been so long.

"I don't want supper." She hugs herself by her elbows and shivers. "I want my mommy." This is going to be hard for her in the beginning, but it will get better. I'll love her like she's my own. So will Dot.

"I know you do," I say, "but she's busy right now, so she wanted you to stay here with me."

She squints at me and then my house. "Here, and not at school?"

"You don't have to go to school," I say, thinking this will brighten her spirits. What child wants to be in school? I know I didn't, which is why I left after the eighth grade. "We're going to homeschool from now on," I say decidedly.

She frowns so I try something different. "*Or* we can say *no school* and just play like it's summer all year long."

She perks up. That clearly was the A answer. "Can we play at my house?"

Oh dear. We're back to that again. Poor girl.

"No. I'm afraid we'll have to play here for a while." I try to remember what five-year-olds like. Maybe if she's having a good time, that will distract her and make her less homesick. "Do you want to play Parcheesi?" I ask.

"What's pa-cheesy?" Her knitted-together eyebrows melt my heart.

"A very fun game." And just the ticket for a stormy afternoon and evening. We'll hunker down and have a nice time. Maybe I'll make some hot cocoa. With marshmallows. Who cares if it's August? It's as cold as Christmas in Australia. "Come on, Nugget." I wave for her to follow. "I'll show you."

TERESA
THE EX-WIFE

Day Twenty-Three

I'm at a cabin in a state park when I read the news update on my phone. Two Suspects Detained in Stonefield Elementary Kidnapping.

My eyes burn hot with relief.

Thank God. It's over.

I place Sadie's iPod in my purse and prepare to go home.

There's not much in my suitcase but some basic clothing I've purchased from thrift stores on the road. I donated the children's clothing in parcels along the way because I knew I wouldn't be bringing it home. I was also painfully aware that Emma would never get the chance to wear any of it. I'd completely deluded myself into believing that Allen would run away with me. *Run away with us.* I'd planned for us to become a family. Allen, Forrest, Emma, and me.

I never intended to steal Sadie's child, of course not. What I thought we needed was some time away. Just Allen with me and the kids for the weekend. A fun getaway so we could experience our new family unit by ourselves, and without Sadie's interference. I wanted Allen to tell Sadie the truth, that he and I were still in love with each other and wanted to give things another try.

I planned it carefully and rented us a mountain house in Banner Elk, outside Boone. I thought I'd get both kids early at lunchtime so we could make a long weekend of it. Stonefield doesn't do much during that first short week of school anyway. It's more about students getting acclimated and going to assemblies and such. I didn't send an early dismissal note for Forrest because I knew he wouldn't need one with me being his mom.

All Allen had to do was go home and talk to Sadie, pack a few things, and meet me at my house so the four of us could head out together. I was already prepared to pack for Emma. I wanted her to be excited about being with us and have lots of pretty, new clothes to wear. Allen said Sadie would never share custody, but I was certain he was wrong. It's better to share than to lose something completely. I learned that very difficult lesson with Forrest.

When the police closed in, I knew I had to run. They'd seen me on the school bus, and I'd invented the iPod story. I meant to give the iPod to Allen directly so Sadie would never know what Forrest had been up to, but he forgot to take it home.

Then Emma went missing, and I knew it would look like I'd done it. Everyone would figure me for the individual with a motive, the jealous ex-wife. The only person who could vouch for me was Allen, but he wouldn't because he didn't want to admit he'd come to my office to see me that morning and that he'd fallen into my arms.

That, at the instant of Emma's kidnapping, he and I were making love.

O'REILLY
THE COP

Day Twenty-Three

Rodriguez drives me to the old farmhouse on a distant road. We've plugged the address into the GPS. Claremont's with Patel and other squad cars follow, along with FBI. We hope this will be a peaceful procedure. I pray the kid's alive and well. Enough years on the job have taught me people are complicated. Whether intentionally or due to mental compromise, Dotti could have made her whole story up. Yet, the DNA evidence supports it and her timeline clocks.

I don't know how she could have talked herself into doing something so potentially harmful to a child. While she might not have hurt Emma physically, who knows what type of psychological impact a kidnapping might have on a kid? Hopefully, Emma will be okay and wasn't physically or emotionally mistreated. That, in itself, will be a blessing if it's true. A child psychologist rides in Mercer's car. We've got a social worker on the team and a trauma specialist too. An ambulance trails us quietly at a distance. I hope to God it's not needed.

Rodriguez shifts her hands on the steering wheel. "I hope this is the end of it," she says.

"A happy ending." I sigh. "Yeah."

"Happy endings are good. I believe in those." She smiles at me. "You?" She's a very nice-looking woman, but what I like best about her is her smarts. Her good heart. I still feel crappy about having the wool pulled over my eyes by Kate, but never again.

Rodriquez isn't Kate, though. She's her own person. A very lovely one too.

I shrug. "Depends on the circumstances."

Things probably won't end happily for Kate. She's been charged as an accessory after the fact in kidnapping, as well as for concealing and tampering with evidence. I think the latter charges will stick, at a minimum. I'm disappointed in myself for not seeing her for who she was sooner.

Claremont was correct. I should have recused myself from the case. I kick myself for unwittingly sharing information with her about Cass Thomas, who turned out to be completely innocent after all. Same with the ex-wife, Teresa. She forged the teacher note and that was duplicitous, but not criminal. Teresa never had any intent to harm Emma. She was merely in love with Emma's dad and very sadly misread the situation, thinking he was also in love with her.

Allen was no prince, but he also wasn't any kind of kidnapper. The only thing Allen was guilty of was breaking his wife's heart. I wonder if she'll find it in her heart to forgive him? Maybe for the sake of the kid?

"So Rodriguez?"

She briefly takes her eyes off the road to glance at me. "Yeah?"

"I was wondering, when all this is said and done, if maybe you'd like to go for a coffee?"

She laughs. "We have coffee all the time at my place."

"Yeah, about that." I lay my hand on my duty belt. "I think it's time I moved out."

"What?"

"You've been very kind," I tell her, "but I don't want to abuse your hospitality."

"You haven't been abusing, O'Reilly." A hint of mirth sparks in her eyes. "I've liked having you around."

"That's sweet, but I want things to be proper."

She lightly chides me. "Spoken like a good Catholic boy."

"You haven't answered."

She pulls up to a house with a wide covered front porch and parks. The other vehicles park behind us and doors pop open.

"About the coffee?" She grins. "Yeah, sure. I'll go."

MEEMAW
NANA'S MAMA

Day Twenty-Three

Someone pounds at the door. Barbaric. I *do* have a doorbell.

Then shouting. "Open up! Police!"

My heart leaps in my chest and I stare at the child.

She clings to my leg, trembling. "What's happening, Meemaw?" She's got her stuffed doggie with her, and her eyes are huge. Frightened.

"Don't worry, Nugget." I gently stroke her hair. "Your Meemaw will handle it." I point to the kitchen table where I've already made her lunch. Peanut butter sandwiches with the kind of jelly she likes. "Wait here."

She obediently slides into her chair. A worried frown. "I'm scared."

"Hold your Night Doggie," I tell her. She clutches him to her chest. "I'll be right back."

I square my shoulders and walk to the door. There must be some mistake. There's no need for police here. I open the door and two officers stand on the porch. A man with a closely shaved head and a woman with pinned-back dark hair. "Can I help you folks?"

The woman pulls a piece of paper from her shirt pocket. "We've got a warrant to search your house."

"Search it?" I'm flummoxed. "Why?"

"We suspect you're hiding a child," the man says.

"Hiding? That's a new one. Officer"—I read his name tag—"O'Reilly."

"Can we come in, ma'am?" the woman asks.

"Well, I suppose." I step back a few paces. "But there's nobody home but me and my great-granddaughter, Nellie."

The pair of them exchange glances. That's when I notice the arsenal of vehicles parked behind them. Police cars, black sedans, an ambulance too. My heart twists painfully. Have they come to take the child? Take her away?

"What is this?" My voice shakes. "What are you here for?"

"We're here for Emma," the woman says. Her eyes light up and she stares over my shoulder. I turn and see Nugget standing in the hall, Night Doggie pressed under her chin. *Emma.* Didn't Nugget say something about her? It's so hard to think with the fog closing in.

O'Reilly breathes out the words like a prayer, "Thank God." He holds up his hand to the others, sending a signal. None of them move. My eyes burn hot and my brain scrambles. "What's happening?" The woman places her hands on my upper arms. Gently. Kindly. "Meemaw?" she asks, but it's hard to see her. The tears are coming fast. "Okay if I call you that?"

I nod and she tightens her hold, speaking firmly. "Thank you so much for taking care of her, but the child needs to go home."

"But her mother . . ." I'm blubbering out the words. My chin shakes. "Has passed."

"No," the woman says warmly. "I can assure you they're very much alive and missing their little girl." The policewoman's name is Rodriguez and her smile's calm and kind. "But everything's going to be better now," she tells me.

"They won't—" My breath catches. "Won't harm her?"

Rodriguez shakes her head. "I promise you, no."

"Emma?" O'Reilly moves toward her and Nugget backs up like a frightened rabbit. "Come on, sweetie." He holds out his hand. "We're going to take you home."

Nugget races to me and grabs my leg, pressing Night Doggie against it. I look at the police officers and glance at the yard. Something feels very wrong. "Where's my Dotti?"

Another woman steps up on the porch. She's dark haired and in a pantsuit. She's with a man with a closely cropped beard. "Maybe you can ride with us to the station?" she says. "We can talk in the back seat of Special Agent Mercer's car."

My heart stutters. "FBI?" The girl still clings to my leg.

A horrible realization crashes down on me. Nugget might not be Nellie at all. She could be another person's child. She stares up at me with worried eyes, but I can't keep her here if she doesn't belong. I could never do that to a mother. A father. A family. I gently pat her shoulder. "It's all right, Nugget," I say. "Run along."

She slowly releases my leg. "Bye, Meemaw." She reaches out her tiny arms and I bend down to hug her. She looks so sad it breaks my heart.

"Bye, sweetheart. Remember," I say. I breathe in her little-girl scent, absorb her soft sigh. "Meemaw loves you."

She tightens her arms around my neck. "I love Meemaw too."

She lets me go and takes O'Reilly's hand.

"Come on, kid," he says. "It's time to go home."

SADIE
THE MOM

Day Twenty-Three

Claremont calls to say they've found Emma and she's okay. My heart erupts with anguished joy. I cover my chest with my hand to prevent it from bursting. "What? Where?" I'm crying hard now but I don't care. My cheeks are hot and wet. My heart pounds against my palm, faster, faster. Galloping away. This is the day I've prayed for—so many times.

My baby's coming home.

I'm at the kitchen table and staring at her play set.

Yellow slide. Black swings. Blue tugboat.

A cardinal lands on the stern of the ship.

"Dot Gilmore's had her," she says. She sounds overwhelmed with emotion too. A sob chokes my throat. *It's finally over.* Claremont's smart and tough and, very deep down, unbelievably kind. Thank God we have her. *Thank God they've found Emma.* "She's been at Gilmore's mother's house this whole time."

I'm dizzy with relief. Want to hug her through the phone. Hug O'Reilly too. Mercer. Rodriguez, Patel, everyone. They've been so tireless in their efforts. Their whole team has. I love Claremont. I love them all. My heart's so full of gratitude it aches.

I grip my cell phone, need coursing through me. A want so deep it's burning. "When can I see her?" I have to hold my little girl. It's been so long. *Ages.*

"Deputy Chief O'Reilly and Officer Rodriguez are bringing her home. They're on their way to your house now and will be there shortly."

Be here with Emma. I bury my face in my hands and weep again. I *knew* it. I knew this would end well for all of us. That someone kind was looking after her. "So Dotti?" I ask, breathless. "How did it happen?"

She tells me the whole story about Emma hiding in the media room and thinking it was a game. How Dotti and her mom, Meemaw, were kind to her. Gave her ice cream, taught her games. How she'd seemed fine and well treated when they found her.

I take a tissue from my pocket and dab at my eyes. "Thank you, Chief Claremont," I say. "A world of thanks for everything."

I have to tell Allen.

The garage door opens, and he's here.

"Sadie?" His face goes pale. "What's happened?"

I leap out of my chair and into his arms. He holds me fast, so I don't fall. "Allen," I say, breathing hard. "Allen! They've found her!"

He holds me tighter and weeps into my hair. "Thank God."

ALLEN
THE DAD

Day Twenty-Three

Sadie and I sit anxiously in the living room, wringing our hands. We keep a watch on the street out front through the large window in Sadie's office. At last, a squad car.

Sadie and I spring to our feet. "Oh my God, Allen." She grips my arm, trembling. She can't believe it. Neither can I. This is the most amazing day of my life. Better than the day Emma was born, better than the day I married Sadie. Better than when Teri and I had Forrest. All of it put together—and doubled.

I open the front door and O'Reilly climbs from the driver's seat. He opens the back door and Rodriguez steps out. She holds out her hand. A small arm emerges—then Night Doggie.

My heart bursts with joy and my eyes burn hot.

"Emma!" My voice breaks into a roar as I race toward her. Stride after leaping stride. My world moves in slow motion, actions creeping to a crawl. Emma stands in the drive, staring up at our house like she's in a dream. Like she's not quite sure where she is, and then she sees us. Her mommy and daddy. She grins.

Sadie reaches her first, hugging her tightly. Sobbing.

"Oh, my baby," she says again and again. "I'm so sorry. So, so sorry."

"Mommy? Daddy?" Emma peers into our eyes. "What's wrong?"

"Nothing, sweetie." Sadie strokes her cheeks and kisses her head. Hugs her again. "We're just so happy you're home."

Thank God she's okay. Nothing's happened. Just look at her. Just look at my precious little girl in her shirt full of balloons. *She's alive. She's well. She's home.*

I squat down and take my girls in my arms, kissing the tops of their heads and holding them close. The two loves of my life, Sadie and Emma. I press them to my chest, my heart beating and beating *so hard* I'm sure they can feel it. I want them to feel it so they both know. How much I love them, *fiercely.* How I'll always love them. I embrace them firmly until the world stops spinning. I will *never* let either of them go again.

The sky above is Carolina blue. Warm breezes blow and birds chirp in the trees. Sunshine rains down upon us, bathing us in its glow. My heart's so full it's overflowing.

I look up and O'Reilly's smiling at us. A tear stains his cheek. He discreetly wipes it back. "Well." He straightens his hat. "I guess we'll leave you guys to it."

Rodriguez opens the driver's door to their cruiser and nods. "Y'all take care."

Our family hug breaks apart and Emma gives the police a wave, holding Night Doggie. "Bye!"

"Bye, sweetheart." O'Reilly winks at me and Sadie. "Glad she made it home."

"So O'Reilly?" I hear Rodriguez say before they shut their doors. "About that coffee—"

SADIE
THE MOM

Two months later.

Allen and I stand on the patio with our morning coffee, watching Emma on her play set. October's settling in and we all wear light fleece jackets. There's a nice nip in the air and the breeze is crisp, chilling our cheeks and noses. Leaves turn on the trees, tinged red, gold and brown. Emma pumps herself higher on her swing, her blue-jean legs bending and unfolding as she tilts back her head and smiles. "Look at me! Look at me! I'm flying!" Night Doggie watches from his post at the top of the slide.

I raise my coffee mug and grin. "Yes, you are!" This is the life I hoped for. The life I need. A safe and predictable space with Allen and Emma. Our family.

Teresa returned to Chapel Roads shortly after Dotti was arrested, but she wasn't charged by the police, having confessed her true aim was never to kidnap Emma. She'd expected Allen and the kids to willingly go with her on a family holiday.

Allen told me about their brief affair and begged my forgiveness. It takes time to rebuild trust, but we're getting there. I do believe Allen's sorry and that what he says is true. He's remorseful about sleeping with

Teresa, and it will never happen again. I'm the woman he loves and wants to spend the rest of his life with, if I'll still have him.

Though it broke my heart to learn he'd slept with Teresa, I knew it would break my heart more to lose Allen. It would break Emma's heart too. So I agreed to give Allen another chance. We're going to couples counseling, and Emma's seeing a child psychologist. We're very lucky to have only heard positive reports about her time with Meemaw, and two months out, we don't imagine that changing.

In the wake of Allen and Teresa's brief affair, we've begun the awkward dance of the three of us once more coparenting Forrest together, and it's going okay so far. I'm not sure how Teresa feels about Allen. She seems resigned to how things are, *and* she's started dating someone new, her lab assistant Henry. He's a few years younger than she is but evidently very bright. Most importantly, he's so clearly head over heels for her, his affection shines out like a bright star on the darkest night. Allen and I have seen them around town together, and Teresa always has a smile on her face. That speaks volumes.

Allen wraps an arm around my shoulders. "I'm so happy she's home," he says hoarsely. He sighs, watching Emma swing back and forth. "What a nightmare."

"Yes," I agree. "I'm glad it's over."

He holds me closer. "Me too."

MISS DOTTI
THE GRANDMA

I sit in the jail visiting room wearing a standard-issue orange jumpsuit. Tangerine's never been my color, but it will do. The judge gave me for-ty-four months for first-degree kidnapping, the minimum sentence in North Carolina because Emma was found safe and I fully cooperated.

The police asked me about Emma's stuffed dog, and I explained how the kid had told us about the key. I got it from under the flowerpot but forgot two things in my rush to get away. To put back the key and close the gate. I wasn't stupid enough to park in the driveway while sneaking into the Wilsons' home. Come on. My head's not made of fluff. I did lose my cool very briefly during that episode, it's true, and that's something I'm not exactly proud of.

After creeping up the back stairs to avoid detection from the street, I found Emma's room just where she told me. I wore gloves to keep from leaving prints on the doorknobs and such, and my first thought was to grab the stuffed animal and go. But then I tripped over this little toy horse and picked it up. It looked so real, like an actual horse in miniature, and there were others, a small set of stables too.

I saw this *very fancy* dollhouse, frilly curtains, nice dresses in her closet . . . and this silent rage overtook me. I had a view into Emma's pampered world, the kind of life I never could have afforded to give our Nellie. And so—I lost it, and messed up her room a bit.

I won't lie. Smashing her things up felt *good*, like further retribution against Allen. I could imagine his face when he walked in and found Emma's room in shambles. Would it break his heart? Worry him further? Make him crazy with fear over what sort of horrible monster had snatched his precious child? I hoped the fuck so.

Then I heard a car outside and I realized I'd been there too long. The press conference must have ended. I peered out Emma's front window. Damn. Sadie and Allen were climbing from their SUV and headed toward their front door. I scooped Night Doggie up and raced down the back stairs and out the patio way before they entered, hurrying through the gate.

In some ways, I'm glad for the entire ordeal to be over. Although my mom was initially very heartbroken and disappointed in me when the police explained the truth to her, she got over it the next day. Now, all she recalls is that "Nugget" lived with her briefly, and they had great fun drinking hot cocoa and playing Parcheesi. I guess her dementia is a blessing in that way.

I'm giving up less than four years of my life, but that's no big deal. I was coasting down to retirement anyhow and the payoff is worth it. I've got books to read and a job in the prison laundry that earns me some petty cash. I was worried they'd make me cut my hair and was grateful they didn't.

A guard opens a door on the far side of the glass, and a woman walks in with a little girl.

My heart twists.

Nellie.

She's so pretty with long blond pigtails and pink cheeks. Her mama wears a patterned blouse and black slacks, low heels. She's plump and has short curly black hair. She dyes it. The child sees my face through the glass and her eyes light up. She can't know who I am. Chelsea must have told her.

Chelsea sits in the chair opposite me and pulls Nellie into her lap. "Dot," she says, "how are you doing?"

I sweep my hands down my jumpsuit and say, "Just dandy."

She laughs and jiggles her knees, bumping the child up and down in her lap. "Nellie," she says, leaning forward, "this is your nana."

Nellie grins so big my heart hurts. "Hi, Nana." She's apparently unfazed that her nana is in prison. Chelsea must have prepared her somehow, though I'm not sure what she's told her.

Not long after I took Emma to Meemaw's house, I sent Chelsea a letter by regular postal mail. I didn't want to risk using electronic communications like email or text, because I knew Chelsea wouldn't like that.

Chelsea doesn't like for folks to know where she lives or to dig too deeply into her background. That's why she had to leave when Caleb's case became so public. She never faulted Caleb for what happened, but she couldn't have her old life come back to haunt her either.

Caleb wasn't going to leave North Carolina when he got out of prison. He wanted to stay with his roots and his family. His pa was living at the time he decided this. Meemaw and I were here too. So he and Chelsea parted on amicable terms and made an agreement about Nellie. Chelsea wanted a clean break if Caleb stayed behind. And so, he made his choice. In some ways, I think he believed it was better for the child.

I can't believe how she's grown.

She's got cute dimples and big dark eyes.

My insides ache because I wish I could hold her. I don't even know if Chelsea would allow that, but I still harbor that prayer in my heart. I press my hand to the clear wall between us, flattening my palm against the cool glass. Reaching out, hoping.

And then, the child does the same.

She scoots up in her mommy's lap and fits her tiny hand against mine.

My eyes burn hot. "Thank you," I whisper to her mama.

She's a kind soul, my Chelsea.

But Chelsea wasn't always Chelsea.

DIANE
THE OLD GIRLFRIEND

Allen tried to kill me. He wanted to have sex. I didn't. I was only fifteen, but Allen was used to getting what he wanted. So he was plenty pissed off. He pushed down on my shoulders and held my head underwater while I kicked and flailed, gurgling, gurgling, battling the angry ocean. Fighting for my life. Choking. Gulping in sea water. Writhing. Trying to break away.

Then, mercifully, a riptide.
Yanks me from his grasp and hurls me out to sea.
My body turns over and over.
Violent tumbles.
Knees, elbows grating against shells and sand.
Water getting colder. Deeper.
My stomach whirls with pressure, like a giant rubber band's wrapped around it.
Pulling me back like a pebble in a slingshot going taut.
I'm dizzy. Blacking out.
I lose time.

Icy waves lap my ankles, bare feet, bare thighs. I vomit up sea water and wrench sideways, landing on one elbow. Breathe, breathe. Wheezy, shuddered breaths.

It's night. A million stars.

I sit up and hug my arms.

Freezing.

I'm topless. In my underpants.

Where?

I look around. I don't know this beach.

My parents were both alcoholics. Verbally and emotionally abusive. Allen's were, too. That's probably why they couldn't swim when their fancy sailboat capsized. They were drunk and not wearing any life vests. Or maybe Allen murdered them. If they were sniffing around a bit too much about what had happened with me, he might have. He was attending a great college and had already been recruited for his first job postgraduation. I'm sure Allen wouldn't have wanted anyone messing that up for him. One thing I learned about Allen. He doesn't like messes.

He likes leaving things neat.

After the ocean sucked me in and then spat me back out like a giant wad of gum, I got my bearings and found a group of kids smoking weed under the pier. One girl gave me her jacket. Another a pair of sweatpants. They were runaways and pretty cool. It took me less than five minutes to decide I didn't want to return to my family. As fucked up as they were, I was glad to be free of them.

Well, except for Kit-Kat. Although she always did have a bit of a *twisted sister vibe* about her, to be honest. Like she wasn't one hundred percent right in the head. Considering the parents we had, no small wonder.

It took me a long time to realize Allen had done me a favor.

I wanted to return that favor.

So. I decided to mess things up a bit for him. He'd already fucked with my life majorly. It's *really hard* to top trying to drown someone, it really is. But wrongly convicting an innocent man probably comes in a close second. They do *not* treat people accused of sex crimes well in prison, especially when those purported crimes are against minors. And Caleb is a good guy. He didn't deserve that.

When Dot saw Emma on her class roster, she got a bright idea. I knew she'd terribly missed seeing Nellie, but I didn't want anyone to discover where we lived. Didn't want my maniac parents tracking us down and attempting to be asshat grandparents. God no. Not with Dad's temper. My dad beat the crap out of Mark a lot. Since I followed Mark in birth order, I figured I was next. Dad didn't discriminate based on gender. I watched him choke my mom once until her whole face turned blue.

When I registered at the teen shelter, I told them if I got sent home, my dad would kill me. I guess they'd seen enough of that shit with other kids that they took me at my word. So they helped me build a life, get back on my feet.

One of the shelter volunteers was Caleb. He was in college when I met him and volunteering in that campus's community. I was nineteen then and helping run some shelter programs. We clicked and later, we married. My heart stuttered when I learned he was from Chapel Roads and intended to live there. I was afraid of being recognized, but I'd already changed my hair and gained some weight. Everyone assumed Diane was dead, and I guess she was essentially.

I never told Caleb about Diane. A lot of shelter kids hide their backgrounds, and he never pressed me on mine. I did tell Dot when I was in the throes of childbirth. It was an emergency home birth and Caleb didn't make it in time. But Dot was like some kind of freakishly amazing doula delivering the baby. I don't know how she knew to do all the stuff she did.

She tried to be modest, saying she just followed the directions of the nine-one-one operator. Whatever. I told her my truth. Because.

Hell. What if I died and nobody knew? After Nellie was safe and I regained my sanity in the ambulance, I begged Dot not to tell Caleb or anyone—ever. *Please.* There was no reason he had to know. I never wanted anyone to know.

In the end, I'm glad I told Dot.

She took a chance and called me from a burner phone the day she got her new class list at Stonefield Elementary. She said Emma looked so much like Nelllie that Meemaw wouldn't know the difference. What did I think about her snatching Emma for a while? Not forever maybe, but long enough to put her parents through a scare.

Dot was angry with Allen for having served on that jury and furious at Principal Rand for not sticking up for Caleb. But there was only one reason she reached out to me. She wanted me to know she was avenging me too, for what Allen did all those years ago. She and I were the only two who shared that dark truth, and now she hoped we'd share another. That maybe if we did, I'd soften my heart to letting her see Nellie. Despite the risks and complications, and my wanting to maintain a separate life.

When Dot shared her plan and asked my advice, I could have dissuaded her from kidnapping Emma. But. Sorry, not sorry. Payback's a bitch.

So. I gave her some tips.

I scoot Nellie off my lap and set her sneakers on the floor. "Okay, sweetie. It's time to go." The warden's just given us the signal. Our time is up.

Dot's face hangs in a frown. "Will you come back?"

I'm not sure about that. Coming here once was dangerous enough.

I lift a shoulder. "Maybe when you get out, you can visit Arizona?"

Her eyes mist over. "I'd like that."

ABOUT THE AUTHOR

Camden Baird writes fast-paced, emotionally gripping stories that keep you up late turning pages. A *New York Times* and *USA Today* bestselling author, she's published more than forty works of fiction under different pen names. *The Last Morning* is Baird's debut psychological suspense thriller. The author lives in North Carolina.